BOOK WORM
The Curiosity of George Crosby

To Lita & Maris from David xx

BOOK
The Curiosity of

Copyright © 2021 Da.

The Moral right of the author ha

All rights reserved.

Apart from any fair dealing for the purpose
or private study, or criticism or review, as p
under the Copyright, Designs and Patents Act
publication may only be reproduced, stored
transmitted, in any form or by any means, with the
permission in writing of the author, or in the case
reprographic reproduction in accordance with the ten
of licences issued by the Copyright Licensing Agency

-o-o-o-

The characters herein other than the obvious figures,
historical or contemporary, are the product of the author's
imagination and any resemblance to real persons, living
or dead is purely coincidental. Events are the product of
the author's imagination.

-o-o-o-

BOOK WORM
The Curiosity of George Crosby

-o-o-o-

'To save a mayd, St. George the Dragon slew,
A pretty tale if all is told be true;
Most say there are no Dragons, and 'tis sayd,
There was no George; pray God there was a mayd.'

~ *Anon.*

Dan Tunnelly

Titles by Dan Tunnelly
(all available on Amazon)

NOVELS:

Black Joke Omnibus ~ *Hell's Bells Unleashed*

Book Worm ~ *The Curiosity of George Crosby*

Jagga's Limelight ~ *All the Stages are a World*

Myre Hamlet & the Ice Wolf

Spikey and the Green Wasp ~ *A Tale of Two Wheelers*

What in Blue Blazers? ~ *A History in Education*

NOVELLA:

Shooting the Bridge ~ *A Story of 17th Century Intrigue*

POEMS:

Behind the Silvered Cobwebs ~ *Reflections in the Flash of Time*

Chasing Life's Coat-tails ~ *Poems New & Old*

To 'B'

with love as always

BOOK WORM
The Curiosity of George Crosby

1) The Diabolical Maskquerade...1

2) Orford Mess...23

3) London Spurning...46

4) Lym in Stir..66

5) Book Worm...87

6) Be Stern..112

7) Kilve Beast..142

8) On Edge..161

9) Up Lowland..176

10) Loschy Way...188

11) Whitby Jet Wyrm...198

12) The Whirled Serpent...211

13) Tail Ends...220

14) Epilogue - *Ten Years On*...224

1) The Diabolical Maskquerade

George Crosby stares absently at the twirl of cream that floats atop his fresh poured coffee.

"Penny for your thoughts, dear," offers the old lady who's shuffling herself onto the chair opposite him at his corner table in the café of the British Museum. She carefully ledges her wet umbrella against a vacant third chair and unfastens the see-through plastic hood of her raincoat: "It's chuckin' it down out there, dearie," she informs him.

The weather is wetter, colder and windier than even a mid-November day should be.

"Oh, sorry. I didn't see you," says George, apologetically.

He pushes back his chair and stands to help the weather-refugee, who seems to have migrated into the museum purely to escape the rain.

"No need for that, dear. I'm in now."

George sits back down, looking to return his attention to his coffee.

"Looks to me," says the old lady, "that your thoughts might be worth *more* than a penny."

"Err, yes. Perhaps they are," agrees George. "This here twirl in my coffee… it reminds me of a dragon. Look, there are its wings, and that's its tail. And see the steam snorting from its nostrils? My name's George, by the way."

She peers into his cup: "Can't see it myself, but then *I* don't drink coffee. It's tea for me every time. I can read the tea leaves you know, but I've never seen a dragon in them. I've seen a few pretty terrifying things though, what with wars, murders, and a couple of hangings. But look on the bright side, I say. I've seen lots of love too; weddings and new-born babies, and so on. Not necessarily in that order, you understand."

"Ah, well," replies George. "Truth to tell, I've been studying,

BOOK WORM ~ *The Curiosity of George Crosby*

among other things, a particularly intriguing etching here in the museum: '*The Diabolical Maskquerade, or the dragons-feast as acted by the Hell-Fire-Club, at Somerset House in the Strand*'. That's what the etching's called."

"Oh, dear. That sounds a bit dramatic. What gives you such an interest in dragons and suchlike? The only dragons *I* like are snapdragons... *you* know, Antirrhinums. I grow them every year in my little garden. My mother used to do the same."

"I'm not all that keen on flowers myself," says George. "I do like soil though. There's a lot to be said for soil, but I like dragons more." He sips at his coffee, obliterating his dragon-like twirl. The caffeine hits, and he adds: "So do you live in London then? I didn't catch your name by the way?"

"Now there's a reason for that, young man. I didn't throw my name, so you won't have caught it, will you."

"Ah, Sorry. I didn't mean to pry."

"Don't you worry, lad. I'm quite partial to a bit of prying myself. I'm here to search for something I read in Old Theophilus Moore's Almanac about the predicted return of youth and beauty to the world. I could do with some of that, it's a fact."

"Well, everything and everyone in the world has *some* beauty, if you can only find it," suggests George.

"That's as may be, but it's the youth bit *I'm* looking for. It seems to have deserted me a while ago. I've turned eighty-five, you know."

"Well I'd have said you weren't a day over seventy."

"It's true. I *weren't* a day over seventy... about fifteen years ago."

George smiles and finishes his coffee, making to leave. He's intending to catch the 4.30 train back to Leicester: "It's been nice talking to you. Sorry, but I still don't know your name."

"It was nice talking to you too, George," she answers as her pot of tea arrives. "I'll let you into a little secret. My friends call

2

1) The Diabolical Maskquerade

me Natalie, but I won't tell you my real name. I like to keep people guessing. As to where I live? London is no particular place to be except when I want to be in a particular place."

George rises from his chair and picks up his trilby hat from the table. As he squeezes by the old dear, he spies the protruding name-tag sewn loosely into the back of her mackintosh.

"You take care now, Thalia. And keep on searching for that youth. It's still out there somewhere."

Not realising that her name-tag is showing she looks quizzically at George, wondering how on Earth he knows her true name, but nevertheless lets it pass.

"Don't you go a worrying about that," she says. "Old Moore, the Irish Merlin, will see me right on that score. He's never wrong. And you take care too. Good luck in your quest… like you say, there's beauty in everything so don't you go slaying any of those dragons, George."

He smiles again as he waves her farewell. She waves back with one hand whilst pouring herself a cup of tea from the heavy teapot with the other.

At St. Pancras station, George boards his intended train, having traipsed the length of the platform to the foremost carriage. The engine is snorting steam and belching flame, dragon like, from the well-fed firebox, keen to head for the heathen north, beyond the Midlands, where the wind bites as bitter as a cruel blade on battlefields of yore. On its way north, the mighty beast, all bold brass and bright green livery, will deign to interrupt its progress at a few places, including Leicester. There, George will be disgorged with the prospect of a walk through darkling streets and on across the park beyond the station in the darkness of a moonless night.

George removes his sodden trilby and his soaked overcoat in the corridor, shaking off what rain he can. Entering a crowded compartment as the train lurches into motion, he folds the coat and places it carefully on the overhead rack along with his hat. It's Friday and its rush hour, so he's lucky to have secured a seat. The other five seats are taken: To one side of him sits a man in a suit and bowler hat, with briefcase and furled umbrella; to the other side slouches a slovenly, gum-chewing youth with gabardine mac; and opposite are a couple with a young boy of about eight years of age. The bowler-hatted gent is reading his copy of the Evening Standard. The youth is chewing, ruminant in his slovenliness. The couple are talking to each other about their intended booking of an exotic winter break in Spain and suggesting that young Jonathan can stay just around the corner from home in Kettering with aunt Edna for the two weeks they'll be away. None of them acknowledge George, except for the boy.

"*That's* a funny hat, mister," he declares, picking his nose vigorously.

"Well, *I* quite like it, lad," replies George, smiling nervously at the boy's parents.

"Jonny. I've told you before... don't speak to strangers. You don't know where they've been," admonishes the boy's mother.

Jonny's father looks out of the window at the passing gardens in the gathering gloom, as the train clatters over points.

"That's alright, my dear," reassures George. "I've only been to the British Museum to see a picture I'm interested in."

The woman shuns the conciliatory comment that George offers, turning to her husband and rehearsing her excitement at the prospect of languishing under the hot sun of Torremolinos.

"If *I* want to see pictures, I go to the Savoy cinema," says young Jonny to George.

"What did I just tell you about strangers, Jonny?" his mother asks him, overbearingly.

Father looks out of the window even more intently.

'*Right*,' thinks George. If she wants her overprotected Jonny

1) The Diabolical Maskquerade

to ignore me, we'll give her some food for thought."

"Well, Jonny," says George, "the last boy I knew who picked his nose like that was sent on a very strange adventure. Mind you, instead of wiping his bogeys on the sleeve of his pullover the way you do, he used to eat them. Then one day, one of his bogeys, a long slimy green one, suddenly grew into an enormous fire-breathing dragon with a roar louder than any steam train. Fortunately for the boy, who was called Arthur by the way, the dragon was friendly. It flew off, taking Arthur with him on a long journey right round the world… and that's much further than Torremolinos. He brought the boy back in time for tea though, but because he flew west much faster than the Earth was spinning, it was teatime on the day before they'd left. So for all that day, Arthur could tell what his mother was going to say before she said it."

"Wow!" exclaims Jonny. "Does that mean if *I* pick my nose enough, I'll go on an adventure right around the world and meet myself coming back?"

"Only if you *eat* the bogeys, Jonny."

Now Jonny's mother is exasperated, almost lost for words, and nudges her husband in the ribs: "say something, Cecil."

"Alright, Ethel. Give me a chance. Look mate, I think you've said enough about bogeys and dragons. *Don't* you?" says Cecil, turning away from his nocturnal garden-gazing.

"Yes, I suppose so, Cecil. I'm sorry. It's just that I find dragons so fascinating. I'll shut up now."

"I think you'd better had," says father.

"See, I told you, Jonny," says Ethel. "Strangers will only fill your head with silly ideas… and stop picking your nose."

Cecil returns to his garden-gazing.

"Sorry, mum," says Jonny, "but I *knew* you were going to say that," he laughs.

'*This boy will go far,*' thinks George, smiling contentedly.

The man with the newspaper turns the page and the slovenly

youth replenishes his chewing gum with a fresh stick, thinking for a moment that it's texture is rather bogey-ish. Nothing more is said all the way to Kettering, where three of the occupants get up to leave the train.

"What was the dragon's name, mister?" asks the boy, as he and his parents slide through the compartment doorway into the corridor.

"That's for you to find out, lad. There are hundreds of dragons all with different names. I know a few of them, but there are lots more to find. Just be sure to wear your fireproof gloves when you're looking for them."

"Thanks. I shall," says Jonny. "And your hat isn't so bad after all," he shouts back, as his mother whisks him away down the corridor.

George stands up to stretch his legs, then sits down in the seat that Jonny's father has vacated so that he can stare into the darkness of the night: *'Dark already, and it's not yet five o'clock.'* he thinks. *'Still, it is November. I can't believe that nineteen sixty-four is almost gone'*.

For the rest of the journey to Leicester, George sits in virtual silence. The bowler-hatted man has now graduated incongruously to a magazine for motorcycle enthusiasts, whilst the youth appears to be fast asleep and yet still chews his gum vigorously.

George gazes out of the window, reflecting on the picture he'd seen in the museum, wondering quite why he's acquired such a strong interest in dragons recently. He seems to be drawn to them inexorably these days and wishes he could afford to further explore the enthralling creatures: *'The Diabolical Maskquerade indeed,'* he thinks. *'I don't see anything devilish in dragons at all. They seem noble creatures, despite their reputation for being duplicitous. In almost every circumstance, as far as I can see, it's man who's the deceiver... the one who masquerades in much of what he undertakes.'*

1) The Diabolical Maskquerade

Then, his thoughts turn to the hapless young Kettering lad whose mother had seemed so overbearing: '*I do hope I haven't given him nightmares, and that he'll find dragons as benign as I do.*' The boy had reminded George of himself, when *he was a boy*. Thinking back to the time when he and his young schoolmates had played on the old abandoned allotments near to home, a sudden flash of memory comes to him: '*Danny Page! That's it... He used to dig up garden worms and bite their tails off. Leastways, he thought they were their tails. Could have been their heads for all I knew. Either way, it was disgusting but at least he spat them out and didn't usually swallow them.*'

George shudders at the thought but realises, after all these years, it may be why he's developed his interest in dragons: '*I read that wingless dragons are sometimes called worms, or is it the other way round... are winged worms called dragons? Some people reckon if you cut a worm in half, then you get two of them, but I've been told that it's not true. And anyway, I wouldn't like to try that with a dragon. They may be benign, but I think they value their tails above their benevolence.*'

After traversing the park, keeping one eye out for stray dragons but seeing only a giggling courting couple and a six o'clock drunk fresh from the pub so early, George finds home. Inserting his key in the Yale lock he's in, warm and welcoming.

"Is that you, love?" calls his mum from the kitchen.

"No. It's Guy Fawkes on the run from the authorities. It's been about a fortnight now since I escaped from the Houses of Parliament. I think I've shaken them off."

"Don't be silly, love. I know you've been to London, but you're always blowing things up out of all proportion."

"Sorry, mum. Just my little joke. Is dad in?"

"No, love. He's gone down the pub for a swift half. He should be back anytime now."

"Ah, yes. I think I overtook him just now in the park," George replies, jokingly.

"I don't think so, love. He went to the pub just around the corner. You know how he always goes to that one. Anyway how did your day go? Did you see what you went for?"

"I did, mum. And I met a few eccentrics too. There was this old lady in the museum. Very mysterious she was. Her real name was Thalia but she said her friends call her Natalie. She was looking for lost youth, apparently. She reminded me a bit of your aunt Myrtle over in Birmingham."

"Well, we're *all* looking for lost youth, love. But you may as well chase your tail, *I* reckon. Once the day has gone by, it won't come back again, will it, so we should live each day to the full."

"I suppose so, mum."

"It's odd that you should mention aunt Myrtle though, George. I've not been in touch with her for years, but we had a letter today from her solicitor… apparently she died unexpectedly a couple of weeks ago. From what he says in the letter, it was something to do with a low bridge and a lorry loaded with liquorice allsorts. He wasn't very clear, but the funeral's next week. He says he needs to speak with us about the will. She left more than a few bob and he hinted that a large part of it is for you. You always *were* one of her favourites."

"Oh dear. That's a bit sad, mum… sad that we lost touch with her. I haven't see anything about liquorice allsorts in the newspapers though."

"No. neither have I, George. To think that she smoked Woodbines all her long life and then was knocked on the head by a load of errant novelty confectionery."

With the funeral over, the will is read and it turns out that George has been left the princely sum of five thousand pounds.

"I expect you'll put your money in the bank and save it for a rainy day, George," says pop Crosby.

"Well, dad. I *will* put it in the bank, but I have a project in

1) The Diabolical Maskquerade

mind. I'm twenty-eight years old and out of work. It's not fair on you and mum for me to still be at home."

"Well, you could easily buy a house with that sort of money, with plenty to spare."

"I know, but I want to go on an adventure, dad. I'm going on a dragon hunt. I can travel the country searching for them. But first, I'm going back to the reference library. That's where I first came across a reference to *The Diabolical Maskquerade*, so that's where I'll begin my search in earnest."

"Well one thing's for sure, George," says his mum. "It all sounds a bit diabolical to me. You'll spend all that money and then what? You'll be back here expecting a place to live again."

"Don't worry, mum. I won't spend it *all*, I promise. But like you said 'live each day to the full'. And that's what I intend to do."

"Well, chasing dragons is not *my* idea of living life to the full, George."

"Nor mine," chips in dad. "Give me a warm beach and a knotted handkerchief. Now, *that's* living, that is."

"But if I don't do this dad, I'll regret it later in life. I could go on for years living in my house and then go and get knocked down by a lorry full of custard creams or something."

And nothing Mr. and Mrs. Crosby could possibly say would change George's mind, so the very next day he's off to the library armed with pencil and paper to begin his dragon quest. In truth, George knows very little of dragons but he knows in his heart that they really exist. He's convinced that many of those purported by long-standing folklore to have been slain still haunt the hills and valleys of England.

"Excuse me, miss. I'm Mr. Crosby. I came in recently looking for dragons and I'm back to search for more."

"Oh, then you'll want Mrs. Battlebury," the girl on reception replies, sniggering. "She's on her tea break."

BOOK WORM ~ *The Curiosity of George Crosby*

"No. I mean *real* dragons. The ones that breathe fire and supposedly fly around looking for mischief."

"Like I said, you'll want Mrs. Battlebury. She's well versed in that sort of thing. She's been here since the library opened."

"What? All those decades ago?"

"Well, yes. But I meant since nine o'clock this morning. She's the one with the keys. She's very accommodating really, but she *does* like her tea. She'll be down from the staff room in a few minutes. Apart from all her other duties, Mrs. B's also in charge of the rare books section; keeps it under lock and key, she does. In the meantime, you could try browsing the general folklore shelves. They're in section four."

"I shall, thank you, miss. That's where I came across the *The Diabolical Maskquerade*."

"Ah, well, you could have saved yourself the trouble. The whole library can be a bit of devilish show, especially when someone puts a book back on the wrong shelf. Mrs. Battlebury goes a bit nuts when that happens. Anyway, I'll ask her to come and see you in section four when she returns."

"Thank you, miss. I'll go and browse as you suggest."

When George strides into the folklore section, he's greeted by a little chap with a long, grey beard and bushy eyebrows who's just leaving. He looks suspiciously like a leprechaun; he even has a green and yellow jacket peeking out from under his grey winter anorak. Oddly though, the little fellow is wearing black plimsolls and is carrying a plastic bag which is emblazoned with the Tesco logo and bursting at the seams with groceries.

"Top o' the mornin' to yer, my fine man," the 'leprechaun' says.

"*And* to you, my good man," replies George.

"Well, I'm off now to do my shopping," says the tiny chap. "Good luck with whatever it is you're searching for. I was looking for ancient recipes for soup, but all I could find was one for porridge, slow cooked on a peat fire. I'll have to make do

1) The Diabolical Maskquerade

with *canned* soup for the time being."

"Right," says George, bemused, as the leprechaun lookalike skips out through the doorway into the corridor whistling a discordant tune.

George scans the shelves looking for dragon clues, but before he can say 'hoarded gold', Mrs. Battlebury looms into sight. She's an imposing figure, all of six feet tall in her block heels and is truly built for battle, with biceps honed by years of carrying piles of books to and from the shelves. George can't imagine why he hadn't come across her before. Perhaps she was on holiday when he'd been in previously.

"Now then, Mr. Crosby. How can I be of assistance? I gather you may be interested in dragons."

She leans into George as if she's searching for legends of old in the top pocket of his jacket, her voice projecting like the roar of cannon fire, despite the 'SILENCE' notice on the opposite wall. He cowers under the weight of the librarian's presence thinking: *'I do believe I've found a dragon already'* He whispers a timid response: "Yes please," is all he can manage.

"Well, you've come to the right place. Only last week we received an addition to our rare books stock. I'm sure it will be the very thing. Follow me. But before you do, I'll need to inspect your library ticket. I can't let you into the rarities archive without proof of your existence. That would be like blindly believing in dragons, wouldn't it."

"I suppose so," bleats George, blanching in the face of the keeper of rare things, as he fumbles for his library ticket.

"Good. Good. I see it's still in date. As I said, follow me."

Up the stairs they go, their footsteps echoing in tandem on terrazzo treads and bouncing off the gloss painted walls under stark fluorescent lighting.

'Should I be following dragons blithely into their unfamiliar lair?' thinks George. *'I didn't come prepared for this, but if I survive it, I'll survive any amount of potential bother from such exotic creatures.'*

On the next floor, which is devoid of all human activity until they arrive, they're confronted by a heavy oak door endowed with a sign reading 'RARE BOOKS SECTION'.

"This is our rare books section," declares Mrs. Battlebury, proudly yet rather superfluously.

"So I see," says George, finding his confidence a little.

His chaperone fiddles with her cleavage and triumphantly produces a heavy key which is secured on a string placed around her neck. George is put in mind of a magician producing a rabbit from a top hat.

"Now then, Mr. Crosby," she says, "you'll need to sign this card with your further details. Here's a pencil. You'll see that I've filled in what I can myself."

"Please, call me George," says George, getting the measure of her bluster. "By the way, I've got my *own* pencil."

"It's not a 2H is it? Much too dangerous. Before you know it, you could make a bad impression. This HB will be far more acceptable."

"I can assure you, I'm intending to make nothing but a *good* impression, Mrs. Battlebury."

"*All* impressions are bad if they impress our books, Mr. Crosby."

George is rendered speechless.

"Right, George," she offers, now adopting his first name as she reaches for a heavy leather-bound book from a top shelf. "You must be very careful when you're handling this book. You'll need white gloves, like these I have on. I'll get you a pair from my special store in a moment."

George has a discomforting thought that she perhaps keeps the gloves in the same place as her key to the rare books section, but is relieved when she reaches down to open her low-level drawers.

The spine of the book reads:

1) The Diabolical Maskquerade

'The Traditions and Legends of East Anglia'

"You're privileged to be the first member of our public to delve into the pages of this newly acquired treasure. Here are your gloves. And if you're making notes, remember... pencil only. I won't have ink in my rare books section. And rest assured, I now have a note of your details on this card and, when your session is finished, I shall inspect every page for evidence of misuse. I shall now lock you in and I'll be back in an hour to let you out."

George can't help but notice that her own notes on the card are made in ballpoint pen.

"But what about health and safety? And is there a toilet?" George asks.

"If you look over there, you'll see a door with a panic bolt that lets you onto the fire escape. The toilet is in that other corner."

With that, she leaves George to delve. He sits down at the desk on which Mrs. Battlebury has placed the tome on a book support. He's not at all sure why she's locking him in, when there's a panic bolt on the fire escape door. She's provided him with a pair of leaded snake-weights for the holding back of the pages. He turns to the index of sections and scanning down it, his eyes fix on one particular entry:

'Suffolk - The Orford Sea-dragon'

Turning to the page indicated, George carefully places the snake-weights down across the outer margins. He's distracted for a moment as one of the weights rolls onto the desk, coiling as it falls, and he imagines that the weight has fangs like some fitful anaconda protesting at being placed upon the page. He places the snake back in its intended position and sets to reading:

'A monster, measuring all of four feet, was landed from the sea off Suffolk in 1749. It resembled a winged alligator but had two legs with hooved feet. Its body was clad in scales and it had many rows of teeth. This sea-dragon was slain, having first flown into the air after it had bitten off several fingers of one man and having gashed another man's arm. The first man died later that day and the second was disfigured for life.'

George shivers as he reads. He's always acknowledged that dragons could prove dangerous, but has a firm belief that they're generally benign, provided they're given the respect any reasonable *person* would ask for. He decides there and then that his new-chosen quest for the dragons of England would start with this, the Orford Sea-dragon. In the meantime, he delves further into the book's pages, carefully repositioning the snake-weights as he turns each page, careful not to awake the fangs again.

After an hour, Mrs. Battlebury returns as promised to release her captive from her lair. After George's literary encounter with the sea-dragon, the librarian seems rather more benign herself.

"Did you find what you were looking for?" she asks.

"Yes, thank you."

"Well, if you come again, you can call me Samantha, George. It's not that we get many people returning to the rare books section."

"Samantha. Right," says George. *'I can't imagine why people don't return,'* he thinks, as he gets up to follow Samantha down the stairs, she leading with the book under her arm for close inspection, after locking the door behind them and reinserting the key in her waiting cleavage.

"You intend to go through with it then, George?" asks Agatha

1) The Diabolical Maskquerade

Crosby.

"Yes, mum. I feel that you have to follow your destiny in life. And dragons are in my blood."

"Well if they are, it's nothing to do with me," says Fred Crosby. "I've never been *near* a dragon."

"I'm sure I don't know where you get it from, George," says his mum.

"Worms mum. Worms came to me the other day."

"There are tablets for that, George. Get yourself off to the doctors'. They'll tell you what to do for the best."

"No, mum. You remember Danny Page, don't you? Well, I recalled that he used to bite the tails off them."

"Ugh," shudders Agatha.

"*I* bumped into Danny Page's dad a couple of months ago, George," says Fred. "He told me Danny's emigrated to Ireland. He'd developed a bit of a fear of snakes and apparently there aren't any over there… all thanks to St. Patrick apparently. Plenty of worms though. Aren't snakes called dragons sometimes, George, or is it the other way around?"

"I think you're thinking of worms, dad."

"You mean snakes are called *worms*?"

"Not really, dad. I think it's wingless *dragons* that are called worms."

"I don't think you can get tablets for *dragons*, George," says Agatha. "Or snakes, come to that. Anyway, if you're intent on gallivanting around the country looking for dragons, how are you going to do it? You can't drive, and I can't imagine you walking."

"There *are* such things as buses, mum. I'll go by bus and coach. I can even afford a taxi or two now, if I choose. Maybe I'll walk a bit too, if the weather's fine. The fresh air will do me good. And I'll find somewhere to stay when and where I need to."

"Waste of money if you ask me, lad," says Fred. "You'll come back penniless... if dragons don't eat you first."

"Well, give my regards to Orford Ness when you get there and send us a postcard, George," says mum Crosby. "I've not been to the seaside for years. Not since that time your dad broke his leg when he trapped himself in a deck chair on Ingoldmells beach. He ended up in Boston General. What a nightmare."

"I thought it was Chapel St. Leonards, love," says Fred.

"No. Definitely Boston. I can picture the Stump."

"Blimey. Anyone would think I had my leg amputated, Agatha."

When the appointed day comes for George to set out, the December weather is encouraging for the intrepid dragon-hunter. He's bought himself a new, fleeced topcoat and a rucksack from the Army and Navy stores in Leicester. The rucksack is filled with essentials for his journey; maps, a note pad and pencils, an army canteen of water, a half-dozen sausage rolls and a change of underwear. He's exchanged his trilby for a bobble-hat, thinking it more practical. In addition, he has his wallet and a chequebook but, apart from these few things, he's travelling light with the intention of buying anything else he may need whilst he's actually on his travels.

The coach will take him through Market Harborough and on towards Kettering. There are few people on the coach but an old couple, who'd boarded a mile or two back, sit in the seats immediately in front of him.

'*I wonder how young Jonny's getting on,*' thinks George. '*Maybe he's with his aunt Edna by now, teaching her all about travel through time, and riding on the backs of dragons whilst his parents are in Torremolinos riding back into the past on donkeys... the poor old donkeys.*'

He spies a sign saying 'Geddington, 4 miles'.

"Geddington? That rings a bell," he says aloud.

1) The Diabolical Maskquerade

"You must be thinking of the cross, mate," says the old boy in front of him, unannounced, head turning to reveal that he's the proud possessor of a whisky nose. "It's the only thing of interest in Geddington… apart from the pubs, and the lovely houses, and the peaceful atmosphere and…"

"Sounds idyllic," interrupts George. "Which cross is that then?"

"The Eleanor Cross. King Edward put it there about a hundred years ago."

"Nearly *seven* hundred years actually, Malcolm," his wife corrects him.

"Blimey, doesn't time fly, Annie. You'll be telling me next that it's nearly Christmas."

"Well, Malcolm…"

"Of course. That's it," says George. "I've read about those crosses somewhere. Weren't there about a dozen of them? Something to do with a funeral procession."

"You're right. Edward Longshanks had them erected in memory of his wife, Eleanor of Castile," says Annie, appearing to be an expert on the subject.

"Were there any dragons involved?" asks George.

"Not that I'm aware," she replies.

"There's a Green Dragon pub over Brigstock way," says Malcolm , appearing to be an expert on *that* subject.

George is intrigued, but decides that he mustn't be distracted by a pub detour for the time being, so he sits tight as the coach heads on for Huntingdon and Cambridge. The late morning sun slants its golden rays onto the honey-coloured stone walls of cottages as they pass, reflecting the warm hue in through the coach windows and all is well in the world with George.

Annie and Malcolm alight in Kettering, leaving George sitting in isolation from the three other passengers who are sat right at the front of the coach. He waves to the alighting couple through the window, as the coach driver crunches the gears and moves onwards. Soon, the coach is back in the countryside as morning heads for noon.

George has purchased a ticket that takes him from Leicester to Cambridge, where he intends to sample the delights of the university town, while looking to take a light lunch there. He'd decided that his sausage rolls would suffice, for after all he's determined, despite his newfound wealth, to prove his dad wrong by returning home at some unspecified future date with a healthy balance in his savings account. After Cambridge, he would catch a fresh coach to Ipswich. From there he sees the need perhaps to hitch a lift with some sympathetic coast-bound motorist or other. He's confident that he'll find accommodation in Orford village, despite the inhospitable time of year, or perhaps because of it.

It's past noon now and, alighting from the coach in the midst of the impressively ancient university buildings, George heads for the Cambridge City Information Centre where he's reliably informed that there are no coaches to Ipswich until the following day.

"Apparently, sir," explains the kind lady behind the counter, "it's all due to a lightning strike called by the union at WARCC... the West Anglian Roadrunner Coach Company. I gather that the crews are in dispute with the controller of operations. Sam Yosemite I think his name is. There are more strikes in prospect for next week too. Probably your best bet is to stay here for the night, instead of trying to make it to the coast. It's a bad time of year for it, sir."

"Oh, I don't think so," says a dejected George. "I couldn't possibly stay in the Information Centre."

"Very funny, sir. I meant here in Cambridge, as well you know. I have enough to bear, working in this place, without jokers like you being silly, pardon me for saying."

"Yes, sorry. I didn't mean to be flippant."

"Well, that's alright then. My husband would be very upset if

1) The Diabolical Maskquerade

I returned home tonight all depressed. Last week, I went home distraught after a Frenchman threatened me with a stale croissant because he couldn't find his way to a pissoir nearby. We have some very difficult customers to deal with and it's sometimes hard to remain polite."

"Oh, dear. I *am* sorry," offers George, genuinely concerned for the poor woman.

"Enough of *my* troubles, dear. You go and enjoy a nice stopover in our dear Cambridge."

"Thank you. I shall."

George sidles by a young woman who stands browsing the information leaflets on a revolving stand near the door.

"Sorry, excuse me," he says instinctively, despite having done nothing deserving of an apology.

She smiles, as he grapples with the door latch which is rather in need of a squirt of oil or perhaps a sharp blow administered with a Hobbies magazine. George makes to doff his trilby before remembering it's a bobble-hat, and finds himself out in the street, met by the streetscape of magnificent academic façades.

Sitting himself down on a low stone wall outside one of the colleges, George takes out his flask of water and delves into his stash of sausage rolls. As he pulls out the pack, his wallet slips out with it and falls to the pavement, two pound notes escaping and fluttering away on a rising wind. He jumps down from the wall intent on pursuit, but by now they're several yards away when an approaching pedestrian steps deftly, first on one and then on the other, frustrating their attempt to escape the clutches of their travelling custodian. She stoops to pick up the notes and hands them back to George."

"Thank you. Oh, it's you," he says as he recognises the young woman from the Information Centre.

"I *do* believe you're right," she agrees.

He smiles at the quip: "Of course it is. Who else could it be?"

19

"Oh, *I* don't know. Oliver Cromwell perhaps, or David Attenborough, even John Milton. Or maybe Charles Darwin. They were *all* here, *I* can tell you… each in their time."

"I see. Were *you* here?" he asks awkwardly, holding his retrieved wallet in one hand and two pound notes and a sausage roll in the other.

"I *am* here. Honestly. I'm not telling pork pies."

"No, I meant did you attend university here?"

"I did actually. I studied Natural Sciences, like David Attenborough did, but not at the same college mind you. I'm quite into the evolution of animals."

"Do you believe in… oh, sorry, I'm George by the way. Do you believe in dragons?"

"I'll believe in Martians if you show me a skeleton of one, George. I'm Arabella. Arabella Drake. Everyone calls me Bella."

"Well, *I* believe in dragons," Bella. And I intend to find one that isn't reduced to a skeleton. I'm off to Orford Ness to start with. There's a legend of one there that sounds promising to me."

"Are you sure you don't mean Loch Ness. There's one *there*, so people believe."

"I never thought of that. But I want to search for English dragons. I couldn't cope with a dragon that has a Scottish accent… You're not Scottish, are you?"

"Not kilty, your honour. Not Scottish and hopefully not a dragon."

"Wait a minute… Drake… that's suspiciously dragon-like. But you don't strike me as a dragon. Far too attractive. I mean… well, you know."

"Am I?" she says, smiling at his obvious self-embarrassment.

"Trouble is," says George. "There aren't any coaches to Ipswich today and I was hoping to get over that way and start my investigations."

"You're in luck," says Bella. "I have a brother in Ipswich and I

1) The Diabolical Maskquerade

was planning on visiting him later this week. He wouldn't mind me turning up early. I could give you a lift this afternoon if you don't mind waiting for me to grab a few things from my digs."

"But, don't you have a job to go to?"

"I do, but not for the time being. I'm on holiday until after New Year."

George hesitates, pensive at this offer of abduction by an attractive woman he's only just met: "Well, if you really think…"

"Of course I do. I can come and search for dragons with you. What an adventure."

"Well, if you insist, provided you have room in your car. I wouldn't want to impose on you."

"Actually, it's a motorbike. My dad bought it for me. It's a 1957 Norton Dominator 77; a classic. I told him he has more money than sense… 'I *did* have', he said."

"Well, there won't be much room on that then, will there?"

"Sure there will. It has a sidecar."

"In that case, you're on," says George, now with confidence that it's a good move, without giving a thought to his ending up paying for accommodation for two on the dragon quest.

Half an hour later, the dragon-hunters are speeding along the A14 towards Bury St. Edmunds and Ipswich, George riding pillion. Bella has slipped into her sleek, black, biking leathers which she'd had stowed in the sidecar, George turning to look away as she'd swiftly substituted her Levi jeans. George's rucksack containing his few spare clothes and his remaining sausage rolls are now sharing the sidecar with Bella's travel bag.

"What a lark," Bella shouts back at George over her shoulder. "We'll be in Ipswich before dark and you can meet Ken. You'll love Ken. He's into classical music, hang-gliding and Spanish cuisine… not all at the same time, you understand."

-o-o-o-

2) Orford Mess

"Ken lives north of the town, just off the Henley Road," shouts back Bella to George as they leave the A14.

George has been holding tight for miles with a face full of Bella's long flowing auburn hair, thinking that she really should be wearing a crash helmet: '*I guess I should be wearing a helmet too,*' he thinks, as his leather-clad chauffeuse negotiates every right-hand bend on two wheels.

"If Ken's not in, I have a key. He won't mind us letting ourselves in," shouts Bella.

"Right," George shouts back with brevity, spitting hair, keen not to let go of Bella's waist at any cost.

"I could murder a cuppa," Bella shouts.

"Me too," he calls hesitantly, thinking for a moment she'd said 'I could murder a *copper*'.

They pull up at Ken's, a rather magnificent yet sombre-looking, faux Gothic house. Bella kills the engine and signals George to grab their bags from the sidecar as she skips across the gravel drive to the front porch.

"I'll put the kettle on, George. Sugar?"

Still shell-shocked from the brisk ride, and half deaf from the wind, he thinks for another moment that she called him 'sugar'.

"Err, two spoons, please," he manages.

She disappears inside, leaving the door ajar for him to follow. As he does, he perceives the sound of some classical Italian lament leaching up the hallway from deep within Ken's den. It turns out that Bella's brother is home after all. George is both relieved and disappointed at the same time, his whirlwind motorcycling acquaintance having taken his breath in more ways than one.

"Come in, George. Meet my villain of a brother."

"Hi," offers George to Ken who's seated on an enormous

leather sofa, lounging in a Victorian smoking jacket, with a large whisky in one hand and a smouldering Benson and Hedges cigarette in the other. Bella turns down the record player and carefully lifts the stylus, setting it in its mount.

"Hi," says Ken, returning George's greeting. "You're early, sis... about *two days* early."

"I knew you wouldn't mind, Ken. I thought you'd be out though."

"I came home early myself, Bel. I bought that record on the way home. I was just reading the sleeve notes."

"What is it?" asks George, feeling the need to make conversation.

"Handel. George Frideric. It's Rinaldo... 'Lascia ch'io pianga'. It's rather good, don't you think?"

"It sounds very sad. Is it Spanish?" asks George remembering Bella's suggestion that Ken likes Spanish cuisine. He's rather out of his depth, having been brought up on a diet of skiffle and Frank Sinatra.

"No, no, no. It's in Italian, written by a German: 'Lascia ch'io pianga, mia cruda sorte'... 'Let me weep over my cruel fate'."

Oh, I'm sorry. What happened?"

"No, dear boy. That's a translation of the words."

"I see," says George, apologetically.

"Tea, Ken?"

"No thanks, Bel. Would you prefer a whisky, George?"

"No thanks. Tea will be fine."

And off trots Bella to the kitchen. Ken shows no curiosity as to how and why Bella has arrived on her motorbike with a new acquaintance, prompting George to think that it may be a regular occurrence.

"It says here on the sleeve notes," announces Ken, "that Handel used the aria in several forms. A few years before this version, the words apparently were 'Lascia la Spina, Cogli la Rosa'... 'Leave the Thorn, Take the Rose'. I rather like that.

2) Orford Mess

Don't you?"

George's head is spinning now. He's thinking *'leave the dragons, take the girl.'*

Early next day, George comes down from his makeshift guest room. Ken, not having expected the two visitors, had cleared a pathway through piles of Victorian memorabilia in the unused room so George could get to the plush bed that looks as if it had belonged to Miss Havisham, all lace and cobwebs. After a delightful breakfast in the Victorian conservatory, all Albinoni and aspidistras, George and Bella bid farewell to Ken and resume their three-wheeled journey.

George is getting used to Bella's right bend technique by now, enjoying the thrilling vision of levitation as the unoccupied sidecar lifts off the tarmac momentarily. He even finds enough confidence to take away one hand from her waist now and then to clear his face of wayward hair.

Then, disaster strikes. As they approach the village of Orford, an oncoming lorry swerves to miss a wobbling cyclist and veers into the path of the motorcycle. Taking evasive action, Bella pulls in tight to the road edge, forgetting for a moment the sidecar which meets full on with an innocent bystander... a bystander in the form of a traffic-sign post. Fortunately for the two of them, the bike and sidecar part company cleanly, the sidecar wrapping itself immovably around the post. Bella, with great presence of mind, checks her mirror, does a smart 'u' turn and pulls up at the scene of the collision.

"Oh, dear," she says, quite nonchalantly. "What an awful mess. Still, we can manage without the sidecar, can't we George?"

"I guess so," answers George, shivering with shock.

The lorry driver, having screeched to a stop, leaves his cab and rushes back to check if anyone is injured. The cyclist has disappeared. Bella and the lorry driver exchange insurance details. Someone seems to have called 999, and when the police arrive they take photographs and statements. Bella and George extricate most of their belongings as the local garage mechanic arrives, armed with cutting equipment, and sets to work on the scrap metal that once was a sidecar.

"Can it be repaired?" asks Bella.

The mechanic laughs: "Don't think so, do you, love? I was just considering offering it to the local art gallery."

"Oh, could you?" sighs Bella "I'd be ever so grateful. Ah, well, easy come, easy go."

George chivalrously writes the mechanic a cheque and, overladen with bundled possessions, the dauntless pair set off again, soon arriving at the Jolly Sailor pub in Orford.

"Any chance of a room?" asks Bella of the shifty-looking landlord who's in the process of pulling a pint of something that has the look of treacle.

"*Two* rooms, actually?" enquires George.

"Sorry," answers the treacle-meister, grinning with rationed teeth. "We only have two rooms here and they're booked for the rest of the week. You could try old Harry down on Doctor's Lane. He always has rooms available. Mind you, don't expect the Ritz. He's a bit down-to-earth, is old Harry. Bit of devil too. He believes in all that mumbo-jumbo about sea-dragons and water sprites. He's been here for years but nobody can quite make him out. He's lived on his own in that there cottage ever since I can remember. Anyway can I get you drinks?"

"Two pints of cider," suggests Bella, turning to George with a look that says 'you like cider, don't you?'.

"Fine," agrees George, who's never drunk cider in his life.

"Scrumpy then?" asks the landlord.

"That's fine," Bella confirms.

The landlord grins again, his few teeth shining like yellow beacons at the gateway of his black hole of a mouth. George pays for the drinks and they head towards a corner of the room,

2) Orford Mess

making to pass a character dressed in oilskins complete with sou'wester. Rosy-cheeked, and endowed with a seriously bushy beard, if red beards can be in anyway serious, the oily fellow says: "I overheard Jacob there telling you about old Harry. You want to be careful of the old boy if you go staying in his cottage. He's harmless enough, but I reckon he's a bit bonkers... all them tales about fairies and dragons and sea serpents. He reckons it was his mother, way back, who introduced him to the real world of the sea. She used to insist that she'd been a mermaid in a former life and that her father was a man whose ancestors had witnessed the old Orford Sea-dragon. Harry maintains that *he's* seen it too. I don't believe a word of it, but that's what he'll tell you."

"Thank you for the warning," Bella says.

"Yes," agrees George. "He sounds interesting though. I have a great interest in dragons myself. I'd like to meet him. What's your name by the way?"

The briny fellow bellows a laugh to wake the dead: "Harry. That's my name, young fellow. Old Harry some call me. Now let's talk terms on those rooms you wanted."

Bella laughs at his strange deception, a little nervously for, despite her apparent cavalier attitude to life, she's apprehensive, particularly when she notices the absence of two fingers from the old boy's right hand.

"Oh, dear," says Bella. "How on Earth did *that* happen?"

"Well, young miss. If we can agree on three pounds each a night, I'll tell you all about my two missing fingers, back in the cottage over a nice cup of tea."

"Three pounds each it is," says George, knowing that he'll be picking up the bill for both of them, yet not caring a fig for double-dipping into his nest egg.

It's dark now, and fog is descending, sea mist rolling in off the cold North Sea on a gentle north-easterly breeze. The village seems deserted. All sensible folk are snug in their homes or else in the pubs.

Despite her trepidations, Bella offers to pillion old Harry to his cottage, so as to know where it is, then come back for George. The old fellow grapples with some of the couple's baggage while George starts out on foot along Quay Street towards Church Street with the rest of their possessions.

"I'll put the kettle on, my dear," calls back Harry to Bella, as she starts the brief return journey.

She reaches George and he jumps up behind her on the Norton, holding on with a free hand as she accelerates away again, heading back for Doctor's Lane.

"What a stroke of luck," shouts George in Bella's ear. "All this way and we find the dragon man as soon as we arrive. I bet he has a rare tale or two to tell."

Bella answers with a brief thumbs up, to save from shouting over her shoulder, negotiating the turn into the High Street, then on again to old Harry's home. George dismounts and Bella pulls the bike onto its stand on the short, concreted drive. George knocks on the door and it falls open on silent hinges, revealing a rather messy Aladdin's cave of nautical knick-knacks; an old tarred net hangs from the ceiling, corks and glass fishing floats dangle entangled. Dead crabs, dried starfishes and sea urchins adorn the walls, as does an enormous, preserved dogfish in a glass case entombed and doomed to stare forever down old Harry's hallway.

"Fascinating," says George to Bella.

"A bit creepy though," replies Bella, whispering so that Harry won't hear her.

The kettle whistles merrily in the kitchen at the end of the hallway and entering they find Harry lifting it from the hot, lead-blacked stove.

"Sugar, dearies?"

"Two, please," George confirms.

"None for me, thank you," says Bella.

2) Orford Mess

"Right then, sit you both down through there… on the comfy sofa."

Old Harry follows them into the tiny lounge, carrying a tray laden with three mugs of sweet, spicy tea.

"Now then, you pair of adventurers. Let me tell you about my mermaid of a mother."

The two travellers sip at their tea, Bella making no mention of the unexpected sugar, as old Harry embarks on his fantastical story: "You'll have heard of the Orford Sea-dragon?"

"We certainly have, Harry. That's why we're here," confirms George, looking into his mug, thinking: '*this tea is really heady. It smells of jasmine and tastes of turmeric.*'

"Well, my mother was a mermaid in a former life," Harry goes on, "and her father's ancestors saw it."

"Jacob said as much, Harry," suggests Bella, not intimating that the landlord didn't believe a word of it.

"I know. I heard him. I reckon he says it to everyone I meet in the Jolly Sailor. Well *he* might say it's a load of old tosh, but *I* know different. I'm convinced that my mother had a particular ancestor… an ancestor with claws and with vicious teeth. These here fingers…"

"*Which* fingers?" George interrupts.

"The ones I ain't got," declares Harry, waving the two remaining fingers and the thumb at the couple. "I were born like this. It's hereditary. Handed down as you might say."

"Come off it, Harry. You must have lost them in an accident," suggests Bella.

"Well, *you* think what you like, but I've never had a full set of digits. I swear on my mother's tail. Anyway let me top up your tea, both of you. It's thirsty work listening to an old salt's tale… as thirsty a job as telling it."

Bella and George aren't that keen on the tea but, anxious to hear Harry's tale, they submit to another fill. Bella reminds him about the sugar.

"You see," Harry goes on, as he returns with three mugs of sweet tea, "I've seen it for myself, more than once. So I know for a fact that it never was killed. It survives to this day."

And so Harry tells them more, elaborating vastly on his description of the creature and its habits, then at length says: "I'll show you if you like… down on the flats it comes, at dead of night. We could go and look for it now. It ain't midnight yet is it. That's when I last seen it… at midnight."

Bella, hyped up with sugar and spice, has already put on her coat: "Come on George. You won't get another chance like this. Lead the way Harry," she says, draining the dregs of her second fill of the heady brew.

George follows suit, prompted into action more by Bella than by his burning desire to see dragons.

"Here," says Harry. "Put on these gumboots. It gets a bit soggy underfoot down on the fields near the river this time of year."

George puts down his emptied mug and, once they're all booted and coated, off they head towards the river, some way east of the village and over the fields. As they reach the river's edge, the foggy mist is clearing and the moon is rising way out over the sea. They sit themselves down in a sheltered thicket and wait. Midnight arrives and by now George is shivering, as is Bella who's losing some of her enthusiasm in the cold of the now cloudless night. The two of them are foggy-headed though, Harry's tea having fuddled their minds with its intoxicating scent. Harry is rubbing his hands, warming his incomplete set of fingers.

"I reckon we should get back, Harry," says George, not so enthusiastic now.

"Wait a while longer," insists the old salt.

"Just a short while then. I'm ready for bed," suggests George.

"Me too," says Bella, snuggling up to George, her enthusiasm for the chase defeated now.

2) Orford Mess

"Look, see! There! Beneath the moon. That splash in the water," calls out old Harry.

Sure enough, the silver-threaded path that is the moon's reflection on the restless waters is broken for a moment as some winged thing rises clear of the deep. Higher now it flies, in a sweeping arc above their heads. Looping around the lighthouse, it roars within an inch or two of their upturned faces, all fiery mouth and sea-scales shedding water. Then it darts towards the orb of the moon again and, as if running suddenly on empty, it dips in mid-flight and plummets seaward, parts the waves, and is gone.

"I almost missed it," says George, groggily.

"*I* saw it well enough," says Bella, bright as a button, then swooning in an instant in slumber into George's arms.

"Better wake the young thing up, George," says Harry. "You can't carry her all the way back."

The three of them step out, George and Bella stumbling sleepily over the fields. Before they're truly awake again, George and Bella are in bed, not stirring until morning comes.

George wakes with the coming of daylight, head throbbing. Turning restlessly, he rolls over and, tangled in the bedclothes, he startles at the scream of surprise that emanates from the depths of the blankets.

"George Crosby! What are you doing in my bed?"

"I was about to ask *you* that, Bella. I'm not paying Harry for two rooms. I don't care what he says. Otherwise I've wasted three quid."

"Ow! My head," she says.

"Mine too!" George empathises. "I reckon it must have been that tea."

"So, I'm not worth a pound or two extra then, George."

"Well you would be if you weren't in my bed."

"You certainly know how to pay a girl a compliment."

"I didn't mean it like that, Bella. You know I didn't. I'd have you in my bed anytime. No… I didn't mean it like that either. Look, we'd better get up. I could do with some breakfast to take off this headache. As long as Harry doesn't serve us any of that tea."

"I agree. Mind you, the sea-dragon was good, wasn't it? I was surprised to see it. I didn't believe Harry's tale at all, but maybe his mother really *was* a mermaid after all."

"I'd really like to think so," agrees George.

They rise and Bella goes to her intended room. They gather their things together, ready for a departure after breakfast, and head downstairs together to find Harry… but he's nowhere to be seen.

"Maybe he's gone out to get provisions for breakfast, Bella."

"Right. I'll make us a coffee while we wait for him, George."

They wait for an hour… no sign. They wait for another hour, and another coffee… no sign.

"This isn't good enough, is it Bella, I say we leave him three quid and go over to the Jolly Sailor. They'll be open by now. Jacob's sure to have something he can serve for a breakfast. And you never know, Harry may be there."

"I suppose so, George. But I hope Harry's okay. Anything could have happened to him. I was so groggy last night, I don't even recall him coming back up from the riverside with us. The sea-dragon could have eaten him for all I know."

"I wouldn't have thought so," says George. "That might be incest, Bella. Him possibly being related and all."

"Are you sure you don't mean cannibalism, George?"

"Don't be daft. That involves humans."

"Doesn't incest too?"

"Ah, of course. Mind you, if they *are* related, the sea-dragon might be part human."

"Let's go George. This is getting silly."

"Hey! Bella!"

2) Orford Mess

"What is it, George?"

"My wallet! It's down here on the floor... and look! My cash is gone! There was nearly twenty pounds in here. The thieving bugger!"

"You don't *know* that George."

"I'll have to pay for breakfast at the pub with a cheque. Then, if Harry's not there, we'll come back and find out what's going on with the cheeky sod."

They gather up their stuff and mount the Norton.

"Of course you can pay by cheque," says Jacob, the less-than-jolly landlord at the Jolly Sailor. "I warned you that old Harry is a bit of a devil. I doubt you'll see him down at the cottage. Not for a few days anyway. I reckon he's done this kind of thing once or twice before, but I've never been sure whether it's him or his guests that have been telling tales. He's always disappeared on some urgent errand or two when accusations have been made. He comes back eventually though."

"Well, we can't afford to wait. We're looking to move on today," says George, rather downcast.

"Put it down to experience, George," says Bella, brightly. "Think about it. We did see the sea-dragon. It was worth the cash just for that, wasn't it?"

"I suppose so, Bella," George says, smiling hesitantly.

"Oh, you *saw* the sea-dragon, did you?" says Jacob.

"Yes. We nearly missed it, but it was quite the most magical thing," says Bella.

"Oh dear. I meant to warn you... you drank some of his tea, didn't you. A mug of that stuff and you'll see anything you want to."

"Ah. We had two mugs each, actually," admits Bella, sheepishly.

"My, oh my. And you only saw sea-dragons. You were lucky. There's one or two have come by here and seen the real Old

Harry... the Devil himself. When I say real... that depends on your belief system, I suppose. Some believe he's real. Some even believe dragons are real."

"Blimey. Enough said, Jacob," coughs George. "You mean his tea's hallucinogenic."

"That's about the sum of it, my friend. There *is* one other thing though. You may not know it, but down there on the flats there's that Atomic Weapons Research setup. I imagine they get up to all sorts of things down there. I've always reckoned that's where Harry lost his fingers. I know bloody well that he had them when he was younger."

"Look, Jacob, thanks for all your advice," says George, after the pair have eaten their fill, "but we really must be going. Bella and I have an appointment with more dragons, in London."

"Do we?" says Bella. "That's the first I've heard on the matter, Mr. Crosby."

"I reckon you're screwier than old Harry," says Jacob, polishing his freshly washed pint glasses. "Dragons? They should be banned. They never did anyone any good, real or imagined."

George shrugs his shoulders in mild disagreement: "You just tell old Harry when you next see him that we've marked his card and I might just be back one day to retrieve my cash. I'll have his legs as easy as if I were grasping his mermaid-of-a-mother's tail."

"I'll tell him," promises Jacob. "It's about time someone gave him what for."

Shouldering their bags, George and Bella thank Jacob for breakfast and bid their farewells to the Jolly Sailor.

"So, London is it? Where exactly would you like me to take you now, my lord?" jokes Bella, knowing in truth that she's game for any adventure that's not too cold and foggy.

2) Orford Mess

"Well, I think maybe we could go to the British Museum to start with. I could show you *The Diabolical Maskquerade*. It depicts revellers in masquerade costumes and with partially clothed women. Mostly, they're masked as animals; a lion and a bear and such like. And there's Lucifer, and a Roman god, and a goddess, and there's a monstrous dragon on a ledge. Beyond the scene of this Hell-Fire-Club debauchery is a colonnade and an ornamental garden."

"You know, George, the dragon sounds the least interesting of all that lot. I'd have thought you'd be more interested in the partially clothed women."

"Don't be silly, Bella. You can find *them* anywhere. Well, not partially clothed, but…"

"No need to explain, George. A lot of men look upon women as dragons anyway."

"Well there *is* Mrs. Battlebury, in the reference library, back in Leicester."

"Look, George. If we set out for London now, we can get there in a couple of hours as long as we don't stop on the way. Where are we going to stay though?"

"Oh, we'll find somewhere. There was a place I saw near the museum."

"But it'll cost a fortune, George."

"That's okay… I still have a chequebook, don't I."

"If you insist then."

"In the meantime, thanks to old Harry, we'd better find a bank as soon as we get there, so that I can cash a cheque. We're bound to need some small change."

The Norton is eager to show its paces and they're away like the wind, heading first for Ipswich and Colchester then on to the Capital. They *do* stop, in Colchester, for refreshment, finding a small street café next to the bank and close by The George Hotel on High Street. They park the bike and step across the road.

"Hey, look George. The George Hotel. They must have known you were coming. No dragon mind you... Saint George must have slain him... or was it *her*?"

"I don't know, Bella, but do I detect you're making fun of me and my dragon quest? If so, I might just find my own transport, thank you very much. It's a serious business is dragons."

"Sorry, George. Just having a bit of fun. I wonder if your interest in dragons stemmed from the Saint George story."

"I never thought of that, Bella."

"Now it's *you* that's making fun isn't it, George."

"Did you know, Bella? The dragon that Saint George is supposed to have slain didn't have a name."

"Unless no one knew it or ever wrote it down."

"Well personally, I think it's metaphorical."

"That's a funny name for a dragon, George. It's more likely that it's symbolic."

"That's an even funnier name, Bella," laughs George, going along with the wordplay. "Truth to tell, as you well know, Saint George was supposed to have slain the dragon to save a maiden in distress."

"Not a maiden in *undress* then... like in your diabolical picture."

"Oh, no. I don't think the participants in 'my picture', as you call it, showed any intention of saving maidens, Bella. Quite the opposite, I'd say."

The smart young lad waiting on the customers in the coffee shop looks as if he should be in school serving up solutions to quadratic equations rather than serving up beverages. He comes to take Bella and George's order.

"Two coffees please, young man. And two pieces of that nice sponge cake I saw in the glass jar," says Bella.

"Is that all for now?" the lad asks politely.

"Unless you have any dragon broth?" teases George.

Bella nudges him in the arm: "Don't be silly, George. Behave

2) Orford Mess

yourself."

"I could ask for you, sir. What does it look like?"

"Well, my lad. It's actually distilled dragons' breath that's condensed into a soup-like state. It's fiery, hot as curry," replies George, persisting with his joshing.

"We do tomato soup, sir. That's red, but I don't think it's fiery."

"Just the coffee and cake will do, lad. I'm only joking."

Bella gives George a dagger of a stare as sharp and piercing as any lance that Saint George may have possessed: "Don't be so cruel, George," she smiles, seeing the funny side of it.

The boy soon returns with their tray of coffee and cake. He places each cup and saucer carefully on the table, then the plated portions of cake.

Taking a preliminary bite of his cake, George then gulps his coffee: "What the f…!" he splutters.

"What is it, George?" says Bella, worried that George is having some kind of fit.

The young boy, passing their table with a fresh tray of refreshments for the couple seated at the table beyond George and Bella's, smiles broadly: "That's the fieriest blend I could find, sir. I think it says cayenne on the label of the additional jar, sir. I brought you this jug of water, sir, thinking you may require it."

In a single motion, he places the jug on their table and passes smoothly on his way to the other table. Bella shrieks with laughter as George swallows down half a pint of water in one go, spluttering as he does. He laughs, thinking: *'serves me right.'*

"Better move on, Bella," suggests George, recovering. "If we want to reach London in good time."

"We'll be okay, as long as you can sort out a room at that place you have in mind."

"Just the one room?" he questions. "If you're sure?"

She smiles: "Well, I can't keep on spending so much of your

money, can I."

George pays the bill, leaving a tip under his saucer for the young waiter and they squeeze their way out of the shop which is filling now with ever more customers.

"Must be the attraction of the cayenne," suggests Bella.

"Ha, ha. Don't remind me. I don't think I'll be ordering spiced coffee for a while," says George.

"Looks like rain, George," decides Bella. "You'll have to get yourself a mac, or better still some leathers. Pity about the sidecar… you could have stayed dry in that, regardless."

"I wouldn't say no to a helmet either," says George. "As for sidecars, I could have been wrapped around the post of a traffic-sign by now, so I may give that one a miss thank you, Bella."

They set out, but despite Bella's riding skills and despite giving Chelmsford and Romford the cold shoulder, the two-hour journey to the Capital provides two hours of purgatory, especially for George. By the time they reach London they've stopped in country lay-bys twice for George to dash into the denuded winter bushes for a pee.

"It's all this rain, Bella. I didn't think the sky could hold so much water. I don't know how you've managed without a wee."

"I'm a woman, George."

"Anyway, when we get to London, one of the first things I'm gonna do is to get those leathers. Bloody weather!"

The hotel that George has in mind proves to have an attic room available for two nights, which is just as well for, at half the price of the rooms on the three main floors, it will help George not to spend his entire inheritance before he completes his dragon quest.

"A car, no. But a motorcycle, yes, madam. You're lucky that we have space in the yard, just by the bins, down the alley to the right of our foyer entrance," confirms the man on reception,

2) Orford Mess

Mr. Buncle, who looks as if he applied for the job when the Georgian hotel first opened.

"Thank you," offers George on Bella's behalf, shivering with wet and cold. "Now, what about a bath?"

"Oh no sir, I don't think we have room for a bath."

"No... a bath for me. I'm soaked to the skin."

"Oh, I see. Sorry, sir... I did wonder how you might have arrived on a motorcycle with a bath, unless perhaps it had wheels. I'm sorry your room is not en-suite, but you'll find a convenient bathroom on the floor below you. it's signposted from the lift lobby up there. Have a pleasant stay, Mr. and Mrs. Crosby."

"Thank you, Mr. Buncle," Bella smiles. "You're very kind."

Bella chuckles as she and George ride the ancient scissor-lift to the attic landing in search of their room and then look for the bathroom below.

"I had to bite my lip there, George," she laughs. "I almost said 'a good job we don't have a car, Buncle' to the dear old chap."

"Well it's a good job you didn't. He's a real treasure. Salt of the earth."

George gallantly declines Bella's offer to scrub his back and so she makes herself at home in their cosy little attic room, like some smug artist who's managed to sell her work *during* her lifetime and so moving into an up-market garret. She follows George with a bath, disappointed that there's no offer to scrub her back for *her* to decline gallantly. They decide to venture forth into the streets to find a place to eat. At the reception, they arrange with Buncle for laundry to be undertaken and George explains that they're intending to visit the British Museum the following day.

"How nice for you both. *I* remember when the museum was quite new."

"But it's over two hundred years old, Mr. Buncle."

"No, no. I mean when they reconstructed a lot of it, back in the thirties, just before the war. And, by the way, please call me Carlton. I prefer that to my surname. It's funny, but I think my parents had a rather eccentric sense of humour. You wouldn't believe the number of people who call me Car Buncle."

"Really," says Bella, struggling to contain herself. "Who'd have thought it?"

"Anyway, Mr. Buncle... Carlton, that is," says George. "I was wondering. Do you know of any dragons in this area of London? I'm hoping to find more in the museum, but there must be a few tales down on the streets."

"I can't really say that I do, Mr. Crosby. Mind you, my old dad used to say that Hitler's rockets were the Devil's dragons whereas most people called them doodlebugs. Then again, my old mum used to say that our Mosquitoes and Spitfires were God's winged unicorns, fending off the doodlebugs as best they could, down towards the coast, by tipping their wings to send them off course. But the blighters got through a lot of the time, didn't they."

"Fascinating," says George, "but no *real* dragons then?"

"The doodlebugs were real enough, sir. They did a lot of damage. Killed thousands too."

"Of course. Doodlebugs. I remember them vaguely now," decides George.

"They sound dreadful," says Bella, thoughtfully.

"Just a minute. Ah, yes," says the laconic Buncle. "Dragons! There's an old boy has a shop down on Greek Street. Soho way. Herbert's his name. His little shop is called *Herbie Dragons*. I bet *he* could find you some real dragons. It's only a fifteen-minute walk from here... well, ten minutes for you young 'uns."

"Thanks. Thanks, Carlton. We'll try it tomorrow. Just the ticket."

Over supper in a tiny bistro in Museum Street, George and Bella discuss the adventure that is life.

"I can't believe my luck in meeting you, Bella," say George,

2) Orford Mess

"but I hardly know you. We've been thrown together in such a whirlwind that I'm more intimate with your bed than with your broom. What I'm trying to say is that we're sleeping in the same room, yet I know hardly anything about you, or what you do. All I know is that you have a sophisticated brother, a slick motorbike and nice, long hair."

"What more do you need to know, George?" says Bella, sipping her Beaujolais. "Life should be driven by its mysteries, don't you think. *I* think that if you found your ideal dragon, the fun would be over, wouldn't it? Didn't Oscar Wilde say that it's better to travel in hope than to arrive?"

"I think that was Robert Louis Stevenson actually, Bella. Mind you, I think Wilde did say something about life being far too important to talk seriously about. And anyway, I wouldn't go so far as to think of you as a dragon, even if I did know more about you. You're nothing like that Mrs. Battlebury."

"Well, there you are, George. You don't really need to know about my history, nor I yours. We only need explore what we have ahead of us. That's far more romantic."

"You're so right, Bella. You remind me of something I came across once in the library back home when I opened a book about smallpox."

"What a wonderful literary choice, George."

"Well, there was this aristocrat, a Lady Mary Wortley Montagu. She introduced the idea of smallpox inoculation into Britain after she'd been to Turkey, but the medical profession weren't impressed with the idea. Frustrated by this attitude, she's known to have suggested that if we tell only of what has gone before we're dull, yet if we tell of anything new we're laughed at as being romantic."

"But dragons have 'gone before', George. They're of a bygone age, aren't they?"

"But the belief in them isn't bygone, Bella. I for one believe they still live."

"You're right, of course. Let's see what we can find in the museum."

"But first, a trip to *Herbie Dragons*, Bella," says George, excitedly downing the last of the Beaujolais.

Morning dawns. An eager sun breaks through the drawn-back lace curtains of the attic room, slanting sharp on ruffled, white bedclothes.

Bella heads for the bathroom on the second floor, having finished her light continental breakfast. George is tackling the last of his full-English, intending to follow her with his ablutions before tackling the dragon hunt.

"We'll be out and about all day, Carlton," says George as he and Bella set out for Greek Street. We'd like to eat in this evening. The boeuf bourguignon for me and the chicken parmigiana for Mrs. Crosby, please."

"7.30, sir? That's the usual time."

"Yes, of course. As suggested on the menu placed in our room. We shall look forward to it."

Taking Oxford Street, they turn onto Soho Street and strolling in the sun across Soho Square Garden they come to Greek Street. About a hundred yards down, they find the shop. The frontage is painted in a drab olive green, the Victorian window frames picked out in bright crimson. Above the half-glazed door, a sign projects. It depicts two fierce dragons in full flight, seemingly battling with each other over a maiden who swoons upon an oriental carpet. The dragons' nostrils breathe actual blue smoke onto passers-by, fuelled no doubt by some mechanical smoke-producing contraption set within the bowels of the dark, intriguing shop.

They enter, trepid, to the trill of a little spring-loaded bell at the head of the door frame.

"Wow, George," whispers Bella.

"Blimey, Bella," murmurs George.

2) Orford Mess

They're the only customers in evidence, though a curtained doorway appears to lead to some other room in the nether darkness. Herbie springs up unexpectedly behind the heavy oak counter, seemingly attached by a taut string to the closing door.

"Good day, kind people. Welcome to the realm of dragons. We have all sorts here; large ones and small ones, old ones and young, red ones and green, and white too. We have wyverns and wyrms. We have drakes and serpents and griffons and lizards and snakes. There's Indian dragons, Japanese dragons and Chinese dragons. And best of all, we have Norse dragons."

"Blimey, Bella," George repeats. "I don't think we need the British Museum. We've struck gold, thanks to dear old Car Buncle."

"It's certainly dragon-ish in here, George," she replies.

"May we call you Herbie, Herbie?" asks George.

"There's no reason why not," hisses Herbie… a patronising sort of hiss. "Provided *I* may call *you* Bella and George."

Seeing their surprise at his knowing their names, Herbie adds: "My ears are sharp as needles, my dears."

"Well, do you have any books on dragons?"

"Is the world round, my dear George? Do you have any particular type of dragon in mind, my friend?"

"A *real* one, of course, Herbie."

"They're *all* real as far as I'm concerned," says Herbie.

Bella can't help but notice that all the inanimate models of mythical beasts in the shop appear to be as real as a man with three legs would be: '*pull the other one,*' she thinks.

"But the most real of our beasts," continues Herbie, "is our biggest. He's Norse. He's Jörmungandr, though he's not what you might call a dragon, and we *do* only have him in a book. He's far too large to fit into a small shop like this. He could be anywhere in the world right now. Indeed he could be *everywhere* in the world right now. Some call him 'Ouroboros' and some the 'World Serpent'."

"Blimey," remarks George yet again, mouth open wide, incredulous.

"Follow me into the other room, both of you," beckons Herbie.

Through they go, each in turn waving the curtain aside, passing from dusky room to dusky room. And there they spy the smoke machine, clanking and puffing its vapours to the beat of an oily piston.

Herbie blows the dust from a large leather-bound tome on a corner shelf. The book looks to be long ages old... an antique of antiquity itself:

'Jörmungandr - the Tale of the Tail of a Serpent'

"Four pound ten? That's a bit steep, Herbie."

"Well, George. It's a very rare book. I've never seen the like of it before. You'll see it was printed and published long ages ago."

"1959 it says here. That's not very old."

"That's just my catalogue reference, George... in pencil. If you turn the leaf, you'll see it was published here in London in 1666. The first translation into English from the Icelandic."

"But four pound ten?"

"I could let you have it for three pound nineteen and six, but that's the very best I can do."

"Then make it four pounds, Herbie, and you can keep the change."

"Thank you, George. I'll wrap it for you. Good luck with your search. I'm sure you'll find our Robo the serpent if you search everywhere for him. In fact, I'll throw in this little pocket guide for a pound":

'A Guide to Mythical Beasts of England and Wales'

2) Orford Mess

"There's very little detail in it, but it'll give you some ideas for your searching around. In the meantime, can I interest you in a dragon or two?"

"Not today, Herbie, thank you," George replies. "We're looking for *live* ones."

George hands over a five pound note, places the wrapped books securely under his arm, and he and Bella leave the shop, passing into the bright light of day, heading back to the hotel for their evening meal.

Herbie smiles as the tinkle of the little doorbell signals their departure. Lifting a large leather-bound book looking suspiciously like *Jörmungandr - the Tale of the Tail of a Serpent*, he opens it to the first page and writes 1959 in pencil.

"These are not selling as well as I expected," he whispers to himself, as he takes an old box from a shelf behind him and sprinkles dust on the book. "Perhaps I should reduce the ticket price," he hisses.

-o-o-o-

3) London Spurning

"Did you find your dragon, sir?" asks Carlton Buncle, back at the hotel.

"Sort of," declares George, proudly. "The beast I particularly want to find is in a book... *this* book. A very old book in fact. Now I intend to look for 'Our Boris' the serpent without delay, don't we, Bella?"

"Anything you say, George. I'm along for the ride wherever the Norton takes us."

"You know, sir, your question about dragons set me thinking. I racked my brain and the only other recollection I have of a dragon in London is from a woman who dropped in here last year to see our waitress, Lucy. The woman mentioned that Samuel Pepys once visited an inn called the Green Dragon, over by Lambeth Hill."

"Who's Samuel Peeps," asks Bella. "Does he live near here?"

"I don't think so, Bel," explains George, with great authority. "He was a famous bloke back in the days of King Charles II. He owned a dairy. Famous for it, he was."

"I think you'll find that was a *diary*, sir," suggests Carlton. "I believe that may be the only way it's known that he visited the Green Dragon."

"Ah," says George, somewhat deflated.

"Never mind, George," says Bella. "It could be worth starting the search over that way tomorrow while we're still in London. Let's skip the British Museum, then we'll have all day."

"Oh, I don't think the inn's still there, my dear. That area's a lot different now to what it was back in the day."

"Well, I still reckon we could look," says George. But in the meantime, after dinner, we'll retire to our room and have a good look through these two books. It's all so absorbing."

"Very well, sir, madam. Is it one continental breakfast and

3) London Spurning

one full-English again tomorrow?"

"Yes please, Carlton," says Bella. "In the room again, George?"

"Yes. That's fine," agrees George.

"This little pocket guide is marvellous, George. *A Guide to Mythical Beasts of England and Wales*. It must be older than that massive slab of a book you've had your nose in for the last hour. It was printed here in London in 1470 by William Caxton."

"I doubt it, Bel. *He* didn't introduce printing until later, towards the end of that century. Now Johannes Gutenberg, I could believe."

"Okay, smart arse. So how come your book says 'Printed in Taiwan' on the back."

"What? Where? Oh, yes," sighs George, crestfallen. "That damned Herbie. I bet it was 1959 after all. Still, they probably have loads of dragons in Taiwan. They do in China and in Japan, after all. I'd take the book back to him in Greek Street if it weren't so captivating. I'm not sure I like London so much after all though, thanks to that shyster Herbie."

"Don't be like that, George," Bella says. "These books have given us something to think about, regardless. Something to explore."

"I suppose you're right. This here Norse serpent, Jörmungandr, is colossal. The Nordic stories tell that he's one of the three children of Loki and Angrboda. Then the Greeks called him Ouroboros. It actually says in here that the Egyptians knew of him too, way before. The legends would have it that he circled the world, chasing and devouring his own tail. A symbol of the cycle of rebirth and renewal."

"You mean he met himself coming back?"

"No, Bel. More like he met himself going forwards."

"Sounds a bit pointless, doesn't it? We had a *dog* that chased

47

his own tale constantly, and that never got *him* anywhere."

"Well, that's different. Anyway, much as I'd like to chase him around the world, I think realistically that we can only try to find Our Boris here in England. Even five thousand pounds wouldn't stretch all the way around the world."

"I can't see that we're likely to find Our Boris in England, George."

"I don't need to find him *literally*, Bel. Just evidence of him would do to be going on with. This book covers a lot of the legend, but it doesn't seem to pin him down to anywhere specific. Mind you, Herbie did say he's anywhere and everywhere. Yet then again, the myths all say he was slain."

With that, they fall to reading their dragon literature in silence for a while, then Bella looks up thoughtfully: "That big book is going to weigh heavy in your rucksack, George. And without the sidecar, we'll have a job even to stow any extra clothes. I only have two pairs of knickers and by the smell of you, you only have one pair of underpants."

"That's just silly. You know they're in for laundry with dear old Car Buncle."

"Then I hope you have at least *two* pairs."

"I'll tell you what, Bel. We'll get extra clothes tomorrow. And a new sidecar to put them in as soon as we can."

"It's a deal, George. And I promise to watch out for oncoming lorries."

"*And* traffic-signs?"

"Yes… and traffic-signs, George. And don't forget those leathers either."

They go down for drinks in the hotel bar. George leaves his beast of a book. Bella brings the pocket guide.

"Look, George. There's a place in Sussex called Lyminster that was once home to a Knucker."

"Well, I hope they caught him for it, Bel."

"No. A Knucker is a water-dragon, George. It's said that they lived in ponds called Knucker holes. This one lived near the church and made off with the village girls until a local man killed it and claimed the king's daughter as a prize."

"Fine, but surely that can't be the World Serpent, Bel. Mind you, Jörmungandr is associated with the seas and the oceans, so ponds might have attracted him. As for dragons being killed, my guess is that most of them are invincible. In fact, I'd be surprised if any of them are dead, in truth."

"Well the Orford one was a bit of a disappointment in the end. And I suppose the Knucker does sound a bit small-time to be Our Boris, George. Let's face it, he'd need to be pretty big if he was going to stretch around the whole world. But I guess that it's still worth a look."

"And I bet Lyminster's not far from the sea, Bel. It would be nice to smell the sea air, don't you think?"

"Excuse me, sir," interrupts Lucy, the waitress, setting down a tray with two beers that Bella and George have ordered. "Carlton was just telling me about your interest in the Green Dragon that Samuel Pepys visited."

"Well no actually, miss. I didn't know about it until Carlton mentioned it. Why is it everyone knows about a pub called the Green Dragon, Bel?"

"How do you mean, George?"

"Well, there was a bloke on the bus near Market Harborough who mentioned one that's in a village near there. I ignored him, I suppose."

"Oh, right," says Bella.

"Well, madam," says Lucy, addressing Bella in preference to the dismissive George, "my aunt Vicki lives over Lambeth Hill way. She says her basement shop is on the very site of the old inn. She tells everybody about when Samuel Pepys stayed there."

"You mean that Peeps fellow stayed in your aunt's shop?"

"No, of course not, madam… in the inn, silly. The Green

Dragon has been a long time gone by her account."

"I'm afraid I hadn't even heard of Samuel Peeps before Carlton mentioned that some woman told him about the old inn," answers Bella.

"That's it. That would have been my aunt Vicki. I hardly ever see her these days. She came over to see me last year about a family cake recipe. She bakes and sells cakes you see... down in her basement shop. It's well worth a visit. It's called 'Victoria's Plunge'. If you go, tell her I recommended the shop. She's rather eccentric, but her cakes are delicious."

"Well, what are we waiting for, George? We can call in when we've found you those leathers and we've got our hands on my knickers."

Lucy smiles as she retreats with the empty tray thinking: *'maybe my aunt isn't the oddball one after all.'*

"Oh, yes," declares aunt Vicki, serving George and Bella each a large slice of fresh sponge cake. "The Green Dragon used to be *here* alright. See that deep cut in the stone barrel-vaulting above your head... that was Oliver Cromwell, that was."

"I didn't realise he was that tall," George says, stuffing a mouthful of sponge cake into his mouth.

"No, dearie," It was his *sword* that did it. He and his men came into the inn, towards the end of the Civil War, looking for secret royalists. Brandishing swords and pikestaffs and all sorts they were."

"Doesn't sound very civil to me," says Bella. "And your Lucy told us it was Samuel Peeps that came in here, not Oliver Cromwell."

"Him too," says Victoria. "All the big wigs came in here. Not that Cromwell wore a wig mind you. But Pepys was here about ten years later."

"So what did Pepys think of the Green Dragon then?" asks George. "It's dragons we're interested in more than diarists."

3) London Spurning

"Well," aunt Victoria whispers, with an air of mystery, beckoning the couple to lean in closer. "Other ears may be listening, and dragons have the sharpest ears of all, you know."

George looks over his shoulder, half-expecting to see some terrible winged beast leering at him menacingly.

"You see," aunt Vicki continues, "the history books have it that the Great Fire of London in 1666 was probably started by a spark from the oven of a baker by the name of Thomas Farriner over in Pudding Lane, near to where Pepys lived. I know about these things you see, being a baker myself. The histories tell too of a Frenchman accused of starting the fire deliberately… he was later hanged. Scapegoated I reckon. Now, 'farine' is the French for flour, so I reckon Farriner was French… one and the same."

"But what about the Green Dragon?" asks George. "It's dragons we're after. Not bakers and arsonists."

"Ah, now. This is the rub, my boy. I recovered a treasured document found bricked up in this very cellar that speaks of a mild tempered green dragon that had lived quietly for many years in an attic room above. There was another dragon, an awesome red dragon, that lived over Farriner's bakery. Then, a great rivalry developed between the two of them, for that red dragon was well fed on fresh bread and pies, while the green dragon *here* had little more than beer. Over time, the green dragon became habitually intoxicated; drunk on beer and drunk with envy, the latter of which you might just expect from a green dragon. In a fit of hunger and of anger, it flew high into the air and, travelling to the east of the city, plunged the bakery into devastating flame. The red dragon perished and on that fateful night the envious green dragon flew high and away over the Atlantic ocean never to dwell in London again."

"Can we see this document, Victoria?" asks George excitedly. "It all sounds highly unlikely, and yet fascinating."

"My dears. I would show you willingly, but only last week, I unwittingly lit my stove with it. It is no more."

"Oh, dear. How tragic," says Bella.

"I'm so sorry to hear that, Victoria," adds George. "You must be devastated."

"Not really, love. I still have my cakes... and the memories. And I'm sure I heard the whisper of wings as the old document went up in flames. I guess the old bugger is around somewhere, as quiet as you'd like now that he's been off the beer for all these years."

The couple bid the cake maker a subdued farewell, thanking her for the cake, and as they walk out into the street, George turns to Bella.

"Piffle, don't you reckon, Bel?" he says, spurning London and its green and red dragons.

"Well, *I'm* not so sure. *She* certainly seems to believe it all. It's no more spurious than all the other stuff we've come across."

"Well, if this green dragon exists, or even existed, then I'm sure it's not Our Boris; it might stretch to Pudding Lane, but it would never make it round the world."

Bella shrugs her shoulders ambivalently and, as they make to cross the street, a wisp of a breeze flows out through the closing door. Swirling upwards to the skies, it's gone, and all is calm again.

Back at their hotel, George and Bella find that the laundry has been returned, clean, crisp and dry.

"Well, Lucy," says George to the waitress, "your aunt Victoria was an experience I must say, but I'm afraid her dragons aren't quite what we're looking for. Mind you, her sponge cake was delicious and well worth the trip. As you know, we'll be moving on tomorrow but I wonder, do you know anywhere in the area that sells motorcycle leathers?"

"Funny you should ask, Mr. Crosby. You see my uncle Ben has a shop on Neal Street, to the west of Drury Lane. I'm sure

3) London Spurning

he could fit you in, so to speak. You won't believe it, but he's aunt Vicki's husband. They separated years ago. He was always tinkering with motorbikes and if there's one thing he couldn't stand, it was Victoria sponge cake. He said it was the strawberry jam... He was in a motorcycle accident when he was a young man and it reminded him of the blood. I don't see much of *him* either, but you'd love his shop."

"That sounds just the ticket," says George, grateful for the pointer. "I need some underpants too. I think we have time before dinner to fit in a little shopping spree, don't we, Bel?"

"I guess so, George. I need those knickers, and a few other things as well, but I'm a bit short of cash."

"Don't worry, Bel. We have cash now as well as the chequebook."

"Oh, I nearly forgot," says Lucy. "Carlton has the afternoon off, but he said he'd remembered some more dragons. His memory is getting so bad these days. He'd forgotten that he'd arranged the afternoon off until I asked if he'd played bridge lately. Not like him to swear, but he said 'Oh, bugger! I'm supposed to be in Fleet Street in an hour, meeting the others'. Then off he dashed, telling me about his dragons as he put on his coat and hat."

"So tell us, Lucy. Which dragons are these?" asks George, intrigued, eager to explore any possibilities while the pair are still in London, despite the disappointment of aunt Vicki's Pepysian myth.

"Well, they're down by Temple Gardens on the Victoria Embankment. Carlton says that they were put there last year after the Coal Exchange on Lower Thames Street was demolished. Then he said that there's another one, near the law courts on Fleet Street at the old Temple Bar. It was the reminder about Fleet Street that jogged his memory."

"Sounds like they might be worth a look," says George.

"Does your uncle sell motorbike sidecars, Lucy?" asks Bella.

"I doubt it, Mrs. Crosby, but I'm sure he'd know someone who does."

And with that, after a quick visit each to the second floor bathroom to freshen up, off go Bella and George on another trek.

"Sorry," says uncle Ben. "I'd love to sell motorbikes and sidecars, but I just haven't the room. Now, my best mate Barry is the one you want. He's over in New Malden. It's only about an hour away by bike. What bike have you got, George?"

"It's *my* bike actually, Ben," says Bella, with an air of pride, able to shoot down Ben's innocently misogynistic comment. "It's a '57 Norton Dominator."

"Wow! Lucky you. Smashing bike, Bella. Tell you what. Why don't you give Barry a call, see what he can do?"

"Great. I will. We're thinking of heading that way tomorrow as it happens, aren't we George."

"That's right, Bel. To look for a Knucker… in Lyminster."

"Well, each to his own, George," says Ben. "Anyway, about these leathers. I have some beauties in from Italy; pale blue, lime green, all the colours you could think of."

"I reckon I might just stick with black, thanks Ben."

"If you insist," says Ben. "I suppose the bright colours are a bit pretentious. But this *is* London. You must have heard of the swinging sixties. It's all taking off these days; Carnaby Street, Portobello Road. Life's gonna be a riot of colour."

"You mean a riot of Mods and Rockers don't you?" says Bella. "You wouldn't want to have been in Brighton and Margate back in May. Especially not in powder blue leathers."

"Well, I could do you a nice fishtail parka in army green. I like to diversify where I think there's a market. I'll throw in a bullseye for free."

"Sounds good, Ben," says George.

"Don't think you're getting on my Norton dressed in a parka,

3) London Spurning

George Crosby."

"Only joking, Bel."

After much deliberation, George is kitted up with Italian leathers in a discreet charcoal grey. They each take full face crash helmets emblazoned with dragon-flames. So as not to be cluttered with their bounty, they arrange to pick it up on their way back from their trek to the embankment.

Meanwhile, Bella has a good chat on the phone with Barry who assures her that he can have a sidecar, suitable for the Norton, at his garage before lunchtime the next day.

Down on the Embankment, the couple marvel at the sweeping beauty of the Thames. The river, rolling powerful to the sea, sweeps the history of England, day-by-day, out into the lower reaches of the North Sea. And beyond the estuary, news of those bygone events meets with the history of France and of Belgium and of the Netherlands; a timeless rendezvous of naval conflicts, of trade and everything else that politics and the pursuit of wealth even now dictate.

They stroll a distance, and encounter the pair of London dragons with their Saint George-flagged shields.

"I don't know about you, Bella, but these don't really inspire me to thinking of the World Serpent. They're more like the brainchild of some entrepreneur keen to promote London's image than to acknowledge the true power of dragons in the world. Let's hope the Temple Bar dragon is more sympathetic to the reality. I get the feeling that your Knucker will be rather more promising, don't you?"

"Well it's so nice of you to say so, George. Let's just hope you're right. I'd hate you to be disappointed even more than you are with these *London* specimens."

The Temple Bar dragon proves to be more impressive, but no more suggestive of vivacious dragon-fire.

The pair wend their way back towards Neal Street via several clothes shops which deal in underwear and other rather more desirable but bulkier items. With arms almost full, they then collect their other bulky purchases from Ben the biker, wondering how they'll carry all their retail acquisitions on the bike pre-sidecar. Helmets on, to free up hands and arms, they head back to the hotel and a well-earned rest before preparing to move on in the morning.

They reach *'Barry's Bike Bonanza'* in New Malden and George is sinking under the weight of the parcels strapped on his back with the aid of much strong string and many plastic bags supplied by Carlton Buncle.
 Thankfully, George has mastered the skill of riding pillion 'no hands'. Despite wearing his leathers, there are a good few items desperately requiring the use of a sidecar. To top it all, rain has set in and whilst their leathers and their helmets have provided shelter from the elements, it's a cheer-sapping ride.
 Bella pulls the bike onto its stand and removes her helmet.
 "Hey, guys. Pleased to meet you," announces Barry as he greets them outside his workshop, wiping his greasy hands on a rather oily cloth. He sports a conspicuous 'Elvis' quiff and sideburns to match. "You're nothing like I expected on the phone, Bella," he adds warmly, ignoring George who's dismounting preoccupied with subduing his excess baggage.
 "Is that good then, Barry?" Bella replies, glancing at the mechanic's hand as he reaches to place it on her shoulder, ushering her towards the workshop.
 "Is it good?" echoes Barry. "Is Mahatma Gandhi Catholic? I thought for a minute you were Honor Blackman."
 "Bad then. *She's* ancient. She's about forty, and she blonde."
 "Nothing wrong with that, Bella darlin'. But I suppose it was the leathers that did it. They're almost as impressive as your bike. Anyway, I've managed to find that sidecar, just like I promised. I've just been buffing her up. She's looking like a

3) London Spurning

black diamond with all that wax and elbow grease."

Barry squeezes Bella by her captive shoulder under pretence of excitement at his successful acquisition of the sidecar. Bella, feeling increasingly uneasy, glances back to George, hoping for a rescuing hand. George is red-faced, more from fighting with parcels and backpacks than from anger at slimy Barry's obvious chatting up of his Bella.

"I'll catch up in a second, Bel," he manages, dropping his helmet. "Shit," he adds, frustratedly.

"Just call me Bazza, doll," Barry implores her, continuing with his siege tactics as they reach the sidecar.

"I think you'd better ease off, Bazza," she says, turning to stare him in the eye. "My girlfriend back home might get jealous. And you don't want to meet *her* on a jealous day. She's six-foot three in her stocking feet and she has a black belt in bloke-bashing."

"Bloody hell. Sorry, babe. I didn't mean to…"

Barry the mechanic releases his grip as his response tails off to an anxious silence. George catches them up, breathless.

"Sorry, Bel. Hurry up and agree a price on this sidecar," George says, squeezing her tight and kissing her cheek; having caught an inkling of Barry's behaviour, it's an effort at signalling to the mechanic that she's spoken for.

"I'd look out if I were you, mate. Her girlfriend will be after you," says Barry.

George is not sure what on Earth the mechanic is talking about, but is proud to think that the timely kissing of his girl has put the greasy motorbike vendor off the scent.

"Okay, my lovely," says Bella, deliberately delivering a confusing message to Barry. "How much do you want for it?"

"Sixty quid, love," he suggests timidly. "That includes the spit and polish."

"Oh, dear. I don't think my girlfriend would be happy with sixty quid."

"Err, fifty then," he replies, still unconvincingly.
"Forty," says Bella.
"Sure. Forty's fine."
"George. Write the man a cheque."
"Okay, Bel. Anything to get these packs off my back. They're getting wetter by the minute."
George writes the cheque and hands it to Barry.
Bella shakes Barry's hand and, smiling, turns to George: "Come on, girlfriend," she says to him. "Let's get hitched."
"But…" manages biker Baz, "I thought she… *he* was six-foot three?"
"Oh, that's my *other* girlfriend, Bazza."
"Ah," he mumbles. "That explains it."
George decides not to ask.

The rain has stopped by the time they clear Cobham and by Ripley the roads are dry.

George, free of flowing hair thanks to their helmets, but plagued by a steamed-up visor, is taking in the passing view as best he can. The countryside is December winter-drab now and he wonders why on Earth he'd chosen to start his crusade at this time of year. Then again he thinks: *'If I'd left my quest 'til summer, I may never have met Bella.'*

By Guildford, George is enjoying the throaty sound of the engine as Bella puts the bike through its paces; gear changes, rubber squealing on the bends, throttle opening, sidecar soft-top flapping. He closes his eyes and imagines he's riding on the back of some majestic dragon over far-flung mountain ranges, with the sun going down beyond mist-shrouded, snow-capped peaks.

Come Petworth, they stop outside a quaint old teashop.

"It's a bit nippy now, Bel. A nice hot drink will go down a treat."

"And a couple of rounds of toast I reckon, George… bliss."

3) London Spurning

Inside, chattering Sussex ladies are hobnobbing, retired from the world of teaching, dentistry or perhaps esoteric entrepreneurial endeavours into a world of bridge playing, cheese and wine parties, and amateur philanthropic pursuits. Most are in their sixties or seventies and appear to be dressed for an Alpine clime or even an Alpine climb; expensive walking boots, silk headscarves and warm fleeces with subtle Harrods' logos.

"Two rounds of buttered toast twice, please," calls George over the Sussex chatter and the steaming water dispenser, "and a tea for me… black if you will. What about you, Bel?" he adds, turning to his leather-clad partner.

Bella hesitates as she glances down the blackboard that lists every blend of tea imaginable; black, green (with or without mint), Earl Grey, Oolong, Ceylon… The coffee list is even longer. She deliberates, unable to decide. The queue builds behind them. At last she asks: "Do you do Oxo?"

The Sussex ladies' chatter dies as if they're smitten by a thunderbolt. The water steamer hisses. George nudges her: "Bel, behave."

"But I *like* Oxo, George. It really goes nicely with buttered toast."

"I'm sorry, my dear. I'm afraid the only savoury drink we can offer is Marmite."

"Oh. No, thank you. I'm not even fifty-fifty when it comes to Marmite. I'll have a black tea instead, please."

"Two black teas it is then, thank you," says George, coughing to hide his embarrassment.

"I'll bring them over to you when the toast is ready," confirms the woman behind the counter.

The Sussex ladies' chatter resumes and the water steamer is introduced to George's pot of nascent black tea beverage.

A few miles before they reach Arundel, Bella spies a

commotion ahead and slows down to a halt, kicking down the gears. A farm tractor and trailer has shed its load of hay bales. The bales have spilled across the carriageway and the road is blocked. The pair seem to be the first ones on the scene and pulling onto the grass verge Bella dismounts, removes her helmet and offers assistance to the forlorn farmer who's sat on the back of the empty trailer. George joins them.

"Thanks, lass," says the farmer, easing himself down off the trailer, "but my young 'un has gone up ahead to the top field with a motorist so he can pick up the bale lifter. Far too many here to move by hand. If only I'd tied them on... the lad said as much."

The farmer looks not a day under ninety-five years old.

"Couldn't your lad have lifted them by hand?"

"I don't think so. He's comin' up seventy-five next week himself... and he's got a wooden leg... lost his real one on the Somme. Even the *leg's* nearly fifty years old... I reckon it's got woodworm. I told him he should get a new one, but he says he didn't like the look of the metal one the National Health offered him. He just mutters about it probably goin' rusty, but one day that wooden one'll snap off unexpected... just when he needs it."

"Doesn't he need it all the time?" asks George.

"Well, I suppose he does really, thinking about it. Anyway, he'll be back soon. It's not far."

So who loaded the bales back at the farm if your lifter's up ahead?"

"Ah, that were the missus. *She's* only sixty-nine you see. Built like a brick privy, she is, pardon my French."

George looks at him sideways, his brain calculating the years.

"She's the young 'un's stepmother; my second wife you see," explains the old boy. "The first one ran off to sea with a sailor."

Bella, despite the old chap declining her help, has already loaded four bales back onto the trailer: "Come on, George. We

3) London Spurning

can't wait all day. The traffic will be building."

George hesitates. He's not really built for lifting hay bales, but he sets to, wanting to impress Bella lest she develop a hankering for someone more macho, like biker Baz.

By the time the 'young' lad returns with the lifter, the bales are back in place on the trailer and the accumulated traffic is dispersed.

"So how come you're shifting all these bales this time of year?" Bella asks the farmer's 'boy'.

"Ah, that's a long story really, lass. It's enough to say that we need them to be in the barn in the top field. We were goin' to sell off half the herd you see, but the bottom fell out… out of the market that is, not the herd. Anyway, look, we're grateful for your help. If you want to follow us up to the barn while we unload again, we can go back to the farm after that for a tot of rum. I like my navy rum and I don't normally like sharin' it with anyone, but seein' as how you've been so kind, I think I can spare it. Not sure about your bloke though… he only shifted five bales."

With the bales stashed… and roped this time, Bella kick-starts the Norton. George is safely pillioned and they move off gently, following the Fordson tractor and its trailer on the road towards Arundel. They make out the imposing castle, high on the skyline in the middle distance.

'Now there's a fitting haunt for dragons,' thinks George. *'Worth a visit, perhaps.'*

"Elsie! Visitors!" calls out the old boy.

"What have I told you, Joe? Bringin' back visitors unannounced. I'm in my dishabille," calls a disembodied voice from within the dilapidated Georgian farmhouse.

"Don't you worry about that, Else. They ain't fussy. Just look what they're wearin'… leather fandangly costumes, they are," says Joe. "They look like they've come out of the sixties or somethin'."

Bella smiles to herself.

"We're *in* the sixties, dad. And *I* quite like them," protests young Tommy as he, Joe and the bikers enter the large farmhouse kitchen to be greeted by Big Elsie, who's stoking the wood-burning stove.

"What have I told you, Tom? Don't go messin' with them sixties. They're the bane of civilisation."

"Well it's my choice, Elsie. I *am* seventy-five years old. I can make my own decisions."

"You're *not* seventy-five, Tom. Not 'til next week. And look what the sixties have done to my sister Joanie, down in Lyminster. What with them Beatles and that Mary Quant. It ain't natural. And as for Joanie messin' with fairies and dragons and stuff. What's the world comin' to?"

George's ears prick up at the mention of Lyminster and dragons.

"Can't you tell her to stop pickin' on me, dad?"

"I daren't do that son. More than my life's worth to mess with Big Else."

"Well, I reckon I could get my wooden leg covered with that there leather," says Tom, attempting to assert his autonomy. "Especially the grey. I'd be a real hit at the Young Farmers'."

"Now you're talkin' nonsense, lad," says Tom's dad. "Where have you hidden the glasses, Elsie. I've offered these kind people a tot of my rum."

"Flippin' heck, Joe. Givin' that rum away? You're goin' the same way as your lad, you are. The glasses are in the usual place on the Welsh dresser. Are you goin' blind as well as daft?"

Joe heads for the glasses. He pours them all a tot and raises a toast: "Here's to friendship… and young women with strong muscles."

"And young men with grey leathers," adds Tommy.

3) London Spurning

"I honestly believe the Somme took more than your leg, Tom," says Elsie.

"Go easy on the boy," says Joe, pushing his luck on the Big Else front. "*I were lucky enough to be too old to go to war, but Tom got caught with that first lot. Horrendous it were. I seen it on the telly… all barbed wire and gas it was."

"I know, Joe dear," says Elsie, in a surprisingly conciliatory tone. "Sorry, Tom. I didn't mean to snap."

She raises her glass and toasts: "To Tom and all the other Tommies. We have a lot to thank you for."

Joe, Bella and George raise their glasses and echo her words.

"Tell me, Elsie," ventures George, "what's this about your sister and dragons? You see, I'm on the trail of the World Serpent and I'm hoping to find the Lyminster Knucker. I'm sure it's still alive, living in a pond somewhere down this way."

"I'm looking too, George," Bella reminds him.

"Oh, Blimey. Not *more* of you," says Elsie, raising her arms in disbelief. "You two and Joanie would make fine companions. They *do* say mad people are drawn to each other."

Joe chunters something about the day he'd met Elsie but, fortunately for him, she doesn't hear his mumblings. Elsie doesn't like to admit that she envies her sister's weird indulgences, but likes to talk about them nonetheless.

"Well, it's like this," starts Elsie. "I was brought up in Lyminster, same as Joanie. She was the one who introduced me to Joe at a horse sale we were attendin'. He brought a couple of Shires back here… and me with 'em. His first wife had just run off with a sailor; it were the year before young Tom went off to war, while we had to sit it out. The seaman saw war comin' and bein' the rotten coward he was, he took Joe's wife and buggered off to God knows where, never to be seen again."

"At least he left his stash of rum behind," says Joe, pouring himself a fresh tot.

"Anyway," continues Elsie, "sit yourselves down and I'll tell you more."

"What a pig," says Bella as she and George park themselves on the old threadbare sofa near the stove.

"Too right, love," agrees Joe. "And left me here to sit it out with Big Elsie... *sit* it out? Fight it out more likely. I ask you?"

Elsie ignores the jibe, keen to tell more of her sister.

"Well, Joanie had always been a bit whimsical. She'd started readin' Edith Nesbit books..."

"E. Nesbit? I thought that was bloke. Wasn't it he... she who wrote the 'Railway Children'?" says George.

"That's it, but she wrote horror stories too, you know, and she wrote about dragons. It was soon after that when Joanie heard what she said were intriguin' things about the Knucker, and she's been nuts about it ever since. She even says she's seen it, down by the Knucker hole but I told her she's got more chance of seein' the Loch Ness Monster."

"Well, she won't find that in Lyminster, Elsie," suggests Tommy, whittling a piece of wood with his pocketknife. "It's in Scotland. Everybody knows that."

Elsie ignores him and continues her tale.

"I've told Joanie time and time again that it's all bunkum, but she won't have it. All I can say is that if you two are as daft as *she* is, you'd better look her up if you're goin' to Lyminster. I'll give you her address. She's so full of it that she won't resist spillin' her tales to you."

"Would you, Elsie. I'd be ever so grateful," says George excitedly.

"Fine. Then I must get on. I've a muckheap as tall as the pyramids that needs tidyin' up. Then I have to prepare supper for this pair of layabouts."

"We'd better be off anyway, Elsie," says Bella. Don't want to arrive in the dark. And we need to find somewhere to stay there. Thanks for the rum, Joe."

"You're welcome. It's the least I could do to thank you for

3) London Spurning

your help."

"Yes. Thanks Joe," adds George.

"Look," says Elsie. "If you don't find anywhere to stay, Joanie will put you up… provided you can put up with *her*. She has an old shed that's kitted out with a couple of beds and all her paraphernalia to do with the Knucker. Sounds like it would suit you down to the ground."

'*Wow,*' thinks George. "What could be better, Bel?" he says.

"I can think of a few things, George," she replies, putting on a willing face but dreaming of a comfortable room in a hotel or maybe a pub, "but no… it'll be great."

The pair get up to leave.

"Thanks both of you," says Tommy," fiddling with the pocketknife and eyeing up George's trousers.

-o-o-o-

4) Lym in Stir

As Bella and George ride into Lyminster, darkness greets them kicking twilight into touch. The moon is having a night or two off but, headlamp blazing, they find Joanie's house on Church Lane. Dismounting, they step onto the short cobbled path that leads to the front door. The cottage entrance is bathed in the cold, blue light of a lamp set under the apex of a porch laden with winter-barren wisteria.

"Are you sure this isn't the police station, George?"

"I *am* Bel. This is definitely the place."

They remove their helmets and George tugs at the rusting doorbell chain. They make out a muted response inside, as a door at the far end of the short hallway is pushed wide open. A more inviting light reaches out to the smokily glazed front door, chased by the shadow of the crooked figure that is Elsie's sister, Joanie.

Shooting the bolt, Joanie opens the creaking door and the blue light flees, overpowered by the warm flood that escapes to bathe the visitors. And there stands Joanie in Levi jeans and a multi-coloured, diaphanous blouse worn over a psychedelic tee-shirt. Her wispy salt-and-pepper hair is backcombed in imitation of an out-of-date ball of candyfloss.

"Now, who be you, then?" asks Joanie. "You ain't local and no one calls here at this time of an evening in winter, unless they're after something. You're not from the Council, 'cos they finish at 5 o'clock... 4.30 on a Friday, not that it's Friday. And anyway, *they* don't walk around in trendy leathers carrying crash helmets."

"Sorry to call so late," George offers, "but your sister Elsie said you might help us. We're looking for somewhere to stay and she said you have a shed?"

"That's as maybe, young man, but I like a bit of notice. You can't just go assuming."

"Sorry," says George again.

"We're looking for the Knucker," says Bella.

"Ah, the Knucker," says Joanie, her face lighting up and her back straightening at the mention. "That's different. Why didn't you say?"

"Well, we did… as soon as we could. Elsie told us you're interested in that sort of thing."

"She'd be right, too. She thinks I'm barking mad, but *I* know different. The dragons are every bit as real as *I* am. They're everywhere, aren't they. And I've seen the Knucker… more than once. Lurks round the Knucker hole, he does. Many's the time I've been up by the hole on a moonless night. I take my fiddle and play him some of the old melodies. Ones from way back… two or three hundred years back. Forget Victorian tunes… he seems to like the very old ones. Look, bring your bike in along the drive and park it outside the shed. It's not locked. so put your stuff in there then come in and have a bit of a warm. I'll put the kettle on."

George glances at Bella and smiles. Compliant, they do as Joanie bids.

"So what's brought you on the trail of the Knucker, my dears?" asks Joanie as she pours tea.

"It was me that found it in this little dragon guide," explains Bella, passing the booklet to their host.

"This looks interesting," says Joanie, poring over the booklet. "I ain't ever seen *this* before."

"To be honest," says George. "I'm more interested in Our Boris. I reckon he's the real deal."

"Sounds Russian to me," says Joanie. "Does he live in these parts? Perhaps you should have brought him along with you if he knows about dragons."

"He doesn't *know* about dragons," says George. "He *is* a

dragon... Well a serpent anyway. Actually his name is Ouroboros, or Jörmungandr as the Norse myths would have it. The World Serpent."

"Well if he's a myth, I don't know why you bother. Take the Knucker," says Joanie. "He's every bit as real as I am," she repeats.

George looks at the weird and wonderful lady thinking: *'You're telling us that you're actually real, Joanie?'*

"I reckon old Knucker's favourite tune is Lillibullero," says Joanie, picking up her fiddle from the side of the sofa. "He's come out three times to this one," she adds, and putting bow to strings she sings softly: "Lero Lero Lillibullero, Lillibullero bullen a la, Lero Lero Lero Lero, Lillibullero bullen a la."

"That's lovely," declares Bella, clapping in appreciation. "Though the lyrics sound a bit nonsensical. What do they mean?"

"Oh, that's just the refrain. The verses are all a bit political... something about King William III. I read that 'Lilli' is a familiar form of 'William'. Yet I can't really understand why the old Knucker would like it. You see, I know for a fact that dragons aren't political creatures. A bit cruel at times, though mainly on account of their being misunderstood, but never political. It could be to do with the verse that tells something about an old prophecy found in a bog; the Knucker hole could have been a bog back then."

"Fascinating," says George, enthralled by Joanie's eccentric presence.

"The booklet says the name Knucker could come from the Saxon and would mean 'Water Monster'," says Bella. "Apparently it's referred to in the poem Beowulf."

"So they say," agrees Joanie. "He turns up in the Icelandic too as a 'Water Horse'... and in all sorts of other places. Even as a mermaid over near the Baltic Sea. You won't find anything that I don't know about the Knucker, love. I'll take you up there if

4) Lym in Stir

you like… it's just the night for it tonight."

And with that, Joanie explains more of what she knows of the Knucker.

"They used to say that the Knucker hole is an entrance to the underworld. People told tales of the beast killing livestock and humans alike. A local man is then supposed to have killed the creature. Not so long ago there was a nameless child who would leave snapdragons in the village churchyard on the grave of that man. But I know that none of it is true for, like I said, I've seen the creature. He's alive and well. The people of the village think I'm mad, same as Elsie does. I know that, for I've offered to take them to the Knucker hole and to sing and play my 'Lillibullero' to him. But they just run and hide behind their twitching net curtains, believing that the occasional fiery lights which burst over the hole are nothing more and nothing less than lightning bolts… even on *clear* nights, would you believe?"

Bella looks apprehensively at George, wondering if it's Joanie, or the villagers, or indeed all of them, who might be mad.

'*Snapdragons?*' thinks George, reminded of Natalie who he'd spoken with at the British Museum. '*Thalia and her snapdragons… I wonder, for she was cautious about her name too. And she seemed to be secretive in more than that.*'

Handing a torch to Bella and armed with fiddle and bow, Joanie leads the way along the lane like some benevolent pied piper abducting the last two children in Hamelin on a non-mercenary jaunt. Despite the tea having borne no hints of jasmine or of turmeric, Bella and George follow entranced, the intoxicating fiddle music floating on the chill night air.

"Lero Lero Lillibullero, Lillibullero bullen a la, Lero Lero Lero Lero, Lillibullero bullen a la," Joanie sings softly with a dreamy cadence.

Along the silent midnight lane they go. Here and there net curtains twitch, their twitchers careful not to show an engaged face, yet still curious enough to stir from their sofas after all the years of Joanie's ritual treks to the Lyminster Knucker hole.

Reaching the fields, Joanie and her new adherents clamber over low fences and hop over a rotted and broken stile. Joanie does this without breaking step or missing a note of her tune.

Now, there before them, almost imperceivable in the torchlight, spreads the Knucker hole; deep dark water held in a saucer of ground.

"Some say the hole is bottomless," whispers Joanie, bringing her tune to a close. "People have tried to fathom its depths, so the rumours go, but all have failed."

As the fiddle tune floats away on the still air, all is quiet. George makes to speak, then…

"Hark," cautions Joanie. "Can you hear the rippling? The bubbling of the water? Switch off the torch, Bella," she murmurs.

The three of them stand silent now, eyes wide. A fox barks far off and the hint of a breeze shifts the high, bare branches of a nearby elm. Then, surprising the darkness, the waters cleave and the night is full of wings.

"The Knucker awakes!" declares Joanie. "He was within earshot of the tune tonight, it seems."

Bella gasps and drops the torch, surprised. George takes a step back from the water's edge as the dragon's wake floods to the shore of the hole. Joanie takes up the song once more, trilling in the thin air. The beast flies up, the deluge falling like rain from his scaly wings. No fire, but a hiss he gives… a chill hiss, opining for some lost treasure. Drawn to the tune of the fiddle, he turns and settles on a low branch in the elm tree.

George and Bella look on, open-mouthed, as the creature calls out: "I am here again at your bidding, Joan. Why do you wake me from my sleep?"

4) Lym in Stir

"Naught but curiosity, my dear Knucker," she replies. "We come to ask if you know of Ouroboros, the World Serpent."

"Perhaps I do," hisses the Knucker, "and perhaps I do not. I would not say to you that I do, for I am not sure of your intent. And I would not say that I don't, for the same reason. My father taught me to be cautious in the matter of names. He lives by the sea over in the east."

"Not the Orford Sea-dragon?" asks George, waking from his trance."

"You know him, then?" asks the Knucker, with a hiss.

"So, you're not so cautious with names after all," says Bella, skewering the beast on his apparent indiscretion. "The Orford Sea-dragon is your father."

"Not true... I have nothing but." cries out the Knucker. "You do not win the day, madam, for 'Sea-dragon' is not his actual name. Now, if you search for Ouroboros, you will be a long time looking. I have sought him long enough myself, in vain... and *I'm* a dragon. From Bignor to Bisterne, Kilve to Knotlow, all to no avail, I fear."

"Then thank you, dear Knucker," Joanie calls, by way of a peace offering. "Go now, back to you hole and we shall meet again another day, when perhaps Ouroboros and the world about us are of no import."

"Very well, Joan," says the beast, "but next time, come alone. I do not take kindly to those who would pry. They would do well to keep to their own business, lest an ill fate befall them... your music pleases me, Joan, but I do not like tonight's accompaniment," he concludes, casting a deep-eyed glance at her companions.

And with that, the Knucker crashes clear of the elm tree, with fiery breath now, flies high over his hole and then dives like a plummeting meteor into the water, disappearing into his deep fathoms, all steam and bubbles.

Bella picks up the torch and nudges George: "So much for

you thinking that all dragons are benign, George Crosby. We should proceeded with caution on this quest of yours."

"Well, maybe he's just had a bad day, Bel. We all have them, don't we? And anyway, as you reminded me, this is *our* quest, not mine alone."

"It is, George. I'm only teasing you. We're together in this... from Bignor to Bisterne, from Kilve to Knotlow if that's the path we take."

Following Joanie back across the fields and along dark tracks to her cottage, George and Bella decline the offer of a trawl through their host's archive of Knucker memorabilia and retire to their shed bed. It's gone one o'clock in the morning, and the pair of them are tired and more than a little dazed by the encounter with the Knucker. Joanie herself has turned out to be an experience to grapple with, a throwback to the ancient beliefs, she providing living proof, or so it seems, that dragons really did and still do exist.

The shed is rather cosy, well furnished with a stove and with comfortable chairs sporting plump cushions. The floor is carpeted with exotic rugs and the lamps throw a soft light bathing the walls in warmth. Despite the sleepy lure of thick, winter blankets and pillows to dream on, they settle for mugs of hot cocoa and small talk.

"You know, Bel," says George, reflectively. "Before tonight, despite my hopes and thoughts that dragons really do exist in this living world, I had my doubts. But the Knucker can't lie can it; large as life he was, and undeniably real. And the Orford Sea-dragon, his father by admission, wasn't just a figment of imagination brought on by Harry's tea."

"I have to agree, George. What can't speak can't lie."

"But the Knucker did speak, Bel."

"Well, you know what I mean, George. And anyway, I'm so glad that we bumped into each other back in Cambridge. I've

4) Lym in Stir

been waiting for an adventure like this all my life."

"Me too, Bel. But we still don't know each other."

"It's true. When you said the other day that all you knew was my brother, my bike and my hair, it set me thinking that I owe you a bit more than that. Truth is, my brother and I were brought up in the rarefied atmosphere of a stately home in Oxfordshire. I won't say which one because it's owned by another family now. Our parents separated whilst I was away at a boarding school. Ken had come out of university and was working abroad selling anything and everything to anyone and everyone… not like on the market or out of a suitcase, but real sophisticated stuff. He made a fair bit, but he was living on the edge. The in-crowd became the out-crowd and before he knew it he was out of work, but the money he'd made set him up in his pad in Ipswich. To be honest, I don't know what he does to keep the money rolling in now, but he seems to do alright. Our mum buggered off with some gigolo from Accrington and dad went abroad after selling the family pile. I don't see either of them these days, but dad makes sure I'm okay for a few bob when I really need some extra dosh."

"You said he bought you the bike, didn't you.?"

"That's right. He sent me a cheque from the South of France. That's where he is these days, lapping up the sunshine and the sauvignon no doubt. As for me, George, you may well ask," she says, pausing for George to ask.

Expecting her to go on without prompting, George hesitates and then says: "Tell me. Tell me, Bel. What do *you* do for a living? I know you're on holiday 'til the New Year… you told me that much."

"Well that was a bit of a porky actually. I got the sack the day before we met. I was in the Information Centre looking for possible jobs."

"So, what *were* you doing for work? Why did you get the sack?"

"It's a long story, and a boring one. Let's just say that I didn't see eye to eye with the boss. He was seeing a woman behind his wife's back and I got wind of it. I let it slip to his wife on the phone. I told him my indiscretion wasn't deliberate but he didn't believe me. And he was right not to, the bastard... slipping it out was definitely deliberate. Then, his wife came into the office, hit him with her umbrella and told him not to forget to get the potatoes from the market on his way home."

"You mean that's all she was worried about?"

"No. The next day the other woman came into the office to see him. She had the blackest black eye you've ever seen."

"What? You mean his wife had thumped her?"

"No apparently she threw a potato at her."

"Was it a big potato?"

"I think so, George. I believe he said it was a King Edward. Are *they* big?"

"Big enough, I guess."

"Well I wouldn't know. I do know that the wife came into the office that afternoon and threw potatoes at *him*."

"Were *they* big, Bel."

"No, George. They were mashed."

"Ah, I see."

"It was when I asked him if he'd like a knob of butter on them that he sacked me. I was glad really. He deserved all he got and I didn't really want to work with him anyway."

"So you've no job to go to then. That's good really. We can slow down a bit and enjoy our dragon tour at leisure. My inheritance will see us through for a fair few weeks, and with plenty left over."

"If you're sure, George. I'll get a job when we've done searching and I'll *pay* you back."

"Don't you worry about that, Bel. I'm happy just to pay for your company."

"Is that right, George?" she replies, thumping him on the arm

4) Lym in Stir

in playful protest.

"I didn't mean…" he starts.

"I *know* George. Tell me more about yourself."

"Not a lot to tell really, Bel. As you already know, I live with mum and dad. They're both pretty staid, in a lovely sort of way. They were brought up in a time when things were very different to what they are now, I suppose. Dad was young enough to avoid the first world war but he copped for the second. I did some of my early growing up while he was away in France. And after the war, when he came home, things were tough, what with rationing and so on. But he made a point of us getting to the seaside for a week every summer in the school holidays. I remember one year, when I was about ten it was, we were sitting on the beach at Mablethorpe. Mum had gone to get ice creams, *I* was laid on a beach towel, on my elbows, looking out to sea and dad was sitting in his deckchair… really hot it was… the weather that is, not the deckchair."

Bella chuckles at the vision that George is invoking.

"Anyway," continues George, "there sat dad, with his trousers rolled up and with his customary knotted hanky on his head for a hat against the sun… he burns something terrible without it. And he points out to sea and says: 'look out there, George. Less than three hundred miles away is Germany… not much further than Torquay is from here. All that trouble on our doorstep. You should always keep up your defences is what *I* say. There can be trouble enough on your doorstep without going looking for it further away. Mind you, it's funny to think that if you keep going over that way, beyond Germany that is, on and on, chasing the horizon, you come back to where you started from. All roads lead to Mablethorpe you see, son, so it's a lot easier to stay here in the first place.'"

"He has a good point there, George," says Bella.

"Then," George continues, "mum came back with the ice creams shouting 'Quick, Fred! Here, George! They're melting.

Hurry up!'"

"So, your dad was a bit of a philosopher, George."

"Maybe, Bel. But just then, mum was handing him his cornet and his ice cream fell out and landed on his foot. 'Bugger it, Agatha', he called out… I don't think I'd ever heard him swear apart from then, and once when someone mentioned Hitler. 'Don't *you* think that I'm going back to get you another one, Fred Crosby', said mum. So he got up, rolled his trouser legs down and went off to the kiosk himself."

"Well that little story is more about your dad than you, George."

"I suppose it is really, but it got me thinking, Bel. Regardless of what dad said, every time I look out to sea since then I think of exotic lands beyond Germany; India, China, America then Mablethorpe. And maybe that's why I'm interested to find out about Our Boris. Even the biggest, most adventurous of serpents and dragons seem to end up where they started from. I suppose it makes you think how futile it may be for anyone or anything to spend their lives chasing their tails. Or chasing tales for that matter."

"Don't say that, George. Life should be a big adventure, even if you don't go off around the world. We've only been to Orford and London and Lyminster together, but it has to be worth it, doesn't it?"

"I guess it is, Bel. All the more so for travelling with *you*. I think without you driving me on, if you see what I mean, I could end up in Mablethorpe, with a knotted hankie."

"Maybe in the summer, George. But in the winter, this shed is a much better idea. You can wear a hankie if you really want to though."

And with that warm reassurance, they undress and slide under the beckoning blankets, knowing each other a little more than when they'd returned from their rendezvous with the Knucker.

4) Lym in Stir

Morning creeps up on Lyminster rather than dawning. Bella and George, barely awake, can make out Joanie's cockerel outside, scratching and scraping for worms, too lazy to crow. Then a rat-tat-tat on the door.

"Come on, you lazy pair. Breakfast can't wait for idlers. It's bacon and eggs, for those as want it. Shake a leg."

"Won't be minute, Joanie," a half-asleep Bella manages, as George fights his way free of the blankets.

"George! Who put this knotted hankie on my head?" says Bella, wide awake now.

"It wasn't me, Bel. Must have been the night owls. I think I heard them about two hours ago."

"Twit, George."

"Twit to you twoo, Bella."

Throwing the pillow at him, she climbs from the bed and they hurriedly dress for Joanie's beckoning bacon.

"What's your plan now then?" asks Joanie, pouring tea. "Are you off to find more dragons?"

"That's the general idea," says Bella, spreading butter on her toast. "No hurry though. George is coming round to thinking that if we wait long enough, dragons may come to *us*."

"It's true, in a way," agrees George, thinking of his dad's advice on the matter of trouble and doorsteps. "I have to say, I still want to find dragons, but there's no need to rush. We've nothing to get back to, really."

"You can stay here for a day or two if you like. It's reassuring for me to find someone who doesn't think I'm totally insane."

"That would be lovely, Joanie" suggests Bella. "We can stay awhile and collect our thoughts as to where next."

"Well, I was looking at your little booklet before I called you this morning," admits Joanie. "You left it on the mantel piece. I came across a reminder of the dragon at Bignor Hill. It's not far from here, up beyond Arundel. There's a Roman villa, or at least, what's left of one, south of the village. They do say that the folds in the lie of the land on the Hill were left by the very coils of the beast himself. They seem to think that the dragon is long gone, but what do *they* know? There aren't many of us that know the dragons are all still alive… sleeping maybe, but alive with breath and fire. Being so near, I wouldn't be at all surprised if he isn't related to the Knucker, though I don't think anyone knows his name."

These words reignite the smouldering fire that is still in George's mind, the flame that tells him he must search on for dragons.

"I can't ever see us finding Our Boris," says George. "My inheritance, fine though it is, will never stretch right around the world, especially if I take my dad's advice and keep a lot of it for other priorities. But no matter; these parochial creatures are exciting enough, if the Knucker and the Orford Nessie are anything to go by."

"George, let's stay awhile with Joanie," enthuses Bella. "Then travel on to explore for the Bignor beast in a day or two. In fact, Joanie, you could maybe tag along with us."

"Oh, no thank you, dears. My Knucker is quite enough for the moment. I don't think I could get to know him well in a thousand years or more, and I want to teach him some new tunes."

"It *would* be good to stay for a bit, Bel," agrees George. "I reckon we could get the locals to believe you when you tell them that the Knucker is alive and well, Joanie."

"Heavens no, George! They'd run a mile if they saw him. Probably call in the Army and the Air Force, like in those silly American movies. Better they carry on thinking that I'm a harmless old crank. I suppose I *am*, in a way."

"I wouldn't say that, Joanie," Bella assures her.

"Perhaps you may think it though. *They* do, and they'd probably convince you that you're as mad as they say *I* am.

4) Lym in Stir

They'd say that I conjure up the dragon by some fiendish deception or other. Far better for me and for the Knucker that people ignore us."

"But *we* don't think that way," says Bella

"Ah, but I could tell, as soon as you turned up on my doorstep that *you* were different. George has that light in his eyes, and you have a spirit to match it. You remind me of me when I was younger, not that I ever rode a motorbike."

And so it is that Bella and George stay for two more days and two more nights. George reads and re-reads his hefty book, taking in all the details of Jörmungandr, the mighty worm. He becomes convinced that there's more to the creature than even all the long ages of experts have deduced. A metaphor he's become but, sure as eggs are what they're said to be, there must be a greater truth underling all the myths and legends woven around him.

"We may not be able to chase him all around the world, Bel, but if we can find his true identity here in England, we can expose him, fiery tip to toe and tail."

"Lead the way, George. Our Boris awaits, though I'm not sure he'd appreciate being exposed to the modern world and its ways."

A relaxing day or two later, the pair bid good fortune to Joanie after loading up the sidecar. The Norton fired up, off they ride on the next leg of their dragon crusade.

"Bignor, here we come," shouts back George as they turn into the lane and head for the main road.

The bend in the road takes them north towards Arundel.

Arriving, they cross the river and George spies the cathedral to the east and beyond sees the castle once more: "There *must* be dragons here, Bel. How can there not be with a castle like that? We have to explore."

Travelling beyond the river and taking a turn to the right,

they double back, passing the cathedral, and approaching the castle are staggered by its imposing castellated boundary walls as they skirt the north of the historic town, yard after long yard.

Parking the bike down by the war memorial, they stroll the town.

"George, look. A launderette. Now that's what I call fortunate. If the state of *my* underwear's anything to go by, *your* pants must be on the point of walking under their own steam."

"I'd hardly say my pants are *steaming*, Bel. A bit whiffy maybe, but... well."

"We may not get another chance, George. We have to find somewhere to stay in Bignor and, judging by the size of it on the map, we'll be lucky to find running water, let alone washing powder."

"I suppose you're right, Bel. It's a pity we didn't get Joanie to deal with our laundry."

"Joanie was fired up by dragons panting, George. Not by people's pants. Anyway, look, there's a woman in the launderette in charge of the machines. If we nip back to the sidecar, we can get it sorted. Look, there's only that skinny bloke of a customer in there fighting to load a couple of blankets."

By the time they return and enter with their discreet bundle of washing, the skinny chap is sat in front of his spinning machine with a copy of the Beano, in for the long haul of the '*Superwash-and-Spin - half price as advertised*'.

The woman, middle-aged, overweight and clad in a gaudy flower-patterned pinny is busy cleaning one of the three industrial washing machines. She's armed with a plastic carry-box laden with worryingly strong-smelling powders and other chemicals.

"Morning, my dears," she says cheerily, stubbing out the dying remains of her cigarette in a tar-stained ashtray. "And what can I do for you on this fine Arundel morning?"

4) Lym in Stir

"Is the '*Superwash-and-Spin - half price as advertised*' available for underwear and shirts and such?" asks Bella, taking a lead in the laundry stakes.

"Well, it is, but it's really for heavy stuff like bedclothes. You'd be better off with the '*Mid-range Fresh-and-Go Winter Special*'. It's quite a bit cheaper and it doesn't take as long."

"Oh, I didn't see that on the poster," says Bella.

"No, well, that offer ended yesterday really, but I can squeeze it across the finish line for you... provided you don't tell the boss."

"Right. we'll go for *that* then."

"Are you sure you're okay mixing your underwear with mine, Bel?" says George, timorously.

"Well they've been next to each other more than once now, George, so don't think twice about it."

The skinny man rustles his Beano, turning the page from Lord Snooty to Desperate Dan.

The washerwoman utters an unintentional cough: "Here, my loves. Let me run you through the instructions. They can be a bit complicated when you're not used to them."

"Thank you," says Bella, appreciatively, handing the woman her delicates along with George's unmentionables.

"Don't mention it, love," says the attendant. "My name's Madge, by the way," she adds, lighting another cigarette.

"Right. I won't mention it, Madge... not even to the boss if I see him."

"Oh... *that's* the boss over there, reading his Beano."

"You're kidding," says Bella, embarrassed now.

"I am kidding actually," whispers Madge. "He might as well be the boss though; he's in here a damned sight more that the gaffer. Always reading his Beano, he is, though I did see him once with the Financial Times; I reckon he's got some of them stocks and shares. He don't let on much, but his name's Peregrine."

"Oh, right," replies Bella.

George stands at arm's length, not wishing to get embroiled in the intrigues of washing underwear and the like.

"I'm right aren't I, Perry," shouts Madge. "You're name's Peregrine, ain't it."

"That's right, Madge," he replies, briefly glancing away from Desperate Dan, then returning his attention to the fate of a cow pie that's half devoured already by the stubble-chinned hero.

Madge turns her attention to George.

"You're not from round here, are you?" she asks.

"Er, no," answers George, drawn into the conversation reluctantly. "We're just passing through. We're hoping to find some accommodation for the night in Bignor. We're interested in the Hill, you see."

Peregrine gives up on his cow pie and folds the Beano, distracted by the seemingly unusual event of the launderette having other customers than he.

"You'll be lucky," suggests the comic enthusiast. "Bignor isn't very big, despite its name. There's one place you could try though. It's on the south side, quite near the Roman remains. I'll write the details down for you if you like."

"Thanks," says George, warming to the character.

"You're not chasing the rumours of a dragon up there are you?"

"Well, as a matter of fact, we *are*, Peregrine."

"Call me Perry, if you like."

"Right. *I'm* George and this is Bella."

"Pleased to meet you, Perry," says Bella, the washing now on its way to a pristine state, courtesy of Madge's magic.

"So, do you know about the dragon, Perry?" quizzes George.

"Not really. They say it died years ago... if it ever existed. I don't believe in fairy stories; not unless they're in the Beano that is."

"Or the Financial Times?" quips Bella.

4) Lym in Stir

"Who told you about *them*?" snaps Peregrine.

"Um, no one," says Bella, stepping back a pace. "Just saying."

"That's alright then," says Peregrine, returning to the subject in hand… "Still, there was one bloke who said he'd found something about a dragon, in the library up in the castle. He said there was a reference to a dragon depicted in a stained-glass window too, but *I* never saw one. As far as I'm concerned it's a load of fluff. I used to work up at the castle and I never heard any other mention of dragons. Mind you, there's a lot of books in that library. The castle dates back to the Crusades and beyond and then even further back you've got Saint George. *He* knew a dragon from what the legends say, didn't he. Anyway, what did you say your name is?"

"It's George," says George.

"You're first name's not Saint, is it?"

"No, it's George. George Crosby."

"And mine's Bella," says Bella, presuming Peregrine had not taken in either of their names.

"Oh *that's* a nice name, love," says Madge. "*I* wouldn't have minded being called Bella."

So it is that George and Bella sit on the bench facing their allotted washing machine, Bella next to Peregrine and George next to Bella. Madge steps into the back room for a bit of a break and yet another fag.

George stares into the front-loading machine as the washing rotates; first one way and then the other, trance inducing. The clothes take on the form of a dragon, circling confined to the prison of the drum as Ouroboros might be imprisoned by the heartbeat of the Earth, each revolution a day in the progress of life on Earth yet each counter-turn somehow a denial of advancement. Then, as the fast spin kicks in and progress hurtles out of all control into an unclear future, George is woken from his trance by a sharp nudge in the shoulder from Bella.

"George! Wake up. Perry says he has the key."

"Ow! Don't be daft, Bella. Man's been looking for the key for ever and a day, and still no one knows what the future may bring."

"No, George. The key to the *door*."

"Which door?" asks George, bemused by the comment.

"Which door?" asks Bella, turning to Peregrine.

"The library door," says Peregrine, glancing cautiously at the back room for fear of Madge returning from her puffing session.

"The library door," says Bella to George.

"What? The *castle* library?" says George, still rather befuddled by his spin-cycle.

"What? The *castle* library?" Bella repeats, looking to Peregrine.

"Yes," says Peregrine. "I kept a key to the library, along with a couple of keys for the staff entrances, when I left employment there. I just thought they might come in handy one day. If you really think you could find anything, I could take you up there later, when all's quiet for the night. But take it from me, you'll be wasting your time, most likely."

"So, what's in it for you, Perry? Taking anyone up there, I mean," asks George, bypassing Bella now.

"Nothing really, I suppose. I've always been a tiny bit intrigued by that story of a dragon though. Now there are experts on hand, I just thought... it might be an adventure."

'*Experts?*' ponders George. '*I'm not sure about that, but I don't mind being called an expert.*' "Bella and I need to settle on somewhere to stay first. We need to move on to Bignor. That's our intention."

"If you want to leave Bignor out of it for the moment, *my* place is on Maltravers Street... You can stay there tonight. My cat won't protest... if you ask her nicely, mind."

"It's tempting. The castle library sounds intriguing, but won't

4) Lym in Stir

it be alarmed?"

"Not really. It's used to seeing folk come and go."

"What do you reckon, Bel?" asks George, smiling at the thought of saying 'boo' to a library.

"I'm all for it. Things seem a bit flat since we left Lyminster."

"In for a penny then, Perry," says George. "Let's finish the washing and drying and then go for a spin."

Madge comes back from her tobacco-assisted refreshment break and proceeds to explain the workings of the tumble-drier to her dragon-hunting customers.

Cycles completed, George, Bella and Peregrine gather their laundry and head for the Norton, Bella having decided that there's room in the sidecar along with everything else for Peregrine *and* his blankets.

"Left here!" shouts Peregrine from his overwhelming nest of laundry, gesticulating wildly, realising that his shouts alone are in vain. "About three hundred yards," he adds, as Bella spots his waving and his holding up of three fingers with little hope of being heard.

Bella glances to her left for further instructions after precisely two hundred and ninety yards to see Peregrine screaming, seemingly mute, with one thumb up and a finger pointing at a tiny brick and slated end-terraced house on the right just ahead. They screech to a halt. George dismounts and opens the sidecar door for their prospective host.

"Thank God for air," cries Peregrine as he clambers out from his spin-dried cocoon. "I don't think you could hear me. It was like being in a spaceship with very little space, heading for the planet Mars."

"Well, they *do* say that in space, no one can hear you scream, however large or small the space may be," says George, rather unhelpfully.

Bella turns of the engine and they both remove their helmets and goggles. Once they're all inside, Peregrine introduces them to his black cat, Maggie. George and Bella are entranced by the quaintly furnished enclave that is Peregrine's home.

"Now, as I said, George. You must ask Maggie nicely if you may stay this evening."

George eyes the little black cat rather nervously, he not being at ease with felines in general after a tiger growled at him through the bars of a zoo cage when he was very young.

"Nice moggy. I'm George," he says, expecting rebuke.

The cat squeals in protest.

"Maggie, George. Not Moggy. She'll get upset if you call her Moggy," advises Peregrine.

"Sorry, Maggie. Can we stay here tonight, please?" George asks the cat. She purrs and rubs up against George's leathers, friendly now. George steps back, still anxious.

"There you are, George. She's soft as a kitten really. I called her Magwitch... after the convict in Great Expectations by Dickens, before I knew she was a she. Otherwise I might have have called her Estella. Eventually I shortened the name to Maggie. That seemed more fitting really "

"My goodness, George," says Bella, bending to stroke and fuss Maggie. "You're brave enough to face dragons, yet you seem fazed by an encounter with a little kitty."

"I suppose so, Bel. But cats can be dangerous, can't they. Especially the bigger ones."

"So can dragons, George.

"Well, *I* don't think so. Dragons are far more sensitive than people allow. All that so-called malicious fire-breathing stuff. They can't help having fiery breath, can they. It just comes out wrong sometimes. I think dragons have been maligned by man beyond reasonability. And, a bit like Maggie here, I suppose they only get vicious when they're shown disrespect."

-o-o-o-

5) Book Worm

"To the castle then," calls out Peregrine, as if off to the Crusades.

Maggie the cat squeals with delight and purrs.

"Sorry, Maggie. *You* have to stay here, while *we* go on a little quest to find dragons," says Peregrine.

Maggie purrs all the louder.

Bella and George bring in all their stuff from the sidecar, making better room for Peregrine on his second trip in space.

Dark now, the moon rising over the castle, they cruise as inconspicuously as a motorbike engine will allow. Bella follows the instructions Peregrine has given, riding through the town then finding a secluded lay-by on Mill Road which skirts the castle to the rear of the grounds. Peregrine clutches a torch and pats his overcoat pocket wherein lie his secret keys, excited at the prospect of using them again for the first time after all these years.

'Should we really be trusting a man who names his cat Magwitch, when we've only just met him over a couple of whirling blankets in a launderette?' thinks George. *'Still, in for a penny is what I said. Adventures are what we've settled on, come what may.'*

Through a gap in the ancient hedge they slip, and on into the woods that shield the old fish-ponds from the road. Here and there the moonlight is lost to them, despite the denuding of the winter trees. Breaking from the confines of arboreal shade they follow a grassy path, cross the scar that is a track and plunge into the shadow of yet more trees, soon to be confronted by the boundary wall rising sheer before them.

"This way," signals Peregrine, steering his disciples to the left with the beam of his torch, turning beyond a turret. "There's a wicket gate just around this corner."

"Are you sure this is a good idea, George?" whispers Bella, fearful of being heard by some night creature that may sound the alarm.

"Of course it is, Bel. If we're caught we'll just say we were rambling and got lost."

"What? In the middle of a cold December night?"

"We could say we came out to look at the moon."

"They'd lock us up for loonies, George."

"Look, Bel. Where's your sense of mad adventure? You'd go insane if you weren't mad, in this world. Live for the day is what I say."

"But it's night, George."

"Don't split hairs, Bel."

"Quiet now, you two," whispers Peregrine, as the first lock clicks sweetly in response to his key. "Once we're inside the perimeter, it's just a short dash to the castle wall itself."

"Right," acknowledges George.

Bella clings to George's arm now, convinced that they're about to be apprehended and dragged off to some dungeon, where they'll be broken on the Catherine wheel. Before she can worry more, they dash to the castle wall itself and Peregrine deploys his second key. The inconspicuous door that is the staff entrance sweeps open.

"Good," says Peregrine. "I thought they may have changed the locks before now."

Wending their way along corridors, moonlight slanting in through high windows lighting their way in the relative gloom, they step up, then down again on short flights of stairs. Confronted with a tall, ancient door set on impressive wrought-iron hinges, Peregrine turns back to George and Bella.

"Here it is. The library."

Peregrine produces a third key and, with a turn of the handle and a push, the door cries feebly for oil, swinging open to reveal a torch-lit, awesome sight. Bella forgets her trepidations

5) Book Worm

and, as her eyes adjust a little to the darkness, she casts her gaze first left, then right, then upwards to the balconied perimeter of the magnificent room.

"I don't know where you'll want to look," suggests Peregrine, "but as long as we're as quiet as possible, no one will hear. The occupied rooms are quite a distance away, and thick stone walls have dumber ears than some."

"Wow. This is amazing, Perry," whispers George. "You must have been enthralled to work here."

"I suppose so, but I didn't often get to come into the library, George. You see, I was just one of the odd-job men around the castle; put up a picture here, mend a fuse there... and clean out the drains somewhere else. Now then, here look... there's a bank of light switches behind this panel."

Peregrine twists the turn-button catches of the inconspicuous panel to reveal the switches.

"If I remember aright, this row on the left controls all the subdued lighting for the shelves. If I flick these ones..."

And, click by click, the splendour that Bella and George had perceived in the gloom bursts forth; the vaulted ceiling, the richly panelled walls, the gilded balcony balustrades, and along the recessed walls the sumptuous bookshelves all laden with age upon age of literary treasures.

The history here must be amazing, Perry," says George. "How old is it?"

"Well as far as I remember, this library is only about two hundred years old but, like I mentioned, the castle itself dates right back to well before the time of the Crusades. And then I gather that Richard the Lionheart had his dibs on it once. Now as for the books, I wouldn't like to say much, for that's a whole other story. I do know that a lot of them, new and old, came here when the library was created, but I believe that quite a few really old tomes came from the family archives going back much, much earlier. Some of the documents had been in bundled pages which were stitched together at some point to form books of sorts, often with a clasp to secure them closed. The covers of some were damaged, so they were replaced in leather. Now, as for that bloke I told you about who said he'd found something to do with a dragon here… Well, one or two folk said that when he'd come researching, he'd found a book up there on a shelf on the balcony. When he opened the book he saw a frightening depiction of a really fierce dragon. It was so realistic that when he squealed out in terror it turned its head towards him and threw a fiery spurt of breath off the page so fierce that it completely seared off the poor chap's eyebrows."

"What happened *then*?" asks Bella.

"Well, my dear, they said he slammed the book shut, fastened the clasp and put it back in its place. He ran out of the castle, through the main gate and straight to the pub. Downing a hasty pint, he burbled something of his tale, paid the landlord, dashed out to his motor car and has never been seen in Arundel again."

"Good Lord!" exclaims George. Then, checking his voice back to a whisper, "Fascinating. So didn't anyone know which book it was?"

"If they did, they didn't admit it. By all accounts, there was no evidence of damage beyond eyebrows, but it all went rather quiet and was soon forgotten about by most."

"So the book's probably somewhere up there to this day then. On the balcony."

"That's *my* reckoning, George."

"Right then, Bel. Up we go."

"*You* first, George. I think I'll stay down here and look for books about motorbikes."

"If there are any to be found, they'll be over in the technology section, over there, Bella," suggests Peregrine. "I believe there are quite a few about motorcars, so you may be lucky. I'll stay

5) Book Worm

down here, near the door, just in case anyone's been disturbed by our trespassing. Good fun this, don't you think?"

"Good fun? Oh, yes, Perry," says Bella, unconvinced, turning to emphasize her doubts in that respect to George.

But George is not there for the emphasizing. He's already climbed to the balcony and is commencing to work his way around, bay by bay, looking for telltale clues of dragon tails.

All is quiet except for the occasional flick of pages; ground floor flicks from Bella, first floor flicks from George. Peregrine stands at the door of the library partaking of a Woodbine.

"Ow, y' bastard," shouts George, as the others hear the hint of a roar.

George, having ducked astutely to one side, somehow anticipating the eyebrow-removing burst of flame, drops the book he'd opened onto the floor. This time, the dragon that had been re-trapped by the previous reader has escaped and, after flying twice around the whole extent of the balcony, lands perched on the balustrade, facing his rescuer.

"Thank the gods for that!" it shouts, in out-and-out relief. "Well done, my fine fellow, for release is what I've craved all these years. That clod, who some few years ago impeded my advance, went and closed the clasp and thwarted my dash to escape… when I could have been free. I tried to apologize for his cindered eyebrows, but he gave me no chance, the silly dotard. But oh, the release. At last I can stretch my wings, unfettered."

This beast, escaped from the impressively heavy book, is a sight to behold; modest in size but proud of bearing, despite a present appearance of discarded origami, crumpled after years of entrapment between the pages of an ancient treatise entitled *The Aftermath of the Great Flood*. The creature is no more than three feet long, despite the extending of its magnificent coiling tail. It flashes its fiery eyes, which shine like awakened stars set in a proud, sleek head the like of a noble sea creature. Its glorious mantle of scales is a lustrous green and its crested mane is rich red and gold. It's nostrils flare, smoking still from its prefatorial burst of fire.

"Err?" manages George, recovering from his initial fright as Bella and Peregrine arrive at his side on the balcony. "You mean you couldn't escape from the book without it being opened by someone?"

George inexplicably finds himself holding a serious conversation with an emancipated dragon.

"It's true. There was one occasion when I nearly escaped... it seemed that someone had decided to replace the old cover. I'd been in the deep sleep of centuries and by the time I came to my senses they'd finished their work and re-clasped the damned book."

"*I'm* a bit like that on Monday mornings," says Bella. "When I've got a job, that is."

"In truth, *I* blame that George fellow," says the dragon. "He tried to kill me at one point, until I explained how that damsel was trying to kill *me*. A right brute *she* was. It was a really hot day and I'd only flown down to ask for directions to the nearest cave, so I could cool off a bit. But, I think I startled her and she swiped at me, over and over, with the chains from her chatelaine. Then that nosey George intervened. I tried to explain and at first he and I seemed to be getting on quiet nicely. Then, without warning, he went and slapped me between the pages of that document and fastened its magical clasp when I was off my guard."

"But he *did* kill you. Everyone knows *that*. 'Saint George killed the dragon'. They *all* say it."

"*Saint* George is it? Who made him a saint, I wonder? Well, they're wrong about him killing the dragon, I'm afraid. I think someone must have recorded the event with a degree of erroneousness. After all here I am, living and breathing. It's quite likely someone mistranscribed the crucial word. I fear

5) Book Worm

they may have actually said 'Saint George *filed* the dragon.' now that would make more sense, wouldn't it?"

"Look," says Peregrine, "much as you've convinced me that dragons do exist, George, all that shouting just now would wake the dead. We'd better think about getting out of here. And you, my fine scaly friend, had better think about getting back in that there book."

"If you think that I'm going back in there, you've another think coming," protests the dragon, glancing with an anxious eye at George with Peregrine's mentioning his liberator's name. "How would *you* like to be locked away for centuries without being able to stretch your wings?"

"I heard that a bloke opened the book again, just a few years back,"says Peregrine. "That gave you a chance to stretch your wings and fly, didn't it?"

"You jest, my dear fellow. I'd been holding my breath for ages for fear of igniting my papery prison, and then I had barely a chance to breathe out and in again as he slammed chapters one to four back down in my face."

"Well, we can't let you loose on the public," says Bella. "Not without warning. The people of Arundel would think the end of the world as we know it was coming. And we can't take you with us; we haven't room in our sidecar."

"But, as you can see, I'm not a *large* dragon," insists the dragon. "I mean, as you've seen now, I can fit into small spaces. I don't even suffer from claustrophobia, so I'd be fine as long as there's a handle on *my* side of this 'sidecar' you mention. And if I were forced to fly, then I'd probably prefer it… I can fly very discreetly, I'll have you know."

"We don't even know your name," says George.

"It's Rangvald, George," confirms the dragon. "There. I've said it. Dragons very rarely give their real names, so that shows you can trust me. I'm more than happy to comply with any reasonable etiquette that you suggest. I can turn my flame down to minimum quite easily."

"But how do we know that *is* your real name?"

"You could always ask my brother, the Knucker. He lives quite near here."

"Ah! We've met the Knucker," says George. "We could always check with him, I suppose. But on reflection I don't think that will be necessary."

"Well, there you are then," says Rangvald, triumphantly.

"So the Orford Sea-dragon is your uncle," remarks Bella.

"Oh, you know of him too, then" says Rangvald.

"Yes," says George. "We've seen *him* too."

"So, that's it then. You can trust that I'm telling you the truth."

"Well, I guess so. And it's good that we've found the name of the dragon that Saint George killed," decides George. "No one seems to have known your name before now."

"Hang on a minute, George. I just told you... the other George filed me, he didn't kill me, or I wouldn't be here now. Someone should have put him in his place before he ran riot. For all I know there could be lots of other dragons and serpents and worms trapped in books thanks to him."

"Ah, yes. Sorry, Rangvald," says George, toying with the thought of 'book worms'.

"Well, don't you go telling anyone that I'm that dragon, George, or else they'll reopen the case. I mean, I protested at the time... when they said that I was terrorising damsels. It was only a stroke of luck that I wasn't killed back then. You see, it was only that..."

"Like I said," interrupts Peregrine, "we'd better be on our way. If you're not going back into the book, then we'd better all get out together, but I'm warning you now... if you cause a fuss, then the Arundel constabulary will be down on you like a ton of bricks. By the way, I don't suppose you know anything about a stained-glass window depicting you?"

"Don't be so ridiculous, man," Rangvald replies. "If anyone

wanted to commemorate me, or indeed my demise at the hands of some knight in armour, it would have been *after* I'd been filed, wouldn't it... so how would I know about it?"

"Ah, I see what you mean," concedes Peregrine.

And with that, George snaps shut the clasp on the *The Aftermath of the Great Flood*, and places the book back on its shelf, minus Rangvald. Locking the library door behind them, the three interlopers and the one airborne escapee wend their cautious way back along corridors, those on foot stepping down then up again on the short flights of stairs, back to the staff entrance.

Re-locking doors, onward through the trees by the ponds they go, with the dragon flitting along at the rear of the little band, finding their way to the motorbike and sidecar in the lay-by.

"Let's get back to Maltravers Street as soon as we may. Get the bike started, Bella," says Peregrine, more anxious than the others to keep their low profile intact.

"Look here," says Rangvald. "What ever this infernal contraption is, I feel that it will be most incommodious for me to climb into it, or indeed *onto* it, considering my long years of enforced literary confinement. So, save me the embarrassment, if you will, and allow me to fly stealthily in your wake. That way we can avoid an ill-crossing to this Maltravers Street."

"I see what you did, there," chortles Bella as she straddles the bike. "Ill-crossing... Maltravers. A dragon with a sense of humour. Very good. This is a motorcycle by the way."

"I assure you, young lady. It was not my intention to convey a sense of humour. My incarceration was by no means funny. Many a damsel has met her demise taking such liberties... not at my hands... err, wings, I hasten to add. And further, I trust you will be riding this steed side-saddle, as befits a woman. As regards this prison of a castle I've been freed from... I don't recognise it at all. That other George trapped me when I was visiting a street market in a place called Marrakesh. I'd had an inkling that a distant relative of mine lived over that way and I was innocently looking for documents recording the ancient world of Mesopotamia, before that damsel arrived."

"Sorry, Rango," says Bella, suppressing her sniggering. "Most people would welcome the opportunity to bury themselves in a good book. As for side-saddle... I think not. I need my feet to command this beast."

"The key words there are 'opportunity' and 'themselves'. And *I'm* not 'most people'. However, luckily for you, I do have a sense of humour, even if I hesitate to show it. I'm not sure I like 'Rango' by the way... I could turn very nasty if you're not careful... to the point where killing could be involved."

"Oh, dear. I really had hoped that all dragons would prove to be benign," says George, disappointedly. "I didn't think they really went around demising people."

"Look, George. I was jesting. Like I just said, I *do* have a sense of humour. But all creatures have their limits, so occasionally, in circumstances of great duress, unfortunate and uncontrollable events occur."

"Come on then, Perry," says George, conceding the need for them to flee the environs of the castle. "Into the sidecar. Rango will need to fly on behind. There's not room for both you *and* him in there. It's not far, even for *his* unpractised wings."

"I suppose 'Rango' is going to stick, then," says Rangvald, raising his eyes aloft in resignation.

Rangvald startles at the starting of the engine, but soon is at ease, likening its throaty sound to the purr of some of the larger dragons he was acquainted with of old.

Back at 'Chéz Peregrine', the merry band of dragon and dragon-hunters leave the Norton parked outside under a streetlamp and file into the little terraced cottage.

"Be sure to wipe your feet, all of you" insists Peregrine.

5) Book Worm

Rangvald casts him a glance and says: "don't you be so rude, my friend. My feet have not the benefit of mud, seeing as how I've flown everywhere since leaving the castle."

"Well, I'm sorry, Rango. It was George and Bella I meant really," says Peregrine.

Peregrine leads them to the rear lounge, opening the door cautiously, knowing that Maggie the cat is in there, queen over her queendom, certain in her knowledge that *she* decides who may enter her domain and who may not. Having happily sanctioned Bella's presence and having warily accommodated George's, she purrs now as they re-enter. Rangvald flutters in behind them and Maggie jumps up, not in protest but in welcome, as if the two are friends long-parted.

"Hello, little black cat," says Rangvald.

Maggie purrs.

"Her name is Magwitch… sorry, I mean *Maggie*," explains Bella to Rangvald.

"Do you two know each other?" Peregrine finds himself asking the dragon in a friendly tone, against his previously sceptical intuition.

"I think not, Perry," replies Rangvald, hesitantly. "Unless it was in another life. Dragons may perhaps have long lives… almost immortal one would say. Cats have nine of them and, contrary to the beliefs of mankind, those lives may not necessarily follow each other year-on-year. So, with many years between lives, it could be that she and I have met before. By the way, what year *are* we in?"

"1964," confirms George. Soon it'll be Christmas and then 1965 will follow."

"Hmm," ponders Rangvald. "A thousand years and more locked inside that curséd book. All those centuries!… I can understand then, why things have changed so; motorcycles and sidecars, lamps on tall poles and that strange red box on the corner of your street, Perry. I can see I have much to acquaint my senses with. As for Maggie? So many years passed? Perhaps Maggie and I have not met after all, though it is possible still; there were many black cats I came across back then."

Maggie purrs ever louder.

And so, Bella and George bed down for the remainder of the night in Maltravers Street in Peregrine's spare bedroom. Rangvald settles contented at the foot of the bed and Maggie too lies there curled snugly in the warmth of the dragon's breathing. In the morning, Peregrine wakes the sleeping couple with a breakfast of cheese on toast.

The dragon declines: "To tell truth, Perry, I prefer to catch my own meals, but somehow I haven't quite regained my appetite fully after my enforced hibernation. I'm sure I shall do so when we're on the road, my friend."

"You're keen to travel with us then, Rango?" asks Bella.

"Indeed I am, Bella. I have much to catch up on and I believe both you and George may help a great deal in that. I may even agree to your advice to travel in the sidecar of your magnificent conveyance at times when it may be appropriate for the sake of prudence."

"Thanks for putting us up, Perry," says Bella, finishing her cheese on toast and pouring a second cup of tea from the replenished pot.

"Hear, hear," declares George. "Well met, Perry. Do *you* have plans for today?"

"Well, I thought I may visit the launderette. I remembered there are a few items I forgot when taking the blankets yesterday, and then there are your own bedsheets to consider."

In truth, Peregrine has a soft spot for Madge and he's visited the launderette at least three times a week for the last three months. He's been plucking up the courage to ask her out to the cinema and feels that today might be the day.

Sidecar and backpacks loaded heavily, and with the little

5) Book Worm

dragon in tow, the three itinerants bid farewell to Peregrine. Maggie looks on wistfully, sat at the front gate. Bella kicks the Norton into life and, with a glance behind, she pulls out into the road and the town of Arundel becomes a passing milestone on their journey, as they head on for Bignor with the address of that accommodation near the Roman Villa, carefully following Peregrine's directions.

"You know, George," says Rangvald, when Bella brings her machine to rest outside the church in the hamlet of Bignor, "Crosby is an interesting name. I know it as *Krossbyr*… from the Norse. You're not from Scandinavia, are you?"

"Not as far as I'm aware, Rango."

"Are you related to Bing, George?" asks Bella.

"Have you heard me sing, Bella?"

"No, George. The nearest you've come to it was when you squealed out at Rango as he jumped out of that book."

"Was I in key?"

"Certainly not, George."

"Then I guess I'm not related to Bing."

Rangvald, baffled by this strange conversation asks: "What is *your* true name, Bella?"

"You mean my *surname*?"

"I suppose so."

"It's Drake."

"Ah, now *that's* interesting too. It's Norse. Old Norse in fact. 'Draki' that would be… it means dragon really, though drakes don't have wings. We might even be distantly related."

"But, *you've* got wings and *I* haven't, Rango."

"I did say 'distantly'."

"I thought it could mean 'snake' too," pitches in George, hoping to show off his smattering of serpently knowledge.

"Don't push it, George," protests Bella. "I think I prefer dragon."

"So do I, Bella. I can't imagine you as a snake," decides Rangvald.

"Sorry, Bel," says George contritely, wishing he'd maintained his silence on the matter.

"I forgive you, George," says Bella. "By the way, I thought there was a Butlin's at Bignor."

"No, that's Bognor, Bel. Bognor Regis."

"Oh, I see. Still, I guess this place could be just as entertaining."

"Butlin? Now there's a very interesting name," declares Rangvald.

"Is that Norse too?," asks Bella.

"I've no Idea, Bella."

"I seem to recall it's Norman French," says George, unable to maintain his brief silence. "You seem to know a lot about names, Rango."

"Indeed I do, George, though you aren't doing so badly yourself. But we dragons make great study of names. We're very interested in the continuity of names in our families."

"I think my brother, Ken, knew a chap called Norman French," says Bella. "Oh, no, sorry… it was Norman *Finch*."

George and Rangvald exchange perplexed glances, the dragon wrinkling his brow and George shrugging his shoulders.

'*I just love sending George up, sometimes,*' thinks Bella, smiling innocently.

The recommended accommodation that George and Bella fall upon here in Bignor proves to be rather disappointing. There are no hints of dragon rumours, or of quirky owners to heighten their sense of adventure. With Rangvald hidden in the sidecar for the moment, they arrange to stay for two nights and settle into a rather mundane room decorated throughout with magnolia paint and furnished with beige carpet, as are all the

5) Book Worm

rooms of the house. The owners, a Mr. and Mrs. Stark, are as stark as their name, and indeed as stark as their magnolia and beige might suggest. Mr. Stark reveals that he's a civil servant working in the delightful little town of Petworth some five miles away, where Bella and George had stopped for refreshments. He's as civil as any servant anyone would wish to meet, but Petworth is all the more delightful, even exciting, in comparison with its magnolia and beige civil servant. Mrs. Stark cleans for several local residents who've found it difficult to understand how a broom works and certainly who couldn't activate a vacuum cleaner without intervention from some higher intelligence. Nonetheless, the starkness of the Starks is surpassed by their apparent civility, and even more so by the breakfasts they serve up. Once breakfast has been dispensed on the first morning, Mr. and Mrs. Stark vanish for the day, each off on the routine of their chosen employment, and don't return until late evening. Their absence makes for easier concealment of Rangvald, who seems more than contented with magnolia and beige and is rather taken by the radio broadcast from the set in George and Bella's room.

"So, Rango," says George, "what can you tell us about the dragon of Bignor?"

"As I've already hinted, George, I know very little about him. I wouldn't even know if he's still alive. He is, or was, my nephew, he being the son of my brother, the Knucker, but I lost touch with them, thanks to that bloody George and his collected documents. How am I supposed to know if he's still about when I've been incarcerated between the pages of an unreasonably unwieldy volume of man's scribblings? I do remember though, they called him Micklewhite… not many people know that. He had little white patches all over him. Actually, I shouldn't really be telling you the names of dragons, even those belonging to dragons that might be dead. We like to keep our privacy and we avoid sparrow-like twittering as much as possible, but every now and then, we let things slip. Mind you, I think Micklewhite is only a nickname... not Norse, not Icelandic, as far as I'm aware."

"I think all we have to go on is in our booklet, George," says Bella. "It says in here that its lair was on Bignor Hill, near the remains of the Roman Villa. From what Joanie said, the Hill apparently has strange formations on its surface suggestive of the skinfolds of a coiled creature. It may be Celtic, or even Roman."

"Well, *my* reckoning would say that is simply tosh," suggests Rangvald. "My family possess not an ounce of Celtic. And as for Roman... perish the thought. We are Norse through and through, Iceland is our ancestral home."

"Icelandic?" says George. "Now that's interesting. "My book from *Herbie Dragons* about Jörmungandr, Our Boris that is, explains that the World Serpent is Icelandic."

"Jörmungandr!" exclaims Rangvald. "*There's* a name to bring tears to my eyes. Ouroboros is shrouded in myth, even for us dragons, but he was an adventurer without parallel, so the old tales tell. He circled the whole Earth until he caught up with his own tail. Oh, how I'd love to trace his footsteps and travel to far-off, exotic places again."

"Footsteps?" says Bella. "I can't imagine that he walked. Not all around the world, surely?"

"Well, it's merely a figure of speech, Bella. Let's not split hairs."

"Do dragons have hair, then?" Bella persists.

"Look, Bella. I didn't escape that book to be made fun of. If you're not careful, I'll breathe fire on you. Your hair could be removed in a trice with just one breath."

"And *I* thought you had a sense of humour, Rango."

"That's as may be, young lady, but my sense of adventure is far greater. My feet... I mean my wings... are itching for a journey."

5) Book Worm

"Well so are mine," complains George, "but I've already decided that my inheritance is unlikely to fund a trip around the entire world. The whole lot would soon evaporate. If you go gallivanting you'll have to galli your vant alone, I fear. For the moment I shall concentrate on Bignor."

"Then after that we can head for Bisterne, George," suggests Bella. "I always wanted to visit the New Forest."

In the dim morning twilight of the next day, in Bignor, Bella and George commence the trek to the Hill to see the dragonfolds for themselves. Early breakfast means that dawn is still fighting with the crepuscular remnants of darkness. Rangvald, keen to explore the familial hill, but looking to keep a low profile on high, intends to fly self-contradictorily aloft beyond the reach of quizzical eyes. Before he can attain his anonymous altitude, the little dragon encounters a dear old man in the street who's walking his dog. The dog, more surprised than his rather short-sighted owner, barks in protest at the unexpected flutterings of this alien creature, imagining Rangvald to be some maladjusted, winged cat or perhaps a neurotic bat. The dragon startles, flies twice around a lamp-post before regaining his composure, then rockets skyward leaving a trail of smoke and flame hanging momentarily in the air. As George and Bella reach the old fellow, he looks at them nonchalantly.

"Morning," he offers them brightly.

"Good morning," replies Bella, tentatively.

"Morning," echoes George.

"Guy Fawkes night already?" questions the old chap, rather confused at the commotion. "It seems like only a few weeks ago that we had the annual village bonfire. I'm sure time goes faster as we get older, don't you think so?"

"Well, yes. I suppose so," agrees Bella, "but actually it's nearly *Christmas*."

"Well, they must have had some fireworks left over, then.

That was a good one, but I wish they'd give us some warning. My dog, Hubert here, likes to curl up under the stairs when there are fireworks in the air. I might just write to the Council about it."

"Probably a good idea," says George, not wishing to expose the truth behind the explosive episode that the old chap has just witnessed.

By the time the couple reach the Hill, Rangvald has been sitting there waiting for quite awhile.

"What kept you, sluggards?" he taunts.

"You nearly took that fellow's eye out, Rango," says Bella. "He thought you were a firework."

"Did he really?" says Rangvald. "I *love* fireworks. They were invented in China."

"So they say," says George.

"I was on speaking terms with Emperor Wang, I'll have you know, George. It was two or three hundred years before your namesake came along and trapped me in that wordy prison. He used to put on a really good fireworks display, did Wang."

"Hobnobbing with royalty then," says Bella, intrigued by this dragon tale.

"Oh, yes. He was a nice chap... ruthless in many ways, but nice all the same... as far as rulers go, anyway. I'd really like to visit China again."

"I think you'd find it's changed quite a bit," says George. "But then everywhere has changed in the last thousand years and more. In fact everywhere has changed in the last hundred years, truth to tell."

"I can see that, George, sure enough. What with motorbikes and sidecars and telephones. I can't even get the hang of that electric toaster you showed me back at the place where we've been staying."

"Toasters?" says Bella. "You just watch out for aeroplanes and satellites... and I don't dare mention nuclear power to you."

5) Book Worm

"Ah, yes. Nuclear power?"

"Who told you about *that*, Rango?"

"*You* did. Just now."

"Ah, I didn't intend to mention it."

"Look, you two," interrupts George. "The technology lesson can wait. For the time being, let's concentrate on your nephew, Micklewhite. Let's see if you can find evidence of his still being alive. There's a hole here that's suspiciously like an entrance in the side of the hill… just behind these bushes. Admittedly, the hole is a little small, but maybe the Bignor Hill dragon has taken to living here underground. This could be his front door."

"I'm not too sure about this after all," says Rangvald. " meeting long lost relatives can be a bit disappointing. Distressing even. I mean, what if he's changed for the worse?"

"You seem adventurous enough to go back to China," says Bella, "yet you hesitate to explore a little hole here in Bignor. I've never known such a wimpy dragon… not that I've met many of you."

"China's different," counters Rangvald. It's civilised. I've never lived in a hole under a hill myself. It must be very damp in there, Bella."

"I suppose you're right, Rango. *I* certainly wouldn't relish living down a hole. I wouldn't mind seeing China though."

"I tell you what then, Bella. It's a deal. *I'll* go down this hole if *you'll* come to China with me."

"I can't promise, Rango. I mean, I'm with George. All I can say is that I'll think about it. In any case, I don't see how we could get there."

"George could come too, Bella. I could carry both of you. I'm stronger than my size would suggest."

"Er, no thanks, Rango," says George who's been listening to the conversation with misgivings. "First of all, I couldn't afford it. Secondly, I've more or less set my heart for now on finding out about dragons in *this* country, thanks all the same. And I'm certain that you'll find Bella to be of like mind if you ask me, Rango."

"Well, it was just a thought. I'll nip down this hole anyway, just for you, George, seeing as how you brought about my escape from the library."

And with this, Rangvald disappears behind the bushes squeezing his way into the hole and on into the dark depths of the hill.

"Good luck in there," calls Bella after him.

She's answered by a whoosh as Rangvald belches flame to light his way.

"You wouldn't *really* consider going to China with a dragon, would you, Bella?" pleads George. "We're doing alright touring the country *here*, aren't we?"

"I'm tempted, George. But I must admit, it wouldn't be very practical, would it. As for touring here, I can't say that we're finding the Norton the best way to do our travelling, are we."

"I've been thinking the same, Bel. Maybe we could get a campervan."

"I guess a campervan would make sense, George, but if we did get one, I couldn't bear to part with the bike. As you know, my dad bought it for me and it's close to my heart."

At that very moment, the ground rumbles and shakes beneath their feet. A spurt of fire and smoke belches forth from the entrance through which Rangvald had disappeared, setting fire to the bushes beyond its confines outside. The belch is followed by a shudder as Rangvald forces his way out of the hole, takes to the air, and pirouettes around the burning bushes, settling back to Earth again next to George and Bella.

"Ugh!" exclaims the petit-dragon. "It was horrible! As horrible as horrible can be."

"What, Rango? What is it?" asks Bella. "Have you found Micklewhite?"

"Well, yes… and no. There's a pile of bones in there that look

5) Book Worm

suspiciously like a dragon demised. There's a lump on its skull, between the eye sockets... a family trait, I fear. Poor old Micklewhite... I suspect he is no more. But that wasn't the horrible bit."

"Then why all the fuss, Rango?" asks George. "You frightened us half to death with your rumbling and belching."

"I'm sorry, but it was horrible... I saw a worm... I *hate* worms."

"But you *are* a worm, Rango. *All* dragons are worms, aren't they?" suggests George.

"No they're *not*, George. Worms don't have wings for a start. And as for little worms... they make me shiver. What would *you* do if you came across a little, three inch tall man, George? That would give you the shivers, wouldn't it?"

"I've never really thought about it, Rango, but now you come to mention it, it would be a little unnerving I suppose."

"A little *unnerving*, George? It would probably make you shit yourself."

"Then think about it, Rango," suggests Bella. You're not so large yourself, are you, and if you were to meet with Our Boris, *he'd* be quaking in his boots, for sure."

"I'd let *him* worry about that, Bel. And anyway, dragons don't wear boots. I can tell you now, I'm quite prepared to be selfish here... I'm not going down that hole again. Not for any money."

"We weren't offering you any money, Rango," says George, patting his wallet, with a reflex action to his breast pocket, making sure his cash is still where it's supposed to be.

"It was a figure of speech, George."

"Well, if you're so afraid of worms," says Bella, "I can't see you surviving a trip all the way to China. And just think of all those silkworms. You'd be frightened all over again."

"Silkworms are different. They don't lurk in dark holes in the ground."

"From what I've read," rejoins George, "lots of dragons live quite happily underground. Look at Micklewhite for one."

"That's my point, George. Look at him... living in a hole didn't do him a lot of good, did it. It was probably that very worm that killed him. Ugh!"

"You're being very silly now, Rango," Bella says firmly, attempting to bring the dragon back to reality. "Little worms don't kill majestic beasts such as yourself."

Bella's flattery seems to do the trick and Rangvald calms down. They decide to accept that Micklewhite, the Bignor dragon, is dead and to head back for their room in the village, so as to prepare for the next move on the dragon quest.

As the three of them reach their magnolia and beige den, Rangvald executing a holding pattern high over the house, Mr. and Mrs. Stark are walking up the garden path towards the front door. This is in stark contrast to their usual weekday routine, for they wouldn't normally be home so early. It transpires that Mr. Stark has been summarily sacked from his job of some fifteen years; his immediate boss at the Petworth authority had caught him stealing rubber bands from the stationary cupboard and Mr. Stark had metamorphosed, in a brief moment of madness, into the most uncivil servant in the town. When his boss had been attended to by the first-aid officer, who'd managed to staunch the blood pouring from the boss's nose, Mark Stark had been ordered to leave the building immediately and told that paperwork would follow in the post... post-haste. Muriel Stark had broken off from her vacuum cleaning two doors down and nipped into town to collect the poor man, escorting him home personally, in view of how upset he was.

Bella and George, having followed the Starks up the path, now stand in wonder as the pair discuss the episode oblivious to their queuing guests.

"I told you your temper would flare up again, Mark," complains Muriel. "It's all the pressure of that roadworks job

5) Book Worm

you're working on. I *did* warn you, didn't I."

"Yes, Muriel, but I only took the rubber bands to hold up my trousers. Here, look, my belt's snapped. But that old fart-brain of a boss wouldn't listen... I think he's had it in for me for a long time. That's when I hit him. It felt good though. He's been getting on my wick for years."

"Well, *I* think you should appeal, Mark," says Muriel.

"Oh, I don't know, I'm not really the appealing type."

"He can say that again," whispers George to Bella in an aside.

"Well, if you won't appeal, what are we going to do without your salary, Mark? We can't live on thin air you know."

"Look, Muriel, there's no way I'd go back there to work under *him*. I'll find something."

Whilst all this is going on, Rangvald has decided enough circling is enough, so down he flies and perches on the roof of the front porch, landing in a flutter of wings and a scratching of claws on the shingles.

"What the...!" Muriel cries out loud.

"For crying out loud!" adds Mark. "I've had enough of today already, without mythical creatures descending on me from the heavens."

With that, the not so civil servant jumps up endeavouring to swipe Rangvald from the roof. The dragon steps aside niftily and darts a short burst of flame at the irate civil servant.

"Don't you go burning my husband, you dragon you," shouts Muriel. "He's had enough to cope with today without *you* butting in."

"Excuse me, sir, but I am *not* mythical, I'll have you know," complains Rangvald. "I'm as real as a creature can be. You ask my friends here."

"Is this thing with you two?" says Muriel, in surprise. "I hope it's not been staying in our house."

"Yes, I have, actually," Rangvald decides to admit. "And I've looked after your furniture with great care. I even put down the toilet seat when I used it... George taught me to do that. So please don't call me an it... I'm a him."

"Well you can all just pack your bags and leave," rages Mark Stark who's lost the plot now, thanks to his 'fart-brain of a boss'. "I've bloody well had it up to here today. Sod off... the lot of you," he insists.

"Don't you go punching any noses, Mark Stark," says his wife, sympathetically.

"We were leaving later today anyway, thank you very much," says Bella. "But I don't see why you should take it out on us and our dragon friend just because you're home early. You'll even find that Rangvald here has made the bed... *I* taught him that."

And so, without much ado, and with nothing to keep them in Bignor now they've established that Micklewhite is long gone, George and Bella pack their belongings into the sidecar. Rangvald insists on staying on his porch perch until they're ready to go. George pays Muriel Stark by cheque and bidding her and her smouldering, broken husband a brittle farewell, they're away, heading for Bisterne with the hope of finding another dragon. Rangvald follows, flying in their slipstream, Chichester their first intended destination.

Later that week, news spreads in the town of Arundel that some mysterious intrusion has occurred at the castle. According to police, someone had entered the library and rummaged through some very important books. The local press is reporting that, fortunately, the only damage found was to just one, very ancient specimen which had been put back on its shelf in the wrong place and that mysterious scorch marks had been found on pages seventy-five and seventy-six. The police officer in charge of the investigation, one Harry Fielding, had said that it appeared to be a bungled attempt at setting fire to the whole collection of rare books. He added that the area had

5) Book Worm

experienced a spate of arson around and about recently, though the modus operandi in this case was very different. They were even considering the distinct possibility that it may be an inside job.

"Well, who'd have thought it?" says Peregrine to Madge as they leave the cinema after a showing of Dr. Who and the Daleks. "Intruders and attempted arson at the castle, eh. What's the world coming to?"

"It's all nonsense to me, Perry," suggests Madge.

"What, arson?"

"No... Dr. Who."

-o-o-o-

6) Be Stern

"Hey look, Bel," shouts George. "Just ahead on the right... 'VWs Galore'. It's a sign."

"I know it's a sign, George," calls back Bella. "It's on a bloody great pole."

"No, I mean it's an omen. We said about getting a campervan, didn't we? Well, there's a whole row of them there; blue and white, green and white, red and white... even white and white. Pull over, Bel. It's worth a look at least."

Bella gives George the thumbs up to save further shouting. She runs down through the gears, slowing to turn in onto the forecourt and pulls up at the bank of fuel pumps in front of the showroom. Rangvald is coiled warmly under George's spare coat in the sidecar, having flown a good deal of the way from Bignor. Bella and George dismount and remove their helmets.

"Stay put, Rango," instructs George through the partially opened side window of the sidecar. "Best you keep out of the way in here. One inadvertent flame from you and we could be toasted."

"What on Earth *is* this place, George?"

"It's a petrol station and garage, Rango."

"What's petrol, George?"

"Volatile," explains George. "That's what it is. It's fuel for internal combustion engines."

"I'm sorry I asked... but what's an engine?"

George is minded of an inquisitive child asking a chain of questions, each answer demanding another, and feels ill-equipped to break the chain.

"Didn't you wonder what gives power to the motorbike and all those cars travelling on the road?"

"Cars? Sidecars? Be fair, George. I have a lot to take in. It wasn't top of my list of items requiring an explanation."

6) Be Stern

"Okay. Now, imagine the flames of hell, burning hot and out of control. Then harness them under pressure in a strong container…"

"This is beginning to sound like my incarceration in that book, George."

"Yes, well, suffice it to say that if you then channel those flames into driving the wheels of a vehicle, you can travel about at will."

"Sounds a bit lazy to me. What's wrong with feet… and wings?"

"Ah well, Rango. Seeing as, unlike you, we can't fly, then this way we can convert feet into yards and yards into miles, without blisters."

"Fair enough, George. I'm beginning to understand."

"Anyway, Rango. Like I said, you'd better lie low while Bel and I re-fuel the bike. Then we're going to see if we can find a van to suit our further travels. Let me just close this window."

"A van?," Rangvald chunters to himself.

The proprietor greets Bella and George at the door of his showroom: "Ernest Van Kampe, at your service. Is it just petrol you're after, or can I sell you one of my exceptional campervans?" he asks more in hope than conviction.

"Well, both actually," says George.

Ernest coughs in surprise, searching his grey cells to remind himself of what to say next, he not having sold a vehicle for nearly three months: "Oh, Right. Well, err, lets get you topped up with fuel first, then we can go into my office," he manages, grasping at the opportunity of fuel-filling his everyday obligations, so as to give himself more time to switch to campervan mode.

"Ernest Van Kampe? Is that your real name?" asks Bella in disbelief.

"It certainly is. People don't believe me, but that's what led me into selling campervans. Everyone insists it must have been the other way around, but it's true. My dad's name was Vinnie Van Kampe. People don't believe that either. And *he* didn't sell campervans... he was a wine merchant."

George and Bella accompany Ernest back to the pumps, where the garage owner unscrews the petrol cap on the Norton, lifts the pump nozzle and places it in the tank. He unlatches the pump handle and begins turning, several full rotations per gallon. Bella does her best to distract him from noticing Rangvald, who's fallen asleep partially covered and is snoring serenely as dragons sometimes do. George looks casually to the clear, blue, December sky, whistling strains of Lillibullero, minded of Joanie and her Knucker.

The tank filled, Ernest turns to place the nozzle back in its mount then, fumbling with the bike's filler-cap, drops it inadvertently. It clatters to the concrete with a rattle, Rangvald startles from his slumbers and, banging his head against the sidecar window, lets out a cloud of fiery smoke.

"Bloody hell! What the fuck's that?" shouts Ernest Van Kampe.

"It's alright," reassures Bella. "He's just our pet lizard. His breath is worse that his bite."

"You mean it bites? Oh, my God! Oh, my God! I need a whisky."

"No, really. He wont hurt you. I promise," says Bella.

"It's true, says George," signalling Rangvald to settle down. "Let's go into your office and talk campervan in earnest, Ernest."

"Right you are," agrees Ernest, nervously retrieving the petrol cap and handing it to Bella to deal with.

George pursues the fast-retreating Ernest, while Bella parks up the bike at one end of the line of campervans, then joins the pair of them in the office as Mr. Van Kampe is pouring himself a large whisky. Rangvald settles down to resume his slumbers, dreaming of riding on an enormous internal combustion engine

6) Be Stern

across the vast plains of China, despite being unsure of what in the world a combustion engine really looks like.

"So, what price-range are you looking for, Mr. err...?"

"Crosby," confirms George.

"Well, Mr. Crosby. We have used vans ranging from one-forty-nine pounds up to seven-ninety-nine pounds."

"I really want to stick to three-hundred, top whack," confirms George.

"Well, okay," says Ernest, recovering from his shock and downing the remainder of his large whisky. We have a few nice ones for that sort of price. Lets go out and have a look at what we've got shall we?"

"Fine," agrees George, pleasantly surprised that Ernest seems honest enough not to push him to spend more, but thinking: *'It would have been nice if he'd offered us a whisky.'*

Out on the forecourt, Ernest ushers his customers to the neatly parked line of vans. They're presented in ascending order of price, from left to right, the bike and sidecar being parked at the cheap end.

"Sorry," says Ernest to Bella. "Do you think you could move the motorbike to the other end of the row, love? I don't really want to meet with your lizard again, nice though I'm sure he is."

Bella obliges while George peruses a rather garish campervan, painted a multitude of bright colours and priced at three hundred and fifty pounds. By the time Bella rejoins George and Ernest, her partner has agreed a deal for it at two hundred and seventy-five pounds, plus ten pounds for a suspiciously ancient Calor gas camping stove... cash, no questions asked.

"We'll get off to the bank on the bike and we'll be back with the cash before you can say 'Purchase Tax', Mr. Van Kampe."

"But I didn't mention Purchase T..."

"Precisely," interrupts George.

"You mean you've bought it already, George?" Bella questions. "It would have been nice to discuss it with you first."

"Sorry, Bel, but it was just too good to miss. Don't you think it's a great van? Purple and yellow go so well together, don't they."

"Well, there's hardly a queue for it, is there, George."

"It's true, Bel, but when I decide to do something, I have to get it done, pronto."

"Then how about you learn to drive, pronto, George. Are you assuming that I'm doing all the driving?"

"Ah. That's a point. But *you* can teach me can't you? Tell me you can drive a car, Bel?"

"As it happens, yes, George. You might have asked before now."

"Well, when we mentioned getting a van, I just assumed…"

"And *I* assumed you'd get around to asking beforehand. Anyway, I can't ride the bike at the same time as driving a van, can I. So here's what we do… give the man a deposit and we'll get the rest of the cash later. Before that, I'll take us on the bike and sidecar back to my brother's; he'll stow it and take care of it for me. Then we'll come back here by bus."

"But it's miles, Bella, and it would mean going through London. Why don't we try Barry and his *Bike Bonanza* back in New Malden?"

"That creep?" protests Bella. "I wouldn't trust him with a head gasket let alone a full-blown '57 Norton Dominator."

"I'm sure he'll look after it for you. Let's face it, if he steps out of line again you can always be stern, and threaten him with your girlfriend."

"Well, I suppose he *did* get us the sidecar, George. Did you keep his phone number? It was on the receipt, wasn't it? Anyway, what about Rango? It's best if he stays here, I guess."

"Oh, no," protests Ernest. "I'm not having an unattended lizard on the premises."

6) Be Stern

"But he really *is* harmless," Bella tries to reassure the garage owner. We can lock him in the van. As long as he has water and a few snacks, he'll be okay."

So George hands over twenty-eight-pound-ten to the reluctant Mr. Van Kampe as a deposit and shakes hands on the deal. After speaking on the phone with slimy Barry, the pair reassure Rangvald that the campervan will keep him safe and snug until their return, and they're off back to New Malden.

In the event, slimy Barry proves to be on better behaviour, but insists on a retainer fee of thirty pounds, on the understanding that Bella will collect her bike within three months: "If you're not back to claim it by then, I reserve the right to sell it," he suggests.

"Who do you think you are?" protests Bella. "A bloody pawnbroker? Well that's just a load of balls."

"Just *three*, love, to be prec…"

The bike seller's cut short by a steely grimace from Bella that makes a précis of his precise.

"Well, love, space is money… a bit like time…," he ventures timidly, his words fading away into space and time thanks to another scowl from George's partner.

"Just mark *this*, Bazza," says Bella. "My girlfriend, who you've already heard about is nothing compared to my new boyfriend, Rango. He's like a wild animal with a blowtorch… in fact he is a wild animal with a blowtorch, and unless you have a passion for scorched eyebrows, then my bike will be here when I return, regardless."

"I suppose, being as I know you as a valued customer, I *could* make an exception for such a lovel…"

"Don't push it, Bazza," intervenes George, who'd been silent up to now. "Rango really *is* too hot to handle, mate. Believe me, *I* know."

"You mean *you've* had your eyebrows scorched?

"Almost."

"Anyway," Barry bravely ventures, "you won't get a bus back west until tomorrow now. Next one will be ten o'clock in the morning."

"Bugger," says George. "What shall we do, Bel?"

"We'll be staying here in Barry's showroom. Won't we, Bazza."

"Er. It's highly irregular. I mean it'll cost y…"

"Nothing, Bazza!" Bella glares.

"Exactly, love. As I was about to say, it'll cost you nothing," Barry surrenders.

"Do you think Rango will be okay overnight, George?"

"I'm sure he will, Bel. I'll call Ernest to explain."

"Use the payphone mate," insists slimy Barry, determined not to incur unnecessary expense.

"Thank God you called," are the first words that Ernest blurts out, as George pushes coins into the hungry slot. "You didn't leave me with a number, did you."

"What do you mean, Mr. Van Kampe?" says George, with an air of foreboding. "I'm ringing to say we won't be back until tomorrow. There aren't any more buses today."

Bella picks up on George's note of anxiety and leans in close to try and hear what the garage owner is saying.

"Look here, Mr. Crosby. There's no point you coming back here expecting to find your campervan. It's gone!"

"Gone?" replies George, incredulous. "Gone where?"

"Up in flames. That's where it's gone. Burned to a cinder it is. About half-an-hour after you left, two masked men arrived in a Ford Anglia and one of them got out, pointed a gun at me, insisted I give him the keys to your VW, and made to drive off with it."

"What do mean? What about Rangvald?"

"I was coming to that. That pesky lizard has gone too. It did almost do us a favour though. Took the bloke's hat off with an

6) Be Stern

almighty blast of flames and away the two villains went at ninety miles an hour, if a Ford Anglia can *do* ninety miles an hour. I really thought the whole place would go up in flames."

Bella, looking ever more anxious, catches the words 'gone', 'masked men', 'gun' and 'flames', but not much else. She's about to ask George what it's all about, when he holds up a hand to suggest she let him hear what more Ernest has to say. Barry looks anxious, content to stand at a tactful distance.

"I knew your creature was trouble, what with its fiery flames and all. It spoke it did… it spoke words. It said it was sorry but it was going off to China. A place called Kowloon, I think it was, though it said something about The Holy Land too… said it wanted to find a relative in somewhere called Hebron. By the time I'd realised it was speaking to *me*, it had gone. Flew off to the North East, towards London, as far as I could tell. You'll have to pay for the van, I'm afraid."

"Bella," George utters desperately, turning to his companion. "Rango's gone. He's gone to China. The campervan's gone too."

"What? The campervan's gone to China? But Rango can't drive any more than *you* can, George."

"No. It's gone up in flames and *we've* got to pay for it. At least Rango's safe, but why would he go off without us? We were getting on so well, the three of us."

"Hand me the phone, George," demands Bella, taking it from George's grasp before she's finished asking for it.

"Now then, Mr. Van Kampe," she says assertively, "you listen to me. You can claim the van on your insurance. It wasn't ours yet, was it. And you'd better call the police too. There can't be many armed villains that use a Ford Anglia as a getaway car. Come to that, there aren't many armed villains that would want a brightly painted VW to further their heinous life of crime."

"No, no, I can't call the police. They'd think I'd gone mad saying a fire-breathing lizard had scared the robbers off and they'd start asking awkward questions about purchase tax and things too. As for insurance, well..."

"Right then. Just keep the deposit as compensation, and no questions asked. It'll cover taking the van to the scrapyard, won't it."

"Err, I suppose you're right. Fair enough."

George grabs back the phone and apologises profusely, more worried about the fact that Rango has gone off to the orient without a by-your-leave."

"We won't need to stay over, Bazza," says Bella. "The wheels of the world have turned back a bit, and we'll be using the bike for a while after all."

"Can't say I'm sorry love. What with you wanting to stay over for nothing. Will you be needing the sidecar though? I can always sell it on. I'll give you a good price for it. How about twenty-five quid?"

"You cheeky bastard! We gave *you* forty pounds for it."

"Well it's at least third-hand now, isn't it. And those extra miles on the clock. Well..."

"Well stuff your pony where the paddock don't shine. And anyway we need it, at least 'til we get another campervan."

"Alright, love. Keep your hair on. I was only trying to help."

Bella calms down a little as George steps in.

"Look, Bazza. Let's all settle down, shall we? It's unfortunate that our circumstances have changed, but we'll be heading back for Chichester and Bisterne now, and we need to get moving."

"Right you are, gov," whimpers Barry, still recovering from Bella's admonishment.

"As for campervans," adds George, turning to Bella, "we'll have to see what we can find on the next leg of our travels. We certainly won't be going back to see Ernest Van Kampe and his flaming fleet of VWs."

So, George and Bella are back on the road. George is beginning to wonder if they'll ever find evidence of Our Boris, and Bella is

6) Be Stern

beginning to wonder if the two of them will ever regain their sanity.

"Now then, George," shouts back Bella as they reach the A3, "Much as I love the idea of a campervan, I love this bike more, and I reckon we can manage as we are for a while."

"Suits me, I guess," answers George. "I'm getting to like swanning around in these leathers."

The weather is kind and they make good progress to Chichester, though night is creeping on by the time they arrive.

"We'd better find a pub or something, with accommodation for the night, George. There's bound to be somewhere suitable in a place like this."

They park up in a side-street near the cathedral and venture down to the cross, then along South Street where they're confronted with The White Horse boasting a hand written sign announcing 'ACCOMMODATION' written in a shaky hand on a makeshift piece of plywood.

"Here we are, George. This should do. I wonder if they have room to park the bike?"

They enter tentative, finding a diminutive middle-aged woman behind the bar sporting a smouldering, un-tipped cigarette with a stub of ash that's longer than the remaining stub of cigarette. She's pulling a pint for the only other customer; a spindly, bearded young fellow with a grubby university scarf who's sat in a corner reading a copy of the *Daily Worker*. He already has a full pint glass perched within easy reach of his left hand and a packet of KP salted peanuts near to his right hand.

"Is the landlord in?" enquires George of the woman.

"I'm the landla… drat! Now look what you've made me do," she scolds unbridled, as the plug of ash falls into the half-pulled pint. "That's wasted now, that is."

"Sorry. I didn't mean to…" starts George, only to be interrupted by the lady with the ash-less fag.

"Oh, never mind. It's probably my fault. It's just that I'm rushed off me feet, here. My regular barman if off with apparent tennis elbow. He says it's from pulling pints, but I saw him down the tennis club the other day. I reckon he's pulling the wool more than pulling pints."

Bella looks round at the spindly, socialist bloke thinking: *'rushed off me feet? I wonder how she copes when it's busy?'*

"Well," ventures George, "we were wondering if you had a room for the night?"

"I do. But *you're* not using it. I always sleep on me own. Ever since Archibald left, that is."

"No," protests George, I meant do you…"

"I know what you meant, young man," the landlady interrupts, smiling a wry smile now, as she finishes pouring the replacement pint. "We *do* have a room, and we haven't anyone staying at the moment. You can go up and inspect it if you like. The stairs are through there. It's the one that's first on your left at the top. The toilet's at the far end of the landing. Three pounds a night for the double. Can I pour you drinks while you check it out? I should be able to fit it in, after I've poured this bloke's pint."

She says all this without taking a breath, while the spindly man looks up casually, scratches his stubbly beard, grabs a handful of peanuts and then gets back to his *Daily Worker*.

"Two glasses of cider then, please." confirms Bella. *'Daily Worker?'* she thinks. *'I don't reckon he's done day's work in his life.'*

"Do you have anywhere we can park our motorbike?" enquires Bella. "It has a sidecar attached."

"I'm afraid not, love. The yard's tiny and it's full of empty barrels. It'll be safe leaving it on the streets. Chichester's not London you know. You can't leave anything on the streets in some parts of London. I wish I'd have known that years ago. I would have parked Archibald there, silly old bugger."

After inspecting the room, which turns out to be bijou but

6) Be Stern

spotless, they agree that they'll stay.

"We'll just go and get some stuff from the bike then," says Bella.

"Well, don't be long, or your drinks will go cold," the landlady chuckles. "You can call me Deirdre, by the way."

When George and Bella return, laden with the bulk of their worldly belongings, the spindly man now has two full pints of beer and two packets of KP nuts, Deirdre has poured their ciders and is busy pulling another pint. There are still no other customers.

'Surely not another pint?' muses Bella, casting a glance at the corner.

"Here are you drinks," proffers the landlady. "I'll just finish off priming this new barrel, then I can get you a sandwich if you like. You must be hungry. Where did you say you've come from?"

"Err, New Malden," George answers. "We're looking to go to Bisterne. We're searching for dragons."

Bella nudges George, whispering: "don't go saying things like that. People will think we're mad."

"Don't you worry about that," says the eagle-eared Deirdre. "We get all sorts of nutters in here. Not that I'm calling *you* nutters, mind."

"There's a Green Dragon pub in town," says Deirdre. "That's the only dragon I know about in Chichester."

"What did I tell you, Bel," says George. "Everybody knows a Green Dragon. First that bloke near Market Harborough, then Carlton in London, and now Deirdre. It's obvious real dragons were everywhere once. You can't blame them for hiding though, can you. I mean look at poor old Rango… locked up in that book by Saint George. Makes me almost ashamed to have the same name."

With that, Bella ushers George to a table next to the spindly man who's actually made headway into his first pint.

"I suppose *you* know a Green Dragon too, mate?" George asks. "I'm George, by the way. And this is Bella."

The man in the dishevelled scarf looks up laconically and dibs into one of his packets of peanuts, helping himself to a generous handful: "I *do* know of the one Deirdre just mentioned," he says, "though I've never been in there. I'm told they don't serve peanuts."

"Right," acknowledges George.

"Not that I'm a peanut, you understand." adds the scarved man.

"No, of course not," agrees George. "I didn't catch you name, by the way."

"Derek. Derek Cattermole. Pleased to meet you."

"And pleased to meet *you* too," says Bella, wondering if Derek has been sat in his corner for weeks. *'No one could avoid being spindly living on just beer and peanuts,'* she thinks.

"Damn!" they hear Deirdre call out from the bar. "Another bloody customer coming in. I'll never cope on me own."

"So, what do you do for a living then?" Bella asks Derek, hoping to fathom the mystery of the seemingly permanent fixture of a customer.

"Oh, I'm an atomic scientist," he confirms blandly. "I work over in Suffolk, in Orford Ness, but I'm not allowed to tell you any more than that. I'm back here in Chichester on leave at the moment, where I live most of the time with my mum."

"Orford, eh?" says George in surprise. "We know it well. I bet you know Jacob in the Jolly Sailor. And old Harry, the malingerer who made off with my cash."

"That's old Harry for you," says Derek. "Don't drink his tea, whatever you do. It's lethal. Worse than anything we're working on at the A.W.R.E.... oh, forget I said that. I'm not supposed to mention it."

"Mention what?," says George, complying with the request to forget it.

6) Be Stern

"Do you know about the Orford Sea-dragon then, Derek?" enquires Bella.

"No. No. Never heard of it," Derek says nervously, setting Bella to think that maybe the Orford Sea-dragon is something to do with the A.W.R.E, which they learn from Deirdre is the *Atomic Weapons Research Establishment*.

"We'll leave you in peace to your beer then, Derek," says George. He and Bella shrink back to their chosen table and speak in subdued tones about their next move... to Bisterne.

"Right," says Derek, returning to his *Daily Worker*.

"Whew! Thank God for that," they hear Deirdre whisper, as the other imminent customer does a u-turn and leaves the pub without ordering anything.

Back in their bijou room, replete with cider, Bella and George mull over their strategy.

"Bella? You don't *really* think the Orford Sea-dragon has anything to do with atomic weapons, do you?"

"Well, George. Stranger things have happened at sea, as my old nan used to say."

"But, he's recorded in all the books from ages ago. He's more likely to be related to Our Boris than to Oppenheimer, or Albert Einstein with his $E=MC^2$ or whatever it is."

"I know, George. But it *does* make you think. Relativity could be involved somewhere. For a start, the Orford Sea-dragon is probably *related* to Boris, if you get my meaning."

"Look Bel. We have to focus on our quest for information about Our Boris. All this distraction is a bit off-putting. Bisterne is the place to concentrate on. There may be some real clues there."

"Well, the Knucker didn't have much luck, did he."

"But, he may not have been telling the truth, Bel. Look how sensitive they are about revealing their real names. He could have just been putting up a smoke screen."

"Fair enough, George. *'In for a penny'*, as you've said before."

Next morning, at breakfast in the pub bar, proof is presented that Derek wasn't bolted down to his corner seat. He's left his two peanut packets lying empty on the table, They're floating on a puddle of beer like casualties from the Mary Celeste, drifting on a less-than-heavenly sea.

Deirdre shuffles in, a fresh-lit cigarette on her lips and with two full-English breakfasts to die for, perfectly cooked and presented.

"Morning both. Hope you slept well. I've assumed you'd want black pudding with your fry-up. I'll get you tea for two... we've run out of coffee. Then I'll clear up Derek's debris. He didn't leave 'til midnight, saying that his mother might not let him in so late. But then he don't leave 'til midnight any night. What are men like, eh love?" she says, addressing Bella.

Bella shrugs and smiles thinking better of it than to comment.

"Oh, by the way," adds Deirdre, after placing the meals before them on the neatly laid table. "Derek did say that if you were looking for dragons, you could try the record office. It's just down near the cathedral. He says they've got old books on all sorts there."

"We'll try it out, thank you, Deirdre," says George gratefully, thinking *'if the Library in Leicester can have a resident dragon in the form of Samantha Battlebury, then why wouldn't a record office have a dragon,'* as he tackles a rasher of bacon. "I bet they'll have something of interest," he adds.

"Well, I suppose that depends on what you're interested in, love." suggests Deirdre, with a wry smile.

Bella smiles in return, saying, "We need one more night's stay, if that's alright, Deirdre. Before we move on to Bisterne."

"That's fine," says the landlady. "I'll get you that tea."

When the biking couple arrive at the record office, after

6) Be Stern

checking that their chariot is safe in it's side-street parking spot, they find that the imposing Georgian panelled door is locked. Bella strikes the impressive knocker impressively… once, twice three times like the beat of an execution drum. George exchanges a questioning glance with Bella at the sound of bolts being un-shot within. Bella sniggers, thinking it all a bit dramatic for a record office, while a foreboding, silent pause allows George to return the snigger. The door finally creaks open to reveal in the gloom of the entrance hall a wiry-haired, smiley man in his late thirties.

"S'alright, in't it," he greets them cheerily. "Have you got an appointment?" he adds, looking first at George, then at Bella.

"Err, no," confirms George. "Do we need one?"

"Not really," say the cheerful man. who's as wiry as his hair. "S'alright, in't it. The archivist is never too busy to greet customers. Lovely lady she is. Her name's Allison. I'll tell her you're here. Can I get you coffees?"

"We're okay, thanks," Bella says. "We've just had breakfast."

"I'll leave you to it then," says their greeter, "while I get Allison, that is."

"Thank you. Err, what was your name?" George asks.

"S'alright, in't it. Well, that 's not my *name*… It's James, Jim to my friends… *and* to my mum, when she's in a good mood."

"Thanks, Jim." smiles Bella. "Sorry… James," she adds not wishing to be presumptuous."

"Blimey," says James. "You sounded just like my mum then. It made me wonder what I'd done wrong."

"Sorry," says a confused Bella. "Jim, then."

"S'alright, in't it," says Jim, and off he trots.

When Allison, the County Archivist, arrives she proves to be every bit as nice as Jim had suggested. Fair haired and neatly dressed, she greets the two researchers with a warm smile. They exchange names formally and, armed with an explanation from George of their quest, she escorts them to the search room.

"Now, I do believe we have one particular book that may interest you. We acquired it quite recently from a specialist in London. From memory I think it's called *Jörmungandr - the Tale of the Tail of a Serpent*. Printed in 1666. It's one of only two in existence, I recall. It cost us nine pounds."

"Not from Herbie Dragons?" asks George.

"Oh, I believe that's right. You know it then?"

"Too true. He wanted four pound ten for ours. We paid four pounds in the end. I think if you look a little closer, you'll find it was printed in 1959, in Taiwan."

"Well, good Lord! If I were prone to swearing, I'd say bugger," says Allison. "I've a mind to send Jim up to London to put the frighteners on that Herbie, but he'd probably say 's'alright, in't it'. He's like that."

"Yes, we gathered," says Bella.

"Well, anyway, Herbie Dragons aside," offers Allison, "I'll introduce you to our Cardex system. I doubt you'll find anything here though, but it's worth a try I suppose."

"It's always worth a try," says George. "We're very grateful to you for fitting us in without notice. We're travelling wherever the trail takes us and we're headed for Bisterne next."

"Bisterne? That's in Hampshire, isn't it?"

"That's right," confirms Bella.

"Good. Right, seat yourselves here. I'll get the boxes. Pencils only remember. Here, use this one. You won't need white gloves, whatever it is we can find you. Silly idea that."

George thanks his stars that this Allison seems nothing like Samantha Battlebury.

"You know, our real intention is to find out about Our Boris… Ouroboros to be correct, but we've scoured that book we've both got, *Jörmungandr - the Tale of the Tail of a Serpent*, and the clues are few and far between. I don't think the Taiwanese know much about Iceland to tell the truth. One of the dragons

6) Be Stern

we met, over at Arundel, seemed to know a bit about him, but it was all a bit vague. We just thought there may be more clues over this way. There's a vague mention of Bisterne in the other book we got from that Herbie: *A Guide to Mythical Beasts of England and Wales*, but it's not really very helpful."

Allison looks askance now at the couple thinking she may have made a mistake letting them in without prior arrangement: "I see. So you've met dragons already then?" tending towards humouring George and Bella.

"Not really," says Bella, sensing the air of trepidation in Allison's voice and thinking that the Arundel affair might be best not highlighted. "It's just a figure of speech. George often talks like that. He's *so* keen on dragons, you see."

Allison is reassured and, telling the couple to call for her if they need further assistance, she goes off to the refuge of her office in the depths of the building.

Bella and George are alone, seemingly the only inquisitive people in Chichester on this particular morning. They're still thumbing through the Cardex system to no avail when wiry Jim pops his head round the door. He enters carrying a tray with two coffees and some rather tempting Barmouth thins.

"Thought you might like coffees after all, you two. I bet it's thirsty work, dragon-hunting. All those flames. Make you parched, they will."

Bella thanks him as quickly as she can, hoping he wouldn't say 's'alright, in't it', but he says it anyway, and he adds: "Allison told me about your dragon hunt, and it reminded me that I came across a book a while back that mentioned Bisterne. It's to do with a bloke called Maurice de Berkeley. A knight, I think he was. Might have had something to do with the Crusades. I think it mentioned Burley and Lyndhurst too… they're near Bisterne. I'll dig out the book for you if you like. We should have sent it on to Hampshire really, but we're a bit behind with that sort of thing."

BOOK WORM ~ *The Curiosity of George Crosby*

Before you could say Jörmungandr backwards, Jim is back with a booklet of a book, crimson leather-bound and gold figured. It's titled Baron de Berkeley - from Bolton's Bench to Yew Tree.

"How fascinating," says Bella. "Don't you think so, George?"

"I *do*, Bel. Let's have a closer look."

George opens the little book somewhere at its middle, gingerly folding it back to avoid damaging the spine. He's opened it at a page headed 'Bolton's Bench'.

"Get your hiking boots on, Bel. Looks like Bolton's Bench is another hill. What *is* it about dragons and hills?"

"Well, George. It's probably like birds perching on the highest of branches; for the uninterrupted view of potential enemies. Same as castles and armies."

"I see what you mean, Bel, but the dragons seem to go under-hill rather than on-the-hill. Now, if Rango had've perched himself *on* a hill, Saint George would probably never have caught him."

"Quiet right, George. First rule of dating… 'always meet him, or her, on a grassy knoll'."

Seriously though, Bel, look. It says here that the Bisterne dragon set up home in Burley, a few miles from Bisterne. It was this Baron de Berkeley that actually lived in Bisterne and the dragon was terrorising his village."

"Whatever next?" interrupts Bella.

"And look," continues George. "The dragon was finally killed in Lyndhurst, some distance away, and its body turned into this hill called Bolton's Bench. Then the Baron went mad from the dreadful battle he'd had with the dragon, to the point where he was dying. He went back to the hill, laid down and died and his body took root and became a yew tree."

"Are you sure there's not a bit of mistranscribing going on here, George?"

George takes a sip of his now rather cold coffee and closes

6) Be Stern

the book. "Of course, the dragon might have anticipated the onslaught if Bolton's Bench had been there before he *became* it."

"You know, I don't suppose it's worth going to Bisterne, George. I wonder, if the dragon's dead, what's the point. I guess that the Knucker was right after all. 'From Bignor to Bisterne, Kilve to Knotlow, all to no avail', is what he said, remember."

"I'm *sure* it's worth going, Bel. Truth to tell, dead or alive, all these dragon tales build up a picture. I guess this Bisterne dragon could easily be related to Rango. I don't suppose it gives us any more true clues about Our Boris, but you never know. And anyway, we know we're never going to travel the whole world the way things are going. Let's persevere here in England. Something may yet turn up. I wonder where Rango is by the way? If he's gone back to the Holy Land, he'll find it's changed a bit."

"Hasn't it all, George. Hasn't it all," says Bella rather sympathetically.

Jim pops his head round the door.

"Can I get you some more coffees?"

"Err, no thanks, Jim" says George absently. I think we've seen as much as we'd hoped for, unless you can remember seeing any other dragon books."

"Not really," he says. "We don't see many dragons at all round here. But s'alright, in't it."

Bella smiles, thinking: *'if everyone in the world was like Jim, we'd all be a bit happier'*.

The two researchers bid thank you and farewell to Jim and Allison after handing back the little crimson booklet. Jim retrieves his coffee cups from the table, Allison retrieves her pencil from behind George's ear.

"Good luck with you searches," says the archivist.

Surprisingly, Jim doesn't offer his cheery catchphrase but just says: "cheerio both."

After exploring the city centre for a few hours, browsing the shops then exploring the inner sanctum of the cathedral, George and Bella indulge in a delicious chicken curry in a tiny Indian restaurant they find down along the quiet backstreets. Their meal is as fiery as dragons' breath and they down at least two pints of water each to help it along.

"That was *never* a Korma," says Bella as they head back to the White Horse. "It was a vindaloo... at the very least!"

"Nice though," says George, eyes watering as they reach the pub.

Next morning, despite the aftermath of their curries, they manage another of Deirdre's full-English breakfasts, before packing up their few belongings and making for the mysterious Bolton's Bench on the way to Bisterne.

Forty-odd miles and an hour-and-a-half later, the intrepid pair approach Cadnam, some fourteen miles from Bisterne, after negotiating horrendous traffic in Portsmouth and then in Southampton. There's a turn for Lyndhurst, but they stop to refuel the Norton at a small garage outside Cadnam, just off the A31.

"Well, George. *That* was an enjoyable journey wasn't it." says Bella, as they both remove their helmets and goggles.

"Not bad at all, Bel," says George, not perceiving the hint of sarcasm in Bella's voice.

"You should've come down the A35, mate," says the miserable forecourt attendant. "If you wanted Lyndhurst, that is."

"But then we wouldn't have had *you* to cheer us up, would we," suggests Bella, who's more than a bit cheesed off with the traffic they'd encountered on the way.

"I suppose you're right," says the miserable man, wiping his petrol-fumed hands on his petrol-fumed blue overalls, without a hint of perceiving Bella's acid tone.

6) Be Stern

After paying for the petrol and making a brief visit to the customers' toilets, they remount to cover the remaining few miles to Lyndhurst where Bolton's bench is close by.

"Let's get to Lyndhurst and find somewhere to stay for the night then, George."

"Right you are, Bel. I have a strange feeling about this Bolton's Bench thing. Good or bad?... I wouldn't like to say."

Bella smiles but doesn't answer, thinking: *'strange feeling, George? Why ever would you have a strange feeling about chasing around the country after dragons?'* If there's any hint of sarcasm in these thoughts, she doesn't show it.

"Well, Bel. You said you'd like to visit the New Forest. What do you think of it now you're here? Beautiful, isn't it."

Bella has to agree, her mood lightening as they approach Lyndhurst: "It's certainly pleasant, George. The traffic seems to have evaporated. And look at all the ponies. They're in the streets like shoppers, looking in windows, lying on the pavements. nuzzling each other. Aren't they wonderful. I bet there's even more of them in the summer."

"I don't think many shoppers lie on the pavements, Bel, though a few of them probably nuzzle each other. I imagine it gets busy a lot of the time, even in winter. I've heard that it's very popular, but not today it seems. Maybe the Bisterne dragon's frightened all the shoppers away."

"The Bignor dragon's dead, George."

"Who knows, Bel? You just have to look at Rango. *He's* very much alive, wherever he is."

Parking up near the Fox and Hounds in the town centre, they stop and ask a policewoman who's patrolling the High Street if she can recommend somewhere they might find reasonable accommodation for the night.

"You could stay in one of the cells... if you leave that motorbike where it is. No parking, m' dears. That's what the sign says."

"Sorry," says Bella, apologetic now she's in the relative calm of the place.

"That's okay, love. Only doing my job. You can have a few minutes if you need them. Myself, I'd try the big house just behind the church up the way there. On Church Lane it is, of all things. You can't miss it. The old boy who lives there is a nice pleasant sort of chap, although he's a bit eccentric. Apparently he tells everyone he knows all about dragons. Who'd believe that dragons exist, eh? It takes all sorts I suppose, and I'm sure he's harmless enough. I do believe he has a room that he lets out for accommodation. You could try it, anyway. His name's Maurice Burke or something like that."

"Thank you," says George, excitedly. "We'll give it a try."

"Good luck then," says the super-efficient policewoman as she struts away down High Street towards the co-op.

The pair could walk the distance to the church and the big house if they didn't need to move the bike and sidecar, but instead they mount the machine and head up the street. They find the only really big house in the lane; a brick building with stone-mullioned windows and they pull up on the gravel drive. The curtains in a downstairs room twitch with the curiosity of someone inside. They remove their headgear once more and pace up to the large oak front door. Bella pulls on the bell-pull... the only course of action when confronted with a bell and a pull, unless of course you decide the door they serve is too forbidding. They wait for a response to the distant tinkling within.

"Maurice Burke, Bel? Sounds a bit like 'Maurice de Berkeley' to me. Don't you agree?"

"Can't deny it, George."

The door opens to reveal a smartly dressed man who must be eighty-five if he's a day. Corduroy suit, check shirt, military tie and suede shoes. His silver-grey hair is slicked back with what is probably an up-market equivalent of Brylcreem. A smooth,

6) Be Stern

confident voice with received pronunciation worthy of its Oxbridge origins greets them: "We get very few of your sort up here you know," the old dapper chap informs them. "What can I do for you?"

"Good afternoon, sir," says George, wondering what's meant by 'your sort'. "Mr. Burke isn't it?"

"God damn it no, young man. Everyone always gets it wrong. Who told you that?" Despite the profanity, he speaks with the same measured, mellifluous voice.

"Err, sorry. It was a policewoman just down the road near the Fox and Hounds."

"Not *Beryl*? She *always* gets things wrong. You should hear her at the local Council meetings. Well meaning sort, but a bit imprecise. Wouldn't do in the Army you know. Still, not to worry. I'd be more worried if she started getting things right."

Bella and George turn to each other and exchange glances with a smile.

"It's just that we're looking for dragons… and a bed for the night and…"

"Why didn't you say, young man. I can certainly let you have a room for tonight, but you'll have to vacate it by tomorrow lunchtime. I have a couple of people coming who are looking for the Holy Grail."

"Really," says George, in considerable surprise.

"No, not really. I was just having a little joke. We used to do that all the time in the Army. The laughs we had. First World War, you understand. I was too old for the Second. Some say too old for the First."

"Sounds like you had a very active service then?" says Bella.

"You bet your auntie's tiara, young lady. One time we threw the sergeant's underpants out of the trench. They landed on the barbed-wire, they did. He'd been wearing them for a week… probably a bigger deterrent to enemy than the barbed-wire itself. He never *did* retrieve them."

"Didn't the sergeant put you on a charge?"

"Of course not, young lady. I wasn't a private. I was a major, even then. What larks, eh."

Bella can't help but chuckle at the thought of the soiled 'flag' waving in the wind. *'Good job the pants were dirty, or they may have been mistaken for a white surrender flag,'* she thinks.

"So, what *is* your name, sir," asks George, reminding the old chap that he's neglected to tell them.

"Ah, yes. What is it now? I always hesitate to give that away. You don't know who may be listening. Name, rank and number is one thing... well it's *three* things, actually... but never give your name unless you have to. That's what *I* say."

"Sorry," George says. "But if you don't make your name clear, how can you expect Beryl to get it right?"

"Oh, I never thought of that. Well, I think I can trust you two with it. It's Martin Blake. Major Martin Blake, D.S.O. and bar."

George is lost for words.

Bella bites her lip and asks: "so, do you know much about dragons, major?" hoping to make inroads on George's behalf.

"I *do* know about dragons. For a start, that one up the road had nothing to do with Maurice de Berkeley. Or with a Mr. Burke for that matter. Back in the day, it was my great, great, however many times great, grandfather that fought the dragon. As for it being called the Bisterne dragon? Well, for a start it lived in Burley. But it *was* terrorising the village of Bisterne. I can vouch for that. And it *is* true that it was attacked here in Lyndhurst... by my great, great, wadjamacallit, but he didn't kill it. He just 'gently' persuaded it to move away. Went over to Kilve, In the Quantocks, it did, or so they say. It's over Somerset way. The Quantocks, eh? I always think that sounds like a contagious disease. Don't you agree."

George doesn't answer, trusting that the question is rhetorical.

Bella chuckles again.

6) Be Stern

"Kilve. That's next on our list, isn't it Bel."

Bella doesn't answer, trusting that the question is rhetorical.

George gathers his thoughts and says: "But in our little *Herbie Dragons* book, it says that Sir Maurice de Berkeley *killed* it, and that its body turned into the hill called Bolton's Bench. Then that De Berkeley fellow went mad, returned to the hill and died. Then his body turned into a yew tree on the hill."

"Well I don't know about this *Herbie* bloke, but you won't find a dragon's remains under *that* hill. And you won't find a knight's body on the Bench either, even though you'll find a bloody great yew tree. I'm telling you, everybody gets things wrong around here, young fella-me-lad. The Bench actually celebrates a New Forest Lord Warden from the 1700s, the Duke of Bolton and Master Keeper of the Bailiwick of Burley."

Despite the major's dampener on their hopes, and after agreeing terms, they decide to stay over. Then, before moving on to Kilve to explore the suggested link with the so-called Bisterne dragon, they'd head for Bolton's Bench to see, literally, how the land lies.

The old boy makes them a cold supper of cheese sandwiches and cake. They decline the offer of cigars.

"I'll make sure your room is tip-top for you, then," says Major Martin. "Breakfast at eight o'clock on the pip. Kedgeree alright for you both? Got the recipe from my brother. He was in India, back in the day."

They nod in agreement, not knowing what in the world kedgeree is.

Up in their room, which is a perfect example of regimented order and cleanliness, Bella and George take stock.

"I must admit, George. When I decided to come on this mad adventure with you, I thought I was a bit mad, but I was quite wrong. Now we're here, I realise that I'm *raving* mad."

George glances up from a cup of tea with consternation, only to find Bella smiling.

"I think we've grown together, George. It's probably a lot to do with you clinging onto me on the pillion."

"I'm sure it's more than that, Bel. I think deep down, we're kindred spirits."

"I agree George. We really must stick together when we get back to wherever we're hoping to get back to. Which reminds me... you haven't contacted your parents to let them know you're safe since we've been travelling."

"You're right. I *must* phone them. As for sticking together, Bel, of course we must. I've been thinking about it all along."

"It's a deal then, George."

"But, you're making me feel guilty about my parents, Bel. And anyway, *you* haven't contacted you brother since that day I met him."

"True, George. But he and I have gone our separate ways for years. He knows I'm independent of all that 'sibling ties' stuff.

"I suppose so. I'll phone mum and dad in the morning then. From that phone-box I spotted near the Fox and Hounds."

"Better watch out for Beryl, then," she teases.

"Only if we ride down there on the Norton," George laughs.

And before George can finish his tea, they find themselves between crisp, fresh linen sheets, as tightly packed as if George was riding pillion.

Morning comes, proving warm for the time of year. They gird their belongings before breakfast and marvel at the experience of curried fish and eggs for breakfast; quite a follow-up by way of culinary experiences to the Chichester curry.

"Hello? Mum? Is that you? How are you keeping? I thought I ought to ring to see how you both are, and to let you know that *I'm* okay."

"George? Thank God you're alright. I'm alright too. Where are you, love? I hope you've got some money left in the bank?

6) Be Stern

How's that project of yours going?"

George does his best to answer the barrage of questions.

"I'm in the New Forest, mum. I'm with a girl. Her name's Bella. She's lovely and she's got a motorbike. We've found some dragons, but we're still looking for more. We're going to Somerset next."

"Well, I hope *she's* got some money in the bank. Girls can be very expensive, you know. Pop's always reminding me of that. I hope you've got a helmet if you're riding motorbikes."

"We're okay for money mum. How is dad, by the way?"

"He's fine. Same old pop."

"Good."

"Now then, George. You haven't been to Arundel, have you?"

"What makes you ask that?" answers George, surprised by the question.

"Well, we had a policeman phone us last week. Harry Fielding his name was. He was wondering if we knew anything about an incident at the castle there. Apparently they've arrested some chap in the local launderette and he mumbled something about a scorched book in the library, and a dragon, and a couple with a motorbike and sidecar. I think they've asked for psychiatric reports."

"No mum. We haven't been anywhere *near* Arundel," says George, thinking on his feet, anxious to hide his anxious tone. "And we don't have a sidecar."

Bella, who's outside the telephone-box with the door held partially open with a motorbike boot, looks at George quizzically, catching only one side of the decidedly odd conversation.

"I'm glad about that, George," says mum. "I didn't realise that looking for dragons on a motorbike was so popular. Not that dragons ride motorbikes of course."

"Look mum. I've got to go now. We need to be on our way. Love to dad. And don't mention to anyone that we're off to

Somerset. We want to keep our little quest to ourselves."

"Well, I'll have to tell your dad, George. I don't hold any secrets from pop."

"Okay. But no one else mind."

"Right you are, George. Bye now. Call again soon."

"Will do mum. Keep safe. Love to dad."

And with that, George replaces the receiver and turns to Bella.

"What, George?"

"Err, nothing really. The police have arrested Perry and they've contacted mum and dad somehow, thinking we were involved in the Arundel affair."

"Nothing? We *were* involved, George. What are we going to do?"

"Not much we *can* do, Bel. And anyway, it wasn't a *serious* amount of damage, was it."

"We could give ourselves up, George."

"Don't be daft, Bel."

"Morning you two," says a familiar voice.

It's Beryl on her morning beat. George crosses his fingers, hoping she hasn't heard Bella suggesting they could give themselves up.

"I see you left the bike at home today. Very wise. Did you stay with that Maurice Burke up at the big house then?"

"Martin Blake, actually."

"Oh, really? Where does *he* live?"

"Oh, never mind," says Bella. "Thanks for your help anyway."

"Always here to help," says Beryl, as she turns on her regulation heels and resumes her measured pace down High Street.

Back in Church Lane.

"Be good now," calls the strangely affable Major Martin Blake, as Bella kick-starts the bike. They traverse the gravel driveway

6) Be Stern

to the gate and melt away from the major's benign garrison on their way to Bolton's Bench.

When they arrive at the Bench, they're very disappointed. The hill is not very awe-inspiring. Large though it is, it's no more than a shallow mound, an undulation in an open grass area. The most impressive thing about it, apart from the yew tree at it's top, is the fact that the wild new forest ponies are not distracted by the tourists, who are out in numbers now despite the season. There's not even a hidden entrance to the under-hill that might reveal the ancient last resting place of a dragon.

"Come on, Bel. Let's head off for Kilve. Our luck searching for Our Boris has to change sometime."

Dejected, they briefly consult their map to remind them of the best route to their next destination, and off they go again.

-o-o-o-

7) Kilve Beast

Three-quarters of an hour into their journey to the Quantocks, they hit the A303. In summer, it would be busy with holiday traffic heading for Exeter and on into the deep depths of Cornwall, but today it's quiet, with little traffic to hinder them. Nevertheless, they decide to stop for a break in Wincanton.

The town is hilly and, apart from the High Street, unremarkable, so they stretch their legs and move on.

Reaching Kilve an hour later, they find it even more unremarkable except for the pub. In fact the Hood Arms looks extremely interesting, surely steeped in history. They park up outside and notice a smartly dressed woman, probably in her forties, attending to the cleaning of windows.

"Why do we always end up in pubs when we have questions about dragons?" asks Bella.

"It's because they've always been the social focal point for villages and towns... and cities, come to that." suggests George. "Not that we'll be asking questions in here. It's closed, look."

"Surely, George, the focal points in communities *before* pubs were the churches." Bella points out. "I wonder if there's a church here?"

"If there is, that'll probably be closed too."

"No, dearie. It'll be open," chimes in the window-cleaning woman, who'd edged nearer so as to clean a window within convenient ear-shot. She points across the road to a side junction, taking off a rubber glove as if to emphasise her point. "Up there, it is. Up Sea Lane. The Church of the Blessed Virgin Mary. You can't miss it. And the vicar's always there at this time of morning... has been for years and years, long before *I* came into the area. And if it's dragons you're after, he'll tell you all about Blue Ben."

George turns to Bella and smiles at the unsolicited

7) Kilve Beast

community guidance: "Pub and church working hand in glove eh, Bel?"

"Or even hand out of glove," says Bella.

"Thank you," calls George to the smartly dressed woman who's put her glove back on and has already moved on to the next window.

"Don't mention it," she shouts back.

"Ah, yes," says Benjamin Green, long-standing vicar of Kilve. Benjamin is a short and dumpy, smiley man who looks to be at least ninety years old and would probably look ten years older still, if he were thin and wrinkle-faced. "Do you mean Blue Ben, the promontory, young man?"

George is rather flummoxed by this question: "The what?" he replies.

"The promontory… the sticky-out-bit of the coastline up there a way. East Quantoxhead is the place," the vicar explains, pointing to the west.

"Well, says George, I suppose so, but I thought Blue Ben was a drag…"

"Ah yes," the vicar repeats. "A dragon. Blue Ben's that too. People say Ben might be found over that way, around the promontory."

"The sticky-out bit?"

"Well, yes. although the creature would live in the sticky-*in*-bits. The caves, that is. Even a dragon needs shelter, doesn't he." suggests the vicar. "I'm Benjamin, by the way. Benjamin Green. Green Ben some call me. It's a good job old Bernie Brown never moved here to the village," he adds, with levity.

"Oh, err, *we're* George and Bella," replies George. "Pleased to meet you."

"Pleased to make your acquaintance," offers Bella.

"And I yours," replies Benjamin to the pair of bikers. "If you want to see Blue Ben the sticky-out-bit, then you'll have to walk

143

there. It's only about half-a-mile. But if you want to meet the other Ben, you'll have to fly," he titters.

'This is all we need,' thinks Bella. 'A comical vicar.'

"So, this Blue Ben actually exists then, Benjamin?" asks George. "I wonder, is he still alive?"

"Depends what you mean by *alive*, George. If the dragon's living, then it's alive. And if it's dead, then it's alive in people's minds. And if people have a mind, then it's wanted, dead *or* alive, if you see what I mean."

Neither Bella nor George *do* see what he means by this rather cryptic statement, but they're well versed in going along with the reality of myth by now.

"Well, continues the vicar, "Blue Ben, the dragon, is said to have dwelled in the caves along the coast and to have often bathed in the sea to cool off from breathing fire. I've heard it said that it came all the way from Bisterne, in Hampshire. Some say the beast was captured here by the Devil who'd decided to use it as his fiery steed. It's said that Ben later escaped from the Devil and from Hell but that, in hurrying back to its lair, it trampled through the mud flats and got stuck, sinking out of sight. Others say that the creature built a causeway to *avoid* getting stuck."

"And what do *you* believe?" asks Bella, entranced by the mystical picture the vicar is painting.

"Seeing is believing, and believing is seeing. And I believe I *did* see the dragon once not so long ago, alive to that day at the least. I saw him just the once, mind you. It was just after I'd walked back from the Hood Arms. *I'm* sure it's still about the place."

"Well, we'd better book in to the pub when it opens, if there's room at the inn, that is. Then we could walk up there tonight and see if there's anything to believe," says Bella, trying to play Benjamin's little game.

"I should add," says Benjamin. "Someone, way back, found a

7) Kilve Beast

fossilised dinosaur skull and there are those who've decided that it was Ben's. But I don't think Ben could have been that old, you know."

"Well that's what I'd prefer to believe... that it's not Ben," says George, determined to make progress in his search for extant dragons and maybe find a lead to the mystery that is Ouroboros.

When the pair get back down to the pub, it's open and they find that the smart lady with the gloves and squeegee is the landlady. She tells them that there's a room available, so they take up the offer, with one night's stay.

"Do you want an evening meal then?" she asks them.

"Could you pack up some sandwiches for us, please? We'd be more than grateful. We're going out tonight you see, to explore Blue Ben."

"In the dark? You wouldn't catch me out there in the dark. Whatever you do, don't go to the bottom of the cliffs. You could end up sinking in the mud, just like Blue Ben... the dragon that is, not the promontory. And don't go towards the east. They've built that there atomic nuclear power station... Hinkley Point. Opened it just recently they have. There's one or two said they've seen a blue glow from it at night. They've even said Blue Ben's probably shacked up there... warmer than the caves, you see."

In their room, George and Bella decide to leave it until early the next morning to go exploring, in light of the landlady's anxious words, but they make do with the sandwiches all the same. George says to Bella: "I know it's a bit weird thinking it, but how come dragons and atomic places seem to go together? The sea-dragon at Orford Ness and now Blue Ben at Hinkley Point? It has to be coincidence, doesn't it?"

"Well, if linking the two seems weird, George, then how weird is believing in dragons in the first place... unless you've actually *seen* them. Let's face it, love... a few years ago, telling someone you were going to harness masses of energy just from splitting atoms, they'd have thought *that* pretty weird too. I guess weird *is* as weird does."

George scratches his head, and says: "All we need to find is a Nuclear facility on a hill, with a Green Dragon pub next door, and we have it made."

Rising early next morning, well before breakfast, George and Bella quietly leave the Hood, and less than quietly take the Norton back up to the church, parking it in the lane. No sign of Benjamin in the waking light. Having parked up, they trek towards the sea, finding a winding way down onto the beach. They're greeted by a retreating tide, the grey dawn highlighting the up-ended strata of rocks which sit like pushed-over rubble walls populating the inner reaches of the beach. Rock pools left by the tide break up the rocky platform that they cautiously step on and they half expect their weight to tip the stones further.

"This must be part of Blue Ben's causeway," whispers George to Bella.

"Why are you whispering, George?"

"I don't know, Bel. Perhaps I was thinking not to disturb the dragon."

"Do you really think we're going to find him this morning then, George? Apart from the jolly, jokey vicar, I doubt if anyone else believes he really exists, let alone expect to see him at the drop of a hat."

"Well, let's walk along here. Now the tide's retreated, there's a way to the west for quite a distance."

They pick their way along the rocky pavement, gingerly at first then, after half-a-mile or so, they step with more confidence.

"Look, Bel. isn't that shadow ahead some sort of cave?"

"It *could* be, George. But slow down a bit. You're racing ahead

7) Kilve Beast

as if you're climbing Mount Everest after it's just fallen over."

"Sorry, Bel. I'm getting carried away."

They reach the shadow which proves to be a low-slung cave; a headroom at it's entrance low enough to require them to stoop. Crouching, they step over the threshold, and the light falls away as abruptly as an urgent sunset.

"Blast!" shouts Bella. "Why did we forget our torches. We'd better make this as far as we go, George."

"Perhaps *now's* the time to whisper, Bel."

"Sorry, George. I didn't mean to shout."

Tempering their volume is too late, and their voices are picked up by the rocky walls, echoing into the depths and back again, amplified.

They make out what sounds like a third voice, almost imperceptible at first, but growing louder, shrill against the unforgiving stone, yet with a benign tone underlying it.

"Please *do*. Please whisper. I've not been awake long. It takes your senses a while to catch up with the dawn when you get older… and I'm certainly much older than I was."

"Blimey, Bel," calls out George, forgetting his own advice to whisper. "I thought that was *you* for a minute there, but it wasn't… was it?"

"Do you *mind* George. I'm not a harpy."

"Sorry, Bel. I didn't mean…"

"*Sorry*? You *will* be sorry, if you go around waking dragons so harshly," squeals the high-pitched voice.

"Sorry, voice," blurts George. "We didn't mean to disturb you. You must be Blue Ben."

"Too right. I wish they wouldn't call me that. I'm a *female* dragon."

George can't believe their luck. To have found the Kilve dragon so easily. Bella's not sure whether to turn and run, or to just keep her voice down and crouch behind George.

"When you say *they*, do you reveal yourself often?"

"No, I don't. Not if I can help it. That vicar has seen me once, but very few people believe that he has. I'm not aware that others have seen me for many's the year. As for *you*, I'm not going to give you the pleasure. Seeing's believing, but hearing is more than enough."

"Fine, fine," replies George, perceiving a raising of the shrillness. "We'd better go, and leave you in peace."

"Good idea," says Blue Ben, more calmly now. "But I want you to promise not to tell anyone that you've seen... err, heard me. I'm still trying to keep a low profile these days."

"I promise," says George, worried that they might not get out alive. "Just one question though, before we leave you to your waking. Are you related to the Orford Sea-dragon?"

"No I'm *not*! What makes you ask that?"

"Nothing. I just wondered. It's not important. But do you know him?"

"No I don't! and that's *two* questions now. When are you going to stop asking questions?"

"Sorry, Mrs. Ben."

"Well, if you see him, tell him I've not forgiven him, nuisance that he is."

"So you *do* know him."

"Damn! I wish you'd stop asking questions. And that's three questions now, and third time pays for all."

"But that last one was rhetorical, if it was a question at all. And anyway, it doesn't count unless you answer all three questions properly."

"That's not very funny. Anyway, you'd better leave now, before I get annoyed."

With that, Bella grabs George by the arm and wheels him around, prodding him to shift himself: "Get back to the entrance, George. It's time to go."

"Strictly speaking, Bel, it's the *exit*." he protests.

"George!"

7) Kilve Beast

Blue Ben snorts, and falls silent. The echo of voices follows suit. Daylight greets them, brighter now.

"Come on, George. I could murder a hot, buttery croissant and a cup of strong coffee."

George nods: "Pity we haven't got a camera, Bel. No one will believe we found Blue Ben. Except maybe Benjamin Green."

"You *promised*, George. You're not to tell anyone. Not for now, at any rate."

"You're right, Bel. It wouldn't be fair."

When they get back to the bike at the church, who should greet them but Benjamin vicar.

"Morning, you two. Have you been dragon-hunting?"

"No. no," insists George.

"We've just been down on the rocks admiring the beach and the sea," Bella says. "We decided to forget the dragon idea."

"That's right," agrees George. "We're going back to the Hood for breakfast. Then we'll be moving on."

"Well, it's nice to have met you both," says the jolly clergyman. "I'm sure if you'd met Blue Ben, she'd have taken to you."

"It would be nice to think so," says Bel, not even daring to comment on the fact that the vicar know that Ben is female.

At breakfast, after cereal and full-cream milk, Bella's wishes are more than satisfied with two fresh-from-the-oven croissants and a pot of arabica. George is replete with hot toast and tea.

"I've been thinking, Bel."

"You're *always* thinking, George."

"Seriously though. You know we agreed we'd stick together…"

Bella, having taken a bite from her second croissant, hovers in mid sip of her coffee, anticipating that George is about to say something unexpected and thinking: *'where did I go wrong? I've*

gone along with this crazy quest. What more could I have done?'.
"Will you live with me, Bel? You make me so happy and I couldn't bear us parting. I'd be worried as to who'd hold my torch when I'm in dark places? Who'd shine a light on me?"

Bella, not expecting the early morning 'proposal', coughs and splutters, spraying her imminent gulp of coffee all over the tablecloth... and all over George."

"Should I take that as a no then, Bel," says George, mopping coffee from his expectant brow thinking: *'where did I go wrong? I've brought Bel on this ridiculous quest. I could have offered her a better adventure.'*

"Yes, George. Yes!... I mean *no*. I mean don't take it as a no... it's a yes."

"What?"

"Yes, I'll live with you. When and where?"

"Well. We'll sort out the details a bit later. I suppose we already *are* living together in a way. But we ought to deal with all these dragons first, before we plan the future."

Bella, feeling a little deflated by George's calming of her expectations, apologises to the approaching waitress for pebble-dashing the tablecloth.

"No problem, madam. I'll get you another. It happens all the time. Would sir like another serviette?"

"That would be very helpful, thank you," replies the pebble-dashed George. He smiles at Bella, "...not a *lot* later, Bel." he reassures his dragon-hunting partner.

She smiles broadly in return.

"By the way," says the waitress as she moves the breakfast things to one side so as to place the new tablecloth, "I nearly forgot. There was a gentleman in here very early on asking something about motorbikes and Arundel. Fielding he said his name is. I thought of your bike. I told him he'd better come back later, say mid-morning when everyone was free of breakfast. I hope I did the right thing."

7) Kilve Beast

"Thank you," says Bella as the new tablecloth is put in place and the table re-laid.

"Bella," whispers George, as the waitress recedes. "They're on to us. We'll be put in prison if they catch us. What shall we do?"

"Don't panic, George. It was only a bit of damage to an old book. It's not a hanging offence."

"But it was a really *important* book, Bella. After all, why are they putting the force of the British police on the case?"

"I'd hardly call one policeman a whole *Force*, George."

"Well, I think we'd be best to pay up and move on before that Fielding comes back. We said we'd head north next, to the Welsh borders, so let's get moving. Pronto!"

And so, within twenty minutes they were mounted and heading onwards.

It's a clear day and they make good progress, despite a slog of over two hours before passing through Gloucester, hoping to get to Hereford by mid afternoon.

"Is Hereford where Hereford the Wake came from, George?"

"No. Bel. You're thinking of *Hereward* the Wake. I think he used to hang out in Cambridgeshire, over Ely way. He was famous for having punch-ups with the Normans... 1066 and all that. It's been said by some that he's actually the origin of the Robin Hood legends."

"So what's Hereford famous for then, George?"

"I did read somewhere that they have the 'Mappa Mundi', a medieval map of the world. And I think the S.A.S. moved here a few years back. I don't think the two things are linked."

"But the question is, are there any dragons, George?"

"I saw a brief reference in The British Museum to a beast at Mordiford, which is quite near to Hereford, but it suggested that it was a wyvern. Otherwise, nothing in the area, even in our little book from *Herbie Dragons*."

"So what exactly is a wyvern, George?"

"Who knows, Bel. I think wyverns have two legs' whereas dragons have four. I reckon half of these Green Dragon pubs we keep coming across should be called the Green Wyvern. And that's another thing... The Welsh dragon is red, but *I* think it should be green. Apart from anything else, green's a nicer, calmer colour. Red just inflames people's passions and leads to fire-breathing. I mean the Welsh have always seemed fiery to me. Don't you agree, Bel?"

"I'm not sure I've met any Welsh people, George. I'm sure they're very nice, even if they *do* breath fire."

"Well, anyway, I'm sure Our Boris is not a wyvern and he's definitely not Welsh. It would probably be a waste of time seeking out the Mordiford beast."

When they come across Mordiford, they decide it would be better to look for somewhere to stay than to travel on the further few miles to Hereford itself. Their haphazard progress around the country, whilst generally exhilarating, is proving tiring at times.

"That's right," says the postmistress, all bustle in her bustle and grey of hair. Her age suggests Victorian, as does her dress. "Our postman, Wilfred, lets out a room. He's very reasonable. He's been doin' it for ages... postman that is... not lettin' out rooms. If you hang on a bit, he'll be back off his second deliveries soon. Unless he's had another puncture... his bike that is, not Wilfred. Would you like a drink while you wait?"

"That would be lovely," says Bella.

"They're over there, love. There's twenty percent off the lemonade this week."

Before Bella can recover from this rather commercial offer from the diminutive postmistress, Wilfred clatters in, door bell dinging meekly in submission as he fights his way to the counter carrying a rather large parcel wrapped in brown paper.

7) Kilve Beast

Before he can vent his frustration at having to return to the post office with it, The postmistress intervenes: "Wilf. This nice couple want a room for the night. *You've* got one, haven't you. I was tellin' them, you're very reasonable, so they'll be keen if you can accommodate them."

"I wish *all* of our customers were reasonable, April. Unlike that bloody Agnes woman at number seven on Church Lane. When I told her yesterday we'd got this parcel for her, she said *'bring it over tomorrow, second post. I'll be here waitin' for you'*. Was she buggery. It's heavy, that is. I'd have left it on her doorstep, but it looked a bit like rain, so I brought it back. That's how reasonable *I* am, April. I was more than a bit annoyed really though, so I left a note sayin' she'd have to collect it. *I* don't know. Newcomers? She's only been here ten years and she thinks she owns the place."

"I know, Wilf. You *are* reasonable, love. I was sayin' that very thing to May and June, only the other day."

"I'll tell you what, April. I've always wondered about you and your sisters. All born in April, May and June like that. I reckon it was your mother and father both bein' teachers. You know… school holidays in July, August and September."

"Don't be daft, Wilf. They didn't *have* school holidays in their day. Leastways, that's what my mum always said."

George and Bella look on, open-mouthed, as this conversation progresses, not sure that they'd *actually* agreed with April that they wanted a room at Wilfred's.

"Anyway," says Wilfred, "Put this behind the counter if you will. I'm off for me tea."

"Before you go, Wilf, didn't you hear me? This nice couple want a room for the night. You've got one, haven't you. I was tellin' them, you're very reasonable, so they'll be keen if you can accommodate them."

"Oh, sorry. I was a bit preoccupied there, wasn't I. The room's available tonight, tomorrow and the next day, if that would suit. two pound ten a night all in."

"Can we come back with you to see what the room's like, Wilfred?" suggests Bella, non-committally.

"That's *only* one pound five each, you know," says the postman. "You won't find cheaper in Mordiford."

"We'd like to look first though, if that's alright," insists Bella sternly, concerned that Wilfred's accommodation might be as unaccommodating as his chuntering about parcel delivery.

"I'm sure it'll be alright," says George, thinking to bring down the temperature of the debate.

When they see the room on offer, Bella and George are very impressed and agree to stay for two nights.

"You can park your motorbike and sidecar in the garage if you like. It's empty, apart from my gardenin' kit and a few paint tins. But don't touch them, mind... they might be valuable."

"Thank you, Wilfred," says Bella.

"You can call me Wilf, love. Would you believe that Agnes woman insists on callin' me Freddy, of all things. How would *she* like it if I called her Nessy. Mind you, it would fit the bill. She *is* a bit of a monster... I remember when she first came to..."

"Talking of Nessy, and monsters," interrupts George, "Do you know anything about the Mordiford beast, Wilf?"

Having been stopped in his tracks, Wilfred steps back in visible surprise: "You've heard of the beast then. I didn't think many folk outside of the village know about it. Why do you ask?"

"Put the kettle on, Wilf, says Bella, "then George will tell you all about our quest."

"Quest? that sounds a bit dangerous to me," says Wilf reaching for the teapot from a high shelf.

The postman opens up with his considerable knowledge of the Mordiford wyvern without waiting for George to elaborate

7) Kilve Beast

on their 'quest'.

"The legend has it, and it *is* only a legend mind you, that a little girl from the village, her name was Maud, was wanderin' in the nearby forest, the forest of Dean as is. She found a small winged creature snufflin' in the undergrowth. She took it home to show to her parents but, knowin' it to be a young wyvern, they told her to take it back to where she'd found it because it would only cause trouble. But Maud took it only a little way into the forest and fed it each day until it grew enough to fly. Soon it had a great hunger, beyond any food that Maud could bring it and it began to plague the nearby farms, killin' the cows and sheep. The farmers were up in arms. Well, wouldn't *you* be?

"I suppose so," says George.

"Well, the farmers ganged together to try and kill the beast, but it turned on them, and the people of the village as well. Some say it actually ate them. Maud, who the wyvern regarded as a friend, tried to stop its rampagin', but to no avail."

Bella shudders at the thought of being eaten by a dragon.

"But *did* they kill it?" asks George, excited to find that there truly may be, or maybe was, a wyvern in the area.

"Well," says Wilfred, now engrossed in his own story, "the villagers sought help from a nobleman who lived nearby. He tackled the beast in full armour and the wyvern blasted him with fire, enough to roast his potatoes, he bein' encased in a steel pot as you might say."

"But *do* wyverns breath fire, Wilf? I thought that was quite rare."

"Well, this one apparently did, George. And remember, it's only a legend. Anyway, the nobleman survived, then killed the beast with his lance. Maud never recovered from losin' her friend and mourned for the rest of her life."

"So the beast is dead then. Not much point in us looking for him."

"Well, you don't expect to find a live wyvern, do you? I mean, dragons and things... like I said, they're only legends."

"*We've* seen them, Wilf... more than once."

"You did say you're only stayin' for *two* nights, didn't you?"

"Yes. We have to keep moving," says George.

"Like Bonnie Parker and her mate Clyde Barrow," adds Bella, with a nervous laugh. "To keep clear of the long arm of the law."

"She's only joking," says George, apologetically, nudging Bella in the side.

"Only, my wife has some friends comin' to stay soon," continues Wilf, Bella's comment going clean over his head.

"Your wife?" asks Bella. "Is she not here at the moment?"

"What? Oh, April. she'll still be in the post office. She's *always* in the post office."

"April's your wife? But I thought..."

"I know. She *is* my wife, but she always says the room that you're stayin' in here is *my* business. We both live here though."

"Why did you say that thing about Bonnie and Clyde, Bel? It's no laughing matter. That Fielding could knock on the door any time."

"I told you, George. Don't worry. I reckon Fielding couldn't catch a cold, even if it sneezed on him. It'll all blow over, you'll see."

"Well, we really should move on. I'd say we should only stay the one night."

"If you really think so then, George."

George consults his *Guide to Mythical Beasts of England and Wales.*

"Alderley Edge!"

"What, George?"

"Alderley Edge. That's the next place. We'll be well out of Fielding's reach there. It's up north. Nobody goes up north, if

7) Kilve Beast

they've got any sense."

"So, why are *we* going, George? And what's supposed to be at Alderley Edge by way of dragons?"

"It says here that King Arthur and his knights of the round table lie sleeping beneath the hill there, in a cavern."

"But that *must* be just a legend, George. Like King Arthur himself," suggests Bella.

"You can't *say* that, Bel," George replies. "I'd say *you* believe in dragons now, don't you? You've seen them. Surely Arthur is even more feasible than dragons, right?"

"Well, yes George, but…"

"Anyway," interrupts George, "on the subject of dragons, local custom says that a farmer, who was riding a grey horse to market in nearby Macclesfield, was stopped by an old man who suddenly appeared in front of him. The stranger offered to buy the horse, seeming to know that the farmer was intending to sell it at the market."

"And *did* he sell it, George?"

"No, he didn't, Bel. It was a low offer, and the farmer thought he'd get a much better price at market."

"And did he?"

"Hold on, Bella. I'm coming to that. There was lots of interest at the market, but he didn't get a single offer, so he made to head back home, then the same peculiar old man appeared again. This time the farmer agreed a price, deciding to sell the beast. The old man then led the farmer and his horse to the hillside below the ridge and, laying a hand on the rock-face, an iron gate appeared; it was an entrance into the hill. And there within, the farmer was amazed to see King Arthur and the knights, together with their horses, all asleep in a huge cavern. The farmer's horse was intended for one of the knights, and he felt well pleased to have sold it for a bag of gold. He dashed back to the entrance and made haste on his way, the gate clanging shut behind him."

"Wow, George. That's an amazing story. But if the knight had his horse, will they still all be there waiting for some call or other to return."

"I wouldn't like to say, Bel. They could still be waiting for more horses. And I don't recall any new king being in the newspapers. *'The once and future king'*, they call him, so he's been once but the future bit must still be *in* the future, I'd say."

"So, do you think we could find the gate, George?"

"I doubt it. It sounds like it was well hidden. And besides, you'd need that old bloke to help. I think he must have been Merlin. And unless we had a horse to sell, he probably wouldn't turn up anyway."

"Do you think they'd be interested in a motorbike?" says Bel.

"That's not a bad idea. It's worth a try."

"No, George. I was joking. Selling the Norton's not on."

And so ,with no prospect of finding a dragon here, what with Maud and her wyvern supposedly long gone, they tell Wilf that they'll be staying for one night only.

"Fair enough," says Wilf. "I'll let April know."

The intrepid beast hunters consult their map and look to preparing for the next leg of their wild dragon chase.

"You know, Bel. King Arthur's father was Uther Pendragon. From what I've gathered that translates as 'Dragon's Head'… now that's got to be a good sign that there really is a dragon knocking about King' Arthur's court."

"Or *was*, George."

"Well, true. But if we don't look, we won't find."

First thing in the morning, Bella and George load the sidecar, snatch a quick breakfast courtesy of April, and head north. Wilf waves them off and, as soon as they're out of sight, heads for the garage to check that all his gardening kit and paint tins are still there.

"You never know," he says to April. "My galvanised watering

7) Kilve Beast

can must we worth a few bob."

"Don't be daft, Wilf. That pair were lovely. And they've probably never stepped foot in a vegetable plot."

That snowy afternoon, two strangers walk into the post office. April eyes them up from behind the counter. One is dressed smartly in a long winter coat and homburg hat. The other, a shifty looking character, is wearing a gabardine mac and fingerless gloves.

"Excuse me," says the homburg-wearing fellow as he waves a police warrant card under April's nose. "*I'm* Inspector Fielding. This other gentleman is Herbie. He doesn't have a warrant card… he's just helping with my enquiries. We're looking for a couple on a motorbike."

Herbie rubs his fingerless gloves and hisses a smile.

"Where have you parked it," asks April.

"What?" replies Fielding.

"Your motorbike."

"No, you misunderstand. It's the couple who are on a motorbike, not us. That black and white Hillman Minx parked in the road there is ours."

"Oh, I see," says April. "I'm afraid you've missed them. They went off this morning. Up north they were headed. I think I heard them mention Alderley Edge."

"*Did* you now? Alderley Edge, eh? That's definitely up north," chuckles Fielding. Herbie takes a glove off, scratches his head and says to Harry Fielding: "King Arthur territory that is. Makes sense if they're looking for dragons."

"Let's get going then, Herbie my fine fellow. This could mean promotion. For *me* that is, not for you."

Herbie looks at Harry with disdain. Promotion is the furthest thing from his desire.

At that moment, Wilf saunters in from his second deliveries and April explains who the unexpected customers are.

"I hope you've not been near my garage," says Wilfred.

BOOK WORM ~ *The Curiosity of George Crosby*

"You'll need a warrant to go in there. There's some valuable stuff stored inside."

-o-o-o-

8) On Edge

It turns out that the aspiring Harry Fielding has been busy on his important trail. After taking in all the forensic information and witness statements gleaned from the Arundel 'arsonist' episode, the police had released Peregrine from captivity. Then, from speaking with George's parents, Fielding had almost caught up with the pair at the Hood, in Kilve. He'd got the bit between his teeth with a not-inconsiderable amount of champing and had followed a lead that somehow had found him at the door of *Herbie Dragons* in London. He was convinced that Herbie would have special powers in helping to track down the two adherents of 'mythical' creatures. Herbie had tried to sell him a copy of *Jörmungandr - the Tale of the Tail of a Serpent*, but Fielding had rather astutely commandeered a copy as evidence for free. The intrepid policeman had embarked on reading it, hoping to find more clues, before giving up on the tome after the first ten pages. '1959?' he'd queried, and promised not to prosecute Herbie for misrepresentation if he assisted him in his further investigations, despite misgivings about the dragon man's rather shifty demeanour. Now, they're at Mordiford, hot on the trail.

Meanwhile George and Bella are making headway to Alderley. They're travelling on the A49, skirting the Welsh border, George casting the occasional glance over to the west, wondering if Our Boris had ever taken a trip to the land of Celts. With the great number of Welsh dragon tales, there must be a link, but George was yet to find one.

By late afternoon, Bella has delivered the two of them safely to Alderley, having left the A49 at Whitchurch, then having skirted Crewe. The sun is sinking in a clear sky, the air crisp and the clear light making all the world seem fine.

The accommodation they find is situated in a quiet cul-de-sac not far from the church. The proprietor is a nurse, in her fifties, who seems amenable to all their immediate requirements; parking for the bike and sidecar, a hot meal despite it not being hot meal time, and hot water for baths.

"I'm Anne, my loves. Anne Dromeda."

"Seriously?" questions Bella.

"Well yes and no, love. You see when I was girl, I loved stargazing and what with my name being Anne, my schoolmates added the other bit. My real name is Smith. As for stars, I still love them. On a clear night, on The Edge, you can see millions of them."

"Are there any dragons?" asks George. "I wondered if there may be a dragon living down in the depths of the rocks. Rumour has it, I believe."

"Not that *I've* seen. And I've lived here all my life," replies Anne, looking nervously at George, thinking: '*not another nutter, surely?*'

"What about King Arthur then?" chips in Bella, perceiving the nurse's apprehension and hoping that King Arthur would be a half-way house between the idea of 'real' dragons and the perceived reality of '*the once and future king*'.

"Oh, yes love. I'm sure Arthur is down there somewhere, along with Guinevere and Lancelot and Gawain and the whole crew. Mind you, I don't think you'd get that round table down there… not unless you took it down in pieces and put it back together again once it was got in."

Anne attends to the stove and the impending hot meals, then continues: "I met a doctor once who said he'd seen the knights down there in one of the caves. Mind you there's others that have decided all those holes are no more than abandoned Roman copper mines. And anyway, the doctor got carted away to the loony bin a couple of years after… they said he'd tried to ride a horse down one of the holes in full armour… the entrance was only big enough for a pony. Thankfully the horse survived his mad escapade."

"It sounds interesting though," says George. "I reckon Bella and I will still pay a visit."

"Up to you, loves. I think you'll be wasting your time though. Mind you, I'll take you up there if you like," says their hostess, in her affable way. "I've never been down the mines myself and I don't intend to go down anytime soon. I can wait for you above ground and look at the stars. I've gazed at *lots* of stars over The Edge these past years. I could show you galaxies you've never heard of. It looks like tonight is going to be a really clear one, and I could *do* with a change from watching television."

"It's a deal then, Anne. What time?"

"About eight o'clock would be good. You've got torches haven't you? I'll dig out my *big* torch too; I'm sure the batteries are good. We can go on foot. It's only a couple of miles. Maybe a half-hour walk at a brisk pace."

"You know, George. This is all beginning to sound like Joanie and the Knucker back in Lyminster," suggests Bella.

"I know, Bel. That's just what I was thinking. But I don't think King Arthur has much to do with the Norse myths, so I don't suppose we'll find any links to Ouroboros. I wonder where in the world the World Serpent is?"

"I've no idea George. I mean, this dragon-chasing lark is exiting, as far as it goes, but one day soon we're gonna have to think seriously about settling down, and decide where we're gonna live."

"Ah, yes. Of course. Do you reckon we should chose Lillibullero for the church, Bel? We could invite Rango too. I'm sure he'd liven things up in the service. I wonder where he's got to, or if we'll ever see him again?"

"As long as you don't let him near the hymn books," Bella replies, not overtly acknowledging that George appears to be thinking of actual marriage, "or Inspector Fielding will be after us all the more resolutely, for aiding and abetting serial arson."

"Ah, Fielding. Hopefully we've thrown him off the trail, and that'll all die down before we know it," George declares, seeming more confident now that the Arundel affair is shake-offable.

"Maybe, George. I *do* wonder where Rango is though? I hope he's okay."

Up on The Edge, the promised stars have formed a magnificent canopy for the wonderment of anyone prepared to spare a glance. No one could deny the existence of a higher being whilst under their mantle. There are blue stars, orange stars and bright white stars in constellations and in whole galaxies. The myriad of lights has conspired to reach Earth at this particular moment, longer and shorter aeons after each entity had emitted it. The starlight is so intense that it lights the way up to the escarpment of rock, where the three explorers now arrive.

"There are several holes and entrances you can explore," says Anne, "but you'll forgive me for not joining you if you're intent on delving. Just make sure you don't lose your torches. The stars won't light your way down there. If you go deep enough, maybe the Devil's furnaces will brighten your path. Meanwhile, I'll stay up here and admire the star-speckled sky."

"Come on then, Bel. Let's see if we can find King Arthur, and maybe a few dragons to boot."

"Maybe we shall, George. But I'm not booting any dragons. Not even for *you*. I don't want to be burned to a cinder, thank you very much."

The first two holes in the rock they try prove to be dead-ends, petering out after a few yards, presenting a blank wall of stone. The third proves more promising, cracks in the rock yielding to a wider space. On and down they go, gaining confidence from their bright torches. A little way on, the walls

8) On Edge

run away from each other and the roof flees higher above their heads until they appear to be in a cave. A further opening on the far side of this newly-sprung space entices them on, their voices echoing despite their whispering.

"Why are we whispering again, George?" asks Bella, the echo still passing the message on to her companion several diminishing times before dying unanswered.

George is absorbed in guiding them into the nether opening which, to their surprise, opens onto a vast, stony cavern. The echoes become stronger and longer.

"It all seems pretty dead down here, George. I can't imaging a king wanting to stay for more than an hour or two."

"Well perhaps he didn't have any choice, Bella," George replies, emphatically. "He was *once* a king and I suppose he'll be holding his breath until he becomes a *future* king… something like that, anyway."

They amble on, directing their torches alternately onto the path before them and the the roof above. They pass through two more portals and then into a smaller cave that appears to offer no further way forward.

"I hope you can remember the path back out, George. I don't think King Arthur has arranged a reception for us, so we'll get no help that way. And as for drago…"

Bella's whisper tails off to a barely audible whimper, then dies as they hear a clashing of steel on steel and what sounds like shards of rock cascading noisily to the floor of the cave some distance off.

"What the…!?" exclaims George.

"I don't know," says Bella. "I'm not sure that I really want to find out."

George catches a glint of metal at the far side of the cave in the torchlight.

"Did you see that, Bel? It looked like a crown, glittering. Over there."

He points with his torch.
"There. Do you see Bel?"
"Yes, George. I *do* see."
Of a sudden, a light flares up as if responding to the beam of George's torch.
"Hello," bellows a voice from behind the light, with no attempt at whispering. "Is there someone there?"
George replies: "Hello there," waiting for some regal response and expecting to meet Arthur, wondering what you say when you meet a 'dead' mythical king.

There's no response, but the light flickers erratically, seeming to approach the two explorers amid a clattering of metallic regalia. Bella positions herself behind George, peering over his shoulder and flashing her own torch now in the direction of the commotion. She's certain that she can make out chain-mail in the shadows.

The mysterious beam of light is moving towards them now. Then another appears... and another. The sound of shuffling feet on stone grows in the half-light, George's torch beam is now fencing with three combative laser-like shafts of light. The battling duel, or is it a quad-el?, throws shadows dancing on the walls and roof of the cave as Bella's torch joins in.

"Just don't come any nearer," shouts George at the apparent source of the unexpected illuminations.

"Sorry," calls out a deep voice. "Didn't mean to startle you, but we weren't expecting visitors."

George coughs at the prospect of coming face-to-face with King Arthur and two of his knights. Bella braces herself, thinking: '*dragons are one thing, but now we're about to be slain by a sword-wielding ghost.*'

Then, when the cave-dwellers are a mere ten yards from George and Bella, the mystery becomes clearer, if not a little bit of a let-down.

"We've been down here for a couple of hours," says the deep

8) On Edge

voice. "We've gone further in today than we did last time we came. Anyway, I'm Eric... Eric Battersby... president of the *Macclesfield Caving Club*. We only formed the club three months ago, so this is only our third trip 'out in the field' so to speak."

"Oh, right," says George, in a voice betraying relief and disappointment in equal measure.

"Is it a big club?" asks Bella, emerging now from behind George's shoulder.

"Not really. Just the three of us here... This is Sid, and behind him is Carol."

The two other caving companions mutter a collective greeting. Bella and George acknowledge them with a mumble.

"Would you like to join?" asks Eric. "We're always on the lookout for new members."

"Oh, no thanks," confirms George, snapping himself out of his knightly imaginings. "We're not local actually. We were hoping to find King Arthur, and maybe a dragon or two. I don't suppose *you've* seen any sign?"

"'Afraid not," says Eric, humouring George, having thought that the three of *them* were daft enough themselves coming down into caves just for the geology. "I don't think you'll find anything like that down here. A lot of people seem to think you might, but if *you* were a king or a knight, would you want to spend your death in a damp cave? A couple of hours is more than enough. As for dragons... who in their right mind believes in dragons?"

"Well, *we've* seen dragons with our own eyes," explains Bella. "They can be magnificent creatures up close. Intelligent too."

"Right," says Eric, looking now for a sharp exit from the cave and from this encounter with these two mad myth hunters. "Well, good luck. We've got to get away now. I'm due at a parent-teacher meeting at the primary school in the morning, and I think Sid and Carol have a train to catch."

And before George and Bella can ask whether Eric is a parent or a teacher, the three members of the *Macclesfield Caving Club* are up and gone. As the three spelunkers leave the caves and head back for civilisation, they pass Anne, who's perched on a high stone, gazing captivated by a magnificently bright Milky Way.

"Evening," says the deep-voiced Eric.

"Mutter, mutter," agree Carol and Sid.

"Evening," says Anne, nonchalantly, as if three cavers passing by of a clear cold evening is quite the norm.

Back inside the cave, Bella and George are in a dilemma.

"Should we go deeper in, Bel? Or should we take heed of those three and accept that there's no *once* king unless he's still very much in the *future*?"

"I don't really know , George. But I do know that it's getting a bit cold and damp in here. If we did find Arthur, I reckon he'd be pretty rusty by now."

"Let's get back to Anne then, Bel. We can think on things and decide tomorrow morning what to do next."

As they approach the cave's exit, George slips on a loose stone and stretching his hand out for balance finds the wall.

"Ow!" he exclaims. "Bugger. That hurt."

Bella flashes her torch at George's hand.

"You've cut yourself, George. That rock must be razor-sharp. You're bleeding quite badly. We'd better move fast. Anne will have some first-aid stuff back at *her* place."

George flashes his own torch at the place on the wall where he'd cut his hand.

"Blimey, Bel. Look!"

And there, set solid, is what appears to be the shard of a sword blade, projecting from the rock.

"It can't be… can it Bel?"

"Whatever, George. Your bloody hand is a bit more urgent. Hurry on now. Shift yourself."

The two dragon-hunters emerge from the caves to find Anne

8) On Edge

sitting cross-legged, smiling to herself.

"You missed them, my loves. King Arthur and two of his minions have just gone back down the hill," she chuckles.

"Oh, you mean Eric and his entourage," says Bella realising that Anne is taunting them. "You can laugh, Anne, but George has cut himself on a knight's sword. It was sticking out from the rock."

"Oh, dear. Let's have a look, love. See if we can bandage it with something before we get back to the house. Take your coat off for me will you."

"Thanks," says George, in anticipation of this access to his own, exclusive health service.

"I can tell you, Bella," says Anne, as she rips the shirt sleeve clean off from George's shirt and proceeds to make strip dressings, "that won't be a sword. Don't you go thinking that it's Excalibur. It'll most likely be a remnant of equipment from the mining. There's all sorts of crap down there, so they tell me."

George is pensive: *'maybe she's right. No Arthur. No dragon. What are we doing here when we could be settling down together back in Leicester, or better still in Cambridge. We'll get simple jobs in the local library or a coffee shop. I could get an allotment and grow prizewinning vegetables. Bella could become a leading authority on motorbikes in her spare time, while I could learn more about dragons in the comfort of an armchair instead of all this rushing around the country.'*

"Ow!" squeals George, as Anne tightens an impromptu shirt-sleeve based bandage.

The three of them make to head down the sloping path they'd climbed on the way up, torch beams bobbing before them as they go, when George's squeal is echoed by a distant frenetic shout in the darkness below them: "Got you, you slippery buggers."

They can make out a commotion of lights and subdued

cursing, about thirty yards ahead. As they reach the scene of the disturbance, they see that there are two police cars and several policemen grappling with the entire membership of the *Macclesfield Caving Club*. George and his companions can do no more than approach the melee, the path being the only clear way down the hill.

"You were at Arundel *weren't* you," calls out the frenetic voice ahead. "You and that book-burning dragon. We've found out from our intelligence that that's the way the Arundel book was scorched. You're in big trouble, trying to escape the long arm of the law like that."

"No," squeaks Eric in protest. "You must be after those others. They're up there in the caves, looking for dragons… and King Arthur. Look! There they are now," he adds, spying George, Bella and Anne on the path above them.

"Right, after them lads," calls Harry Fielding to his team.

So it is, that George and Bella's aspiring nemesis, one Harry Fielding, has caught up with the dragon liberators. Here he is, mistaking Eric, Carol and Sid for the pyrotechnic perpetrators of the Arundel arson episode. And to crown it all, George makes out in the gloom, the unmistakable form of Herbie, the proprietor of the dragon shop.

"Love a duck," utters George. "It's Herbie Dragons, Bel. They've ganged up to come and get us. What are we going to do? We can't get by them."

Bella is about to utter a reassuring word to her dear George when, like a tiny erupting volcano, a flash of blood-red flame belches up over the stony ridge of The Edge. A flurry of flapping wings against the starry sky descends on Harry Fielding, claws flying. A nearby Herbie Dragons hisses, flapping his arms in a half-hearted bid to fend off the winged creature. Two other police officers dive into their patrol car to avoid the wild aerial attack.

"It's Rango!" calls out Bella. "He's come back. What brilliant

8) On Edge

timing."

The *Macclesfield Caving Club* adherents escape Fielding's 'long arm of the law' en-bloc, dashing downwards, away into the night. Harry and Herbie emulate the other officers, diving into their *own* car. Harry shouts back up the hill at George's party: "I'll be back to get you. We know where you live. Don't think you can get away with this."

With appropriate urgency, the black and white Hillman Minx starts first time, and they're away.

Now, everything is quiet again. Rangvald settles on a nearby tree-branch.

Anne, still nonchalant as you like, says: "Let's get you back to civilisation, George my lad… what ever *civilisation* is. Then you can tell me all about arson and police officers and this here dragon creature. I've never seen anything like it in my life… and I've seen a few things, I can tell you."

"Fine, but we *must* speak with Rango first… Rangvald that is… the dragon."

"Okay, George. So you want *me* to sit and wait while *you* talk to a mythical creature and you bleed to death, right? Well, I suppose that's a bit more exciting than looking at stars… talking to dragons that is, not you bleeding to death. It certainly seems to have put the cat among the policemen. At least it did those cavers a favour. I wonder what the police wanted them for? Come to that, what did they want *you* for? And who was that shifty bloke with the principal plod?"

"We'll explain later, Anne," suggests Bella. "In the meantime, can we bring Rango with us? He's quite harmless really."

"I suppose that's alright then. Here I am, tending two people I didn't know existed before a few hours ago and now I'm being asked to share my house with a mythical beast. I must be stark raving mad, but I suppose a myth is as good as a mile."

"We really must think about leaving right away, Anne," says

George, apologetically, as she cleans and re-dresses his wound, while Rangvald sits perched on the fridge in her kitchen.

George is anxious to explain: "We're very grateful for all you're doing for us, but those policemen are chasing us for something we didn't do, and they didn't look about to give up. That shifty bloke as you call him owns a dragon shop in London and we never *did* trust him much. Now he's here with the police, on our trail... as if it has anything to do with *him*."

"To be fair, George," chips in Bella, "it *is* something we did. Well, something Rango did... although we helped him to do it. But scorching that book was an accident wasn't it. We aught to come clean with the police and hand ourselves in."

"I tell you, Bel. It'll all die down if we make a quick exit with Rango. There's a place I was thinking of heading for next. It's..."

"Don't say it, George," interrupts Anne. "I don't want to know. I think it's a good idea that you move on in secret and take your fiery friend with you. That way, if that silly policeman and his oppo come back asking questions, I can honestly tell them that I don't know where you've gone."

Anne finishes with the medical side of things and suggests that George and Bella have a private conflab with their winged friend as she leaves the room on some contrived domestic chore or other.

"Now then, Rango," says Bella, addressing the little dragon with a stern, yet grateful tone, "where on Earth have you *been*? Or more to the point where have you *come* from? We thought you'd gone off to China or maybe the Holy Land. According to Barry at his bike shop in New Malden you mentioned a place called Kowloon."

"Well *there's* a nice welcome indeed," says the dragon. "I come back here and save you from that pair, and all you do is tell me off for not going to China."

"So, you *didn't* go then?"

8) On Edge

"No, Bella, I didn't. I went to China *Town*... Chinatown in London, that is. I thought better of going to the Middle East and China itself, and found my way to London instead; a fascinating place I found it too. But while I was there, that police officer turned up. Harry Fielding isn't it? I kept out of sight, but I overheard him asking questions about that castle where I was imprisoned. Anyway, that dreadful Herbie fellow happened along and offered to help the Fielding chap solve the mystery of the scorched book, saying he had some sort of intuition about it all. If you ask me, he's more like some malevolent dragon than a man. I've seen his sort before. You can't trust them as far as you could throw a flame."

"Well, I think *we'd* come to that conclusion, Rango," says Bella in an apologetic tone. "I didn't mean to criticise you. You're more than entitled not to go to China, or to go if you prefer, or to go wherever you please for that matter. And we're very grateful that you came back to help us."

Rangvald sits upright on the fridge, proud as punch now for being acknowledged as the hero of the moment.

"This is all very well, you pair, but..." and at this, George looks over his shoulder to ensure that Anne's not in earshot, "I've decided we should move on right away and head for a place called Upholland, about half an hour north-west of here, beyond Manchester... *nobody* goes beyond Manchester, not even the police. Upholland's a quiet place, from what I can see, and we can decide from there where our next port of call might be. I trust you're not about to fly off to some exotic place, Rango? We'll make room for you again in the sidecar."

"Well, I did hear mention of a nice China-clay works in Cornwall. St Austell, I think was the place. It sounds very interesting, but it can wait. I'm happy to be back in your presence, for the time being at least."

So they cut short their intended stay with Anne and take to the road again.

BOOK WORM ~ *The Curiosity of George Crosby*

George is right; not even the police go beyond Manchester if they can help it and Harry Fielding, with his entourage, has hightailed it back to London feeling scorched at the edges. He and Herbie knock on the door marked 'D.C.I. Hector Parrott', at police headquarters.

"Look, Fielding. This is dereliction of duty in *my* book," says his boss. "I've a good mind to demote you here and now."

"Well you can't demote me from the bottom, sir, can you."

"Well you can't demote me from the bottom, sir..." says Hector Parrott, parrot fashion. "Well, just wait 'til you get that promotion. I'll demote you *then*."

"You have to realise, sir. I've never come actual face-to-face with a real dragon before. It's very unnerving."

"Listen, Fielding. You don't expect me to believe all this mumbo-jumbo about dragons, do you? It's most likely a figment of everybody's imagination. Mass hysteria, that's what it is."

"I tell you, it's real sir. *You* ask P.C. Simpkin or P.C. James. They were both there."

"There you go, then. That's four of you... more than enough for a hysterical mass, I'd say. You'll have to pull yourself together, man. I can tell you, *I* didn't get where I am today without confronting my demons."

"But, begging your pardon, sir. This is dragons, not demons."

"Look Fielding. In my book, there can't be much difference. And anyway, who's this rag-bag of a companion you've dragged in here? I don't remember seeing him before."

"Herbie, sir. Herbie Dragons."

"Dragons? Here we go again. What kind of a name is that? It's obviously an alias, let's be frank. Come on now. What's your real name, Mr. Dragons?"

Herbie throws a venomous look at Parrott: "If I had another name, I wouldn't tell someone with a name like Parrott. He'd be repeating it to all and sundry."

8) On Edge

Parrott's face colours up and he looks for a moment as if he's about to explode. Composing himself, he turns to Fielding: "Get yourself organised Fielding. Head back up north and collar those firebrands before all the libraries in the land are a pile of ashes. And if you *must* take this dubious creature with you, then good luck."

"Surely, sir, that would be *piles* of ashes."

Parrott's expression is enough to make Harry turn tail and Herbie follows him, tail between his legs. In the corridor, Harry mutters to Herbie: "If he thinks I'm headed back up there in a hurry, he's mistaken."

"I think we *should* go, Harry, my friend," says Herbie Dragons. "Those lot could do irreparable damage to the dragon community. And anyway, I have a long-standing bone to pick with that Rangvald."

-o-o-o-

9) Up Lowland

Meanwhile, George, Bella and Rangvald have settled in a small, country hotel in Upholland, Rangvald discreetly hidden of course.

"Believe it or believe it not, George," remarks the dragon, "but I've never heard of this place before."

"I wonder if it's related to Holland itself?" questions Bella, poring over their map.

"Could be, Bel," agrees George. "I *do* know that back in the day, some people called Holland 'Lowland' on account of it being below sea level.

"Oh, Lowland," says Rangvald. I *have* heard of that. It's over the sea to the east, isn't it. When I was last free to roam, before that other George decided to incarcerate me, I used to fly over Lowland quite a lot. But that place is more *down* than '*Up*' isn't it, George."

"Well, yes. I suppose if this place were anything to do with Holland, it would be called *Down*holland rather than *Up*holland."

"There you have it, George," says Bella. "Looking on the map there *is* a Downholland, further to the west of here. Remember though... this place is set on a hill, so that would explain the 'Up' bit."

"Well, Bel, up or down, this place is nice and quiet and out of the way. I can't see Harry and Herbie finding us here."

"And if they do," suggests Rangvald, "I'll make sure they wish they hadn't. Coming after you like that, when all you did was a kind favour to a dragon spirit. I won't forget it, George."

"Well, talking of dragons, how come they always seem to live under hills?"

"*I* never did, George. I preferred the mountains... *on* them that is, not *in* them," the diminutive dragon says, sounding

176

9) Up Lowland

more than a little elitist.

"Well, *I* don't trust that pair not to come looking for us here as soon as you like," decides Bella. "They've had their noses put out of joint and they seem to be on a mission, all over a mild case of book burning."

Truth to tell, George had found a reference to Upholland in the little pocket guide that Herbie Dragons sold them for a pound. For all its briefness, *A Guide to Mythical Beasts of England and Wales* has some very interesting insights to the world of dragons, which is perhaps to be expected, since that's the sole purpose of the little volume. It appears there's a cave, the exact location of which seems to have been be a long-kept secret. The booklet refers to the 'Upholland Dragon's-eye Cave'.

"Now then, Rango. I'm afraid we're going to have to leave you here while we go down to the local pub to see if we can find more about this cave. We may as well make use of our stay in this little hideaway-of-a-place to find out all we can about the Dragon's-eye."

"So, *I* stay here while *you two* partake of the alcoholic brew that you've talked about so much."

"Now look, Rango. That isn't the purpose of our visit to the pub, as well you know. I've a feeling from the description in the booklet that this could well be a lead to finding more about Our Boris. The legendary eye seems to be massive... and a World Serpent's would need to be massive, wouldn't it."

"Well, maybe you're right, but I can't imagine Jörmungandr even visiting a place like this, let alone living here."

"Nonetheless, *we're* going, and *you* have to stay. I'll fill the washbasin with water for you, and we'll bring you back some food, offers George."

"And what food would that be, George?"

"How would chicken in a basket suit you, Rango? With chips?"

"What on Earth is chicken doing in a basket? Just bring me the chicken. You can keep the basket. The chips, whatever they are, might be welcome. I could give them a try."

"You'll need the basket then," Bella informs him.

Rangvald reacts to her apparent taunting with a flutter of wings and a sulk.

In the pub, which appears not to have had a lick of paint for centuries, the customers seem not to have had a duster applied for just as long. There's one old girl sat in the corner of the smoke-room who Bella swears has an inch of dust on her shoulders. She's enjoying a bright-glowing Woodbine and has an untouched pint of stout to hand, perhaps more for quenching the cigarette in an emergency than to quench her thirst. She has a black greyhound by her side which is sitting obediently, expectant of a crisp or two from the woman's packet. A couple of ancient blokes: *'probably retired farm labourers,'* thinks George, are propping up the bar. The leather-aproned landlord is topping up their half-empty beer glasses. The chatter of the two sons of the soil subsides and dies as they become aware belatedly that George is trying to get by them to the bar.

"Be with you in a moment, young sir. I'm just watering these two wilted flowers. Sorry if they're in your way but I think they're rooted to the stools. I've been keeping them alive for years, but I really ought to re-pot them... a bit of root pruning would do them good."

The pair sit oblivious to the landlord's levity. Despite their apparent rooting, they seem less dusty that the old girl.

"That's alright," says George. "There's no hurry."

Meanwhile, Bella has sat herself down at the small, round, cast-iron table set next to the eccentric-looking woman. The greyhound is between them, and nuzzles Bella in the friendliest of ways.

9) Up Lowland

"Now then," says the landlord to George, "what can I get you?"

"Err, just a couple of pint of bitter, please. And some crisps, and maybe one of those pickled eggs."

"Oh, you don't want one of them. I ain't sold one of them since VE Day. Even the jar must be pickled by now."

"Just the crisps, then, thanks."

The labourers resume their chatter. George picks up the words 'turnips', 'bottom', 'field', and 'slurry' but little else.

"I was wondering if you know about the 'Upholland Dragon's-eye Cave'," he asks the landlord. "I believe it's somewhere under the hill, isn't it?"

The labourers' chatter ceases again as abruptly as it had resumed. They share apprehensive glances.

"You don't want to go meddling with that place, young sir," suggests the landlord. "No good ever came from meddling with that place. I don't reckon anyone's been up there, or is it down there?, since before I last sold a pickled egg. And anyway, I don't know where it is, do we Billy?"

"No, Alf. Do we Cedric?"

"No, Billy. Do we Alf?"

"Right. Well thanks anyway. It was only a thought… a passing interest, that's all," Replies George to landlord Alf, perceiving the least said the better.

Bella is having better luck with the old Woodbine lady, who's overheard George's request: "Well, love. *I* can tell you a bit about that cave, though I only know what my old aunt says about it. She's a hundred and three. Well a hundred and two 'til next Woden's Day. Or is it Thor's Day, I'm not sure. Anyway, she told me that it's really a mine, known as *The Hall of Giants*. They mined stone there, thousands of years ago. You can only get in where the roof collapsed but, since it collapsed, you can see all different coloured rocks. My aunt says her husband saw it, but that was about fifty years ago. She knows roughly where it is, love, but you'd probably need to be a miner with all the kit to get to see it. And even then, I doubt you'd get out again."

George makes his way over to Bella's chosen table with their beers and crisps. Alf, Billy and Cedric are oblivious to the old girl's revelations and when Bella informs George of the story, he asks her to keep her voice down for fear of setting off ripples of anxiety at the bar.

The old girl downs her stout in one, and beckons Bella and George to follow. The black greyhound leads leadless.

"I should never have sold those books to that pair, Harry," hisses the sibilant Herbie. "I made a serious misjudgement, thinking them to be the usual folk-tourists just after a bit of casual reading about dragons. Now it seems they really are intent on uncovering the deep secrets of Ouroboros. They have to be stopped, or all Hell will break loose in the dragon lairs of the world."

"I thought that dragons lived in *dens*, not lairs, Herbie. It just shows you how wrong you can be. Hang on a minute... it wasn't until the other day that I even believed that dragons actually exist. Now I've seen a real, live one, I'm not sure I'd like to see another. All I wanted to do was bring to justice people who go setting books on fire."

"Well, for my part, I'd prefer the quiet life, selling artefacts to unwary customers. I don't really want to go back to playing a major rôle in the dragon community."

"Community? How many dragons do you think there are then?"

"More than you could imagine, Harry. Would you like to buy a book about them?"

Harry's look is enough for Herbie to briefly put away his innate salesman persona.

At that moment, Parrott pops his head round the door: "Are you pair still here? I've decided all this is more than just

9) Up Lowland

dereliction of duty. Demotion's too good for you, Harry Fielding. I'm sacking you here and now unless you get your skates on."

"You, sir," replies Fielding, deciding he'd better do as Parrott says or else find himself out on the street without even a Police pension.

"Good. Off you go then." And off goes Hector Parrott himself to concentrate on drawing up the list of select invitees to the forthcoming inter-station police golf tournament.

"Back to Alderley Edge then, Harry," says Herbie. "To see if we can find clues to the latest whereabouts of your book heathens."

"This all sounds very exciting, dear," enthuses the greyhound lady's one hundred and two year old aunt Boadicea. "Who'd have thought we'd have dragon-hunters for tea?"

"They're not here for tea, aunt B. They just want to know where the entrance to that Dragon's-eye Cave is."

"'You don't want to go meddling with that place, young sir.'"

"That's odd. They're the exact same words as Alf the pub landlord used," remarks George.

"I know, my dear. I was quoting him… he always used to say that. He's a right misery, he is. So are those two old codgers stuck to his barstools; Billy and Cedric, isn't it?"

"That's right, aunt," agrees her niece.

"Would yo believe that the last time I went in the pub, that Alf refused to sell me a pickled egg. Said they'd been there since VE Day, he did. But I know he was lying… he sold me the first one from the fresh-delivered jar in 1955."

"I do like your name, Boadicea," says Bella. "It means victorious, doesn't it?"

"It *does*, my dear. How knowledgeable of you. Boady here was named after me. Boady's a bit more modern than Boadicea, isn't it. What are *your* names?"

"I'm Bella, and this is George."

"Anyway, Bella and George, I don't agree with what Alf says. Life's for living. You have to make an adventure out of it, otherwise you'll wind up at the Pearly Gates without ever having risked a pickled egg. Now, I have to say that I've never seen a dragon, but I've a fair idea where you might find the entrance to the cave with the 'dragon's eye'. And despite what others say, I was told where to find an easy path down into the depths of the mine. If I were twenty years younger, I'd come down with you."

Without further hesitation, Aunt Boadicea takes up paper and pencil, and draws them a sketch of where she thinks the path lies.

"If you promise not to tell anyone, Boadicea, especially any policemen, we could bring a dragon here to see you," offers Bella. "He's only a small dragon… quite feisty though at times."

"Oh, that would be wonderful," says a delighted aunt Boadicea.

George nudges Bella: "I thought we were looking to be low-key, Bel," he says from the corner of his mouth.

"Yes, George, but I still fancy a metaphorical pickled egg."

So it is that, armed with old Boadicea's sketch, George, Bella and Rangvald find themselves trekking the hillsides of Upholland looking for the mysterious cave of the dragon's eye. Young Boady has declined the offer of joining them, and is off down the pub with her black greyhound. By a combination of the old aunt's sketching abilities and a moonlit night that an aerial bomber would delight over, they find what appears to be a tiny aperture in the rock amid a bramble entanglement of bushes and overgrown grass. Carefully, George parts the vegetation sufficiently for them to filter through what is a camouflaged entrance to the ancient stone mine, Rangvald complaining that his two companions would find it more of a

9) Up Lowland

squeeze if they had wings to contend with.

Then a little way on, in the torch-lit gloom, they make out an enormous sinkhole there before them where the rock seems to have collapsed into a wondrous cavern below.

"Here, look," says George. "There's a pathway around the side of the hole leading down, just as Boadicea's sketch shows. We can use it to get to the floor of the cave."

"I don't need a path, thank you, George. I can fly down," boasts Rangvald.

"Not complaining about having wings now then, Rango?" jibes Bella.

"Well, no, I suppose not," the dragon replies.

On reaching the flat floor of the delvings, the little party, like to pebbles on a beach, stand rooted in awe of what remains of the cavern roof above them.

"One thing's for sure, Bel," ponders George. "This place is big enough to house Our Boris... when he's not circling the world that is."

"I was thinking, George," says Bella, "Boris's true name, Jörmungandr, sounds a bit like 'George and Dragon' doesn't it. Maybe Saint George actually killed Jörmungandr, the World Serpent.

"Must I *really* remind you, Bella," says Rangvald, expressing continued frustration with the expedition down the Upholland cave, "George *filed* the dragon. And that dragon was me... remember?"

"Sorry."

"He's right, Bel. No mere mortal could slay Ouroboros unaided. Boris is huge. I mean, if he can circle the Earth, what chance would George have against him?"

"Sorry," retorts Bella, feeling a bit miffed. "Well, let's hope *this* George doesn't find him then, or you could be in for a shock."

"But I'm not trying to *kill* Our Boris, am I. If I were, I'd be mad to try."

BOOK WORM ~ *The Curiosity of George Crosby*

"You certainly would, George," chips in Rangvald. For a start, I'd defend our heroic Jörmungandr to the death, like a hero."

"I know you would, Rango. You're nothing if not a hero in my book."

"Don't say things like that, George," pleads the little dragon, with a shudder. "Books are not my favourite subject. You should know that."

"Jörmungandr," shouts George without warning, at the top of his voice. "Jörmungandr," he bellows again.

Rangvald takes to the air startled, in a frenetic fluttering of wings, as George's cries echo around the vast chamber.

"George!" exclaims Bella. "You frightened me half to death. What *are* you doing?"

"Sorry. I just thought that if Our Boris *is* here, then we should try and wake him. To be honest, whispering won't find him, for sure."

Once the echoes subside, George comes to the conclusion that there's no hint of Boris to be found here.

"Might as well make tracks back to the hotel, Bel. Then, first thing in the morning, we'd better move on again... keep ahead of that Fielding and his new found Herbie friend, in case they're still on our scent."

"Well, George. At some point we're going to have to confront the situation. I just can't really understand why the law is so concerned over a frizzled book. But if in the end they won't let it go, we could just tell them that it was an accident and that Rango burned the book in a flurry of freedom."

"Oh, thanks, Bella," Rangvald complains. "Think what that would do for my reputation. No self-respecting dragon normally burns *anything* unintentionally. And you can't blame me for being startled into fiery flight when George opened the book after all that time."

"Well anyway, we need to stop talking and make a move," George reminds them. "Let's go."

9) Up Lowland

With these, George's final words on the matter, Rangvald lets out a defiant burst of flame and they make to head back to the pathway they'd come down. Behind them, on the vast far wall of the cavern, unbeknown to the three explorers, the flash of light from Rangvald's mighty belch of flame illuminates momentarily a huge, many-coloured eye. It seems to be set in the rock; a giant, petrified eye looking out on the eternal darkness. Yet that brief flash of light from Rangvald appears to make the eye blink.

Morning comes.

"Surely, we're not *really* moving on again already," Rangvald complains to George. "I rather like this place. That spare bed seems very comfortable. And the view is wonderful."

"You're sounding like a bed and breakfast guidebook," says Bella, resigned to the fact that they must travel on.

"Like I explained, Rango," says George. "Fielding and his new sidekick are probably winging their way towards us as we speak. And I need to move on and clear my head; this dragon malarkey is getting a bit confusing. The records of your family tree are rubbish, Rango. What books there are seem all too fragmentary. I can't see us ever finding more of Our Boris. If only Fielding would go and chase real criminals, we could go at a steadier pace."

Bella feels the need to stick up for Rangvald: "Well, George, don't you think you're being a bit unfair. Books about family trees are always fragmentary, I shouldn't wonder. That's just the way they're bound to be."

"That's right, Bella," Rangvald agrees. "And anyway, books seem to be at the root of all evil. It can't be denied that the one you released me from is still causing trouble, after all these years. *I* could get the blame. I didn't even ask you to set me free, though I'm grateful that you did, otherwise I'd never have learned about motorbikes and sidecars and police cars and things."

"Well," says Bella, "before we move on to wherever you have in mind, George, we'd better get some fresh bandage for that cut of yours. How is it, by the way?"

"Oh, it's healing, slowly. I don't think it's infected but it's still quite sore. I've been wondering if maybe I *did* cut it on Excalibur, despite what Anne thought. Maybe King Arthur didn't manage to pull it from that rock after all. Maybe he just managed half of it."

"No, George. What Anne said makes more sense. It would have been a remnant from the mining works."

"I suppose so. Anyway, I don't think Arthur had any dealings with Norse dragons. He'd have been waving his sword around in the middle-east if anything."

"Well there you are, George."

"Rango," says George, thoughtfully, "you're not a Norse, are you?"

"Maybe I am, George, but I wouldn't admit it. If I admitted to being an 'orse, you'd be wanting to *ride* on me next thing I knew. Apart from my intention to maintain my dignity, I'm just not big enough for riding on."

Bella smiles, realising that Rangvald is being deliberately obtuse: "So where to then, George?" she asks.

"There's a little place right up beyond York called Loschy Wood. There's a legend about a dragon but, from what I've read, that one is long dead. Beyond that, there's the Whitby wyrm and, although it was banished, it's got to be somewhere waiting to be found again."

"Well," decides Rangvald, "I only hope it's not trapped in a book, George. Otherwise that Harry chap with his objectionable partner will be bringing reinforcements to the proceedings."

Bella smiles again and chuckles thinking: '*Am I completely mad? I could be in Cambridge eating muffins and drinking coffee in that delightful little café by the side of the Cam watching the punters*

9) Up Lowland

on the water.'

With that, they make preparation to move on. Sadly, Boadicea never does get to see Rangvald.

-o-o-o-

10) Loschy Way

With a reticent rising sun peeking shyly from behind gathering clouds, the itinerant band of dragon door-steppers finish parcelling up their belongings. Rangvald squeezes into the sidecar reluctantly, with the express intention of escaping it to follow by air at the first prudent opportunity.

"I reckon we could stop off at York, George?"

"What for, Bel?"

"No particular reason. It's just that I've never been there, and I've heard it's a nice place. Probably as nice as Cambridge, and *definitely* nicer than Leicester."

"There's nothing wrong with Leicester, Bel. Some very interesting people come from Leicester. There's that David Attenborough for a start. I expect he'd find Our Boris really easily, him being experience with that 'Zoo Quest' programme. His brother Richard's good too. Then there's Simon DeMontfort... he's got a hall named after him, and he went to the Crusades as well. I bet he knew King Arthur, *and* Saint George. I can imagine they were like the Three Musketeers. Did that George mention Simon DeMontfort or King Arthur to *you*, Rango?"

"Of course not, George. He was too busy persecuting me and before I had a chance to discuss the ins and outs of knightly combat, I was locked in by that clasp."

"Well, of course he wouldn't mention them, George," declares Bella. "*They* were both later, especially Simon DeMontfort. And I bet Rango hasn't even heard of the Crusades. He was stuck in a book at the time."

"Too right, Bella," says Rangvald. "I reckon *your* family tree records are probably worse than mine, George, if your knowledge of dates is anything to go by. As for David Attenborough's 'quest', in just which century exactly did he go

10) Loschy Way

on it?"

"Sorry, Rango. I get easily confused by all these knightly tales and dragon tails."

"If you *must* know, George," Bella retorts, with an air of authority on the matter, "the Attenboroughs weren't *born* in Leicester, they just went to school there. And where did they go to university? Cambridge, remember. Now as for York... well, there's Guy Fawkes for one. And remember there were lots of Vikings in York... and Whitby come to that. Now if it's Norse you're after, what better than to ask a Viking."

"What's a Viking?" asks Rangvald.

"A Norseman."

"Ah. We're back to the Norse, are we?" says Rangvald, deciding this time not to tease George.

"I give in," says George to Bella. "You being such a fount of knowledge."

After avoiding Manchester and Leeds deliberately, and Rangvald having been decanted from the sidecar just outside Leigh, Bella and George arrive in York and turn into a quiet side-street. The dragon, drifting effortlessly on the breeze high above, waits for a sign from George then plummets like a hawk. Landing, he hides behind a dense privet hedge, dislodging a garden gnome from its proud pedestal in the process.

Bella double checks that it's safe for their winged companion to squeeze back into the sidecar, then gives Rangvald his instructions: "Now you stay here, Rango, until we get back. We'll be gone for about an hour. We'll leave the side window open a little so you can get fresh air, but stay under George's coat as much as possible to keep out of sight."

"But why can't *I* look around this place, the same as you? I may never get the chance to explore Jorvik again. If it's good enough for Norsemen, then it's good enough for me."

"Because, Rango," explains George, "people aren't used to seeing dragons, and if you get into the newspapers and onto the television news, Harry Fielding will be onto us like a flash."

"I still don't really know what a television is, George."

"Never you mind. Just stay low, like Bella says."

"I suppose so," Rangvald replies sulkily, like a teenager who's been told he can't go down to the park to play football, "but don't be any longer. I get claustrophobic in confined spaces, as you must know by now. That's why I can't wait to get airborne whenever we're travelling."

"We won't be too long, Rango," Bella reassures him. We just want to see a few places of interest."

Heading along Bishopthorpe Road and on over the river bridge, the couple turn into Tower Gardens and see the imposing Clifford's Tower before them. The raised earthwork on which the tower sits was apparently where a defensive timber structure had been built by William the Conqueror. Then, when York Castle was intact, the tower had formed part of it. The castle was once the centre of government for the north of England, and later it was a Royalist stronghold in the English Civil War.

They spot a signpost for the Shambles.

"That looks interesting, George. I've heard about the Shambles. Lots of gorgeous little shops. Maybe you could find some souvenirs for your mum and dad. I'm sure they'll be missing you terribly."

"I suppose, so, Bel. I must admit, I haven't given them much thought lately. What with all the dragon stuff, and being chased by the book police."

"Well, *you* think on, George. Family is important. They'll be the ones to visit you if you end up in prison."

"Bel. Don't joke about such things," George says, glancing over his shoulder, half-expecting Fielding's police car to be kerb-crawling behind them with the beady-eyed Herbie

10) Loschy Way

pointing them out. He imagines Simpkin and James parked up in the Shambles, eating sandwiches and drinking cold coffee, waiting to pounce on the unsuspecting couple of sightseers.

Up ahead, on a green space on the approach to the tower, a crowd has gathered. A commotion of laughter and applause bursts forth as a loud shout goes up:

"In comes I, old Father Christmas!
Am I welcome, or am I not?…"

As Bella and George approach, gaps in the gathered crowd reveal gaudily dressed players with a parody of Father Christmas wishing everyone good cheer. He then mentions Beelzebub, who arrives on the scene as prompted:

"In comes I, Beelzebub.
Just watch out for this 'ere club,"

…comes the threat from the grizzly personification of the Devil, then more laughter and more applause.

"It's a mummers' play, Bel. How hilarious. We *must* watch."

"But it's not even Christmas, George."

"Well, maybe they're rehearsing. Christmas is not far away, after all. And anyway, you don't wait 'til *summer* actually arrives to watch a play about sunbathing, do you?"

"I suppose not, George, though I can't imagine there are many plays about sunbathing. Let's get a bit closer and enter into the spirit of it then."

The cast proliferates with the arrival of a knight.

"In comes I, Saint George!"

…calls out this third character.

"Hey, Bel. Saint George is going to fight the Devil."

"I suppose it makes a nice change for him, George, though are you sure he's not just going to file him.

"Well, I can't see any books on hand, Bel."

Saint George continues:

"I fought the dragon years before,
in times forgot, in times of yore."

BOOK WORM ~ *The Curiosity of George Crosby*

"No you didn't! He's alive and well and living somewhere about." calls out George.

A tall bearded man is standing in front of George, a little to the side: "Don't be daft mate. Everybody knows George slew the dragon. I saw it on the telly."

Saint George continues, a little unnerved by the heckling:
> "*I searched the world it's limits round,*
> *and seen him off... he's in the ground.*"

"He's *not*, I tell you. Look behind you," calls George.

The bearded man looks round again, with a glare.

"Shush, George," implores Bella. "Don't go upsetting everyone. You're spoiling the story."

"Sorry, Bel, but you *did* say we should enter into the spir…"

At that moment, a sorry excuse for a dragon enters, it's fang-filled jaw clack-clacking in time with the words of its occupant.

> "*In comes I, with dragon breath.*
> *I'll fight this George unto the death.*"

"Told you he's alive," calls out George, triumphantly.

The man with the beard turns around again, fuming now: "I won't tell you again."

Saint George speaks again:
> "*In come you? I thought you dead.*
> *I'll draw my sword and cleave your head.*"

"Breathe on him. Scorch his eyebrows," heckles George, unable to refrain from continuing to join the verbal fray."

The bearded man turns and raises a fist to thump George when all Hell breaks loose. Saint George is staggering backwards as an airborne peril descends on him from the skies, wings flapping, screeching hysterically, belching flame.

The beaded fellow turns back to see what all the noise is about, just in time to see Saint George, Father Christmas and Beelzebub running hell-for-leather across the road and down a side-street. The mechanical dragon limps after them, grappling with his unwieldy costume.

10) Loschy Way

"Rango!" shouts Bella. "Go away! Now! You're supposed to be in the sidecar."

Rangvald darts too and fro for a moment, then heeds Bella's irate command, flying upwards and disappearing from sight over the nearby rooftops.

The residual cast of the mummers' play; a soldier, a blacksmith and a doctor, hurriedly gather their various baggage and follow the escaping players down the side-street.

The audience turn and disperse in various directions, some mumbling, some laughing and one or two children crying. The bearded man is the last to drift away. He turns as he goes and delivers a parting comment: "*Now* look what you've done. I hope you're happy."

All is quiet again. George and Bella think better of going to the Shambles… they've already seen one.

"That *bloody* Rangvald, George. Why didn't he behave himself? It'll all be in the newspapers now. Fielding will hear about it, for sure. And your behaviour didn't do a lot to help, did it."

"Sorry, Bella. I couldn't help it."

"You're as bad as the bloody dragon… Rangvald I mean, not that other one. Let's hope Rango's gone back to the bike and not rampaging through York. We'd better move on, straight away."

"Agreed, Bel."

When they reach the parked motorbike, they find Rangvald curled up, seemingly asleep, window still half down. The dragon is snoring deeply… but with one eye surreptitiously open. He stirs when Bella opens the sidecar door.

"You stupid bugger," says Bella, taking him to task. "We told you to stay put. What on Earth do you think you were playing at."

"You can't let people go around slaying dragons without so much as a by your leave, Bella."

"That's the point, Rango," says George, abruptly. "You weren't supposed to *leave*... the sidecar, that is. Everyone in York will be reporting that they've see a dragon now."

"Well, *you* were making a good attempt at causing mayhem yourself, George... from what little I witnessed, anyway."

"I was sticking up for you, Rango. That fool in the baked-bean-tin helmet with his wooden sword was suggesting he'd killed you."

"Sorry. I suppose you're right. I didn't know him from Adam. The knight who trapped me was much taller."

"Well, we'd better forget the incident and move on. Herbie Dragons will be sniffing us out for Fielding like a bloodhound sniffs out... blood."

Rain is coming on, so as they move off, Rangvald elects to stay coiled up in the sidecar. As they leave the side-street, turning into the traffic at the junction and heading north, a bearded man steps half into the road in front of them, oblivious to the traffic or to the rain, then jumps back just in time to avoid being hit. He seems to be in a trance and glances disbelievingly at a dragon curled up cosily in a sidecar being whisked away into the distance. Back down the alleyways of York there's a pub entertaining a gaggle of brightly-costumed customers all drinking pints, dazed and bleary eyed as if Armageddon has arrived.

Seeing as the rain continues to fall, Rangvald has decided to stay in the sidecar for the duration of the twenty mile journey, though his decision was helped along by the severe chiding that he'd been given.

Now, they arrive at what is no more than a hamlet.

"So, where's this Loschy Wood then, George?" asks Rangvald, peering out from behind the steamed-up glass. All I can see is that thicket."

"That's it, according to the map, Rango. Perched on the hill."

10) Loschy Way

"Hill? You can't call *that* a hill, George. Which dragon do you expect to find? I can't imagine any dragon wanting to live here."

"Well," explains George, "our book says it lived in that very wood. Local folklore has it that Sir Peter Loschy, a famous warrior, killed a huge dragon which had its lair on the wooded Loschy Hill and terrorised the people of the village. None of them could manage to kill it, so they called in the expert and his dog. There's an ancient tomb in the church at Nunnington which is just over there. It has an effigy of a knight with his dog, though there's apparently no inscription, if ever it had one. Anyway, the knight was cunning and covered his armour in sharp blades so that when the dragon attacked, it was badly wounded. But it lived on, so then the knight chopped off the end of its tail before slicing the creature into many bits. Piece by piece, time after time, the dog carried the bits over to a place near the church. Last of all came the head, but it seems the head was poisonous and the poison killed the dog… and the knight too. The monument was erected by the villagers in appreciation of his sacrifice. Maybe the church has a record of the event."

"That's gruesome, George. And so cruel. No dragon deserves that fate, even if it is a terrorist," says Bella. "I can almost sympathise with Rango here for fighting to protect that one in York."

"There you are, George," agrees Rangvald. "There speaks the voice of reason."

"But you have to admit, Rango. A lot of these dragons we've come across *do* seem to like a bit of terrorising. And I always thought that you and your lot were a force for good on the whole."

"We are, George, we are. It's *your* lot that go around whirling swords about, when all we're doing is looking for food most of the time. And treasure of course."

"I suppose so," concedes George.

After scouting around the woods for a while, looking for

clues, the companions head over to Nunnington making delicate enquiries about the legend of the dragon, but to no avail. Even the vicar has nothing to tell them.

"I didn't expect much here, Bel, knowing *that* dragon had, by all accounts, been cut up into little pieces. There seems to be no real clue at all, unless people are keeping quiet about what they do know. I certainly can't see that there'll be any connection with Our Boris, though I still can't help feeling the World Serpent is all around us... impalpable. Maybe Whitby holds out better prospects but remember, Rango, if we come across a group of old salts singing sea-shanties, then don't go attacking them, right? And whatever you do, keep out of sight if you possibly can."

"Fine, George. As long as they don't go mentioning that big sea monster they call the Kraken."

"The Kraken? I've not heard of that. Do you think it could be the World Serpent?"

"I doubt it, George. It's a giant octopus, so the old tales say."

The three of them move on, looking to reach Whitby by teatime. The rain moves on, looking to reach Norway by nightfall.

The motorcycle trio achieve their goal and, after parking up in the town, near the harbour, they find accommodation for the night, repeating their by now familiar ritual of installing Rangvald secretly in their room.

The next morning, waking late, George and Bella ask for breakfast to be brought to their room, ordering extra portions intended for Rangvald.

Meanwhile, back in York, Harry Fielding and Herbie Dragons have turned up, despite it being north of Manchester. They're setting up an interview room in the police station and sending out minions to round up witnesses to the mumming fiasco.

10) Loschy Way

When interviewed, those of the mumming audience who can be found either daren't say anything, or think the affray was intended as part of the act...

All but the bearded man, who confirms to Fielding the attendance of two people dressed in motorbike leathers, one of them being a persistent heckler. He also tells him unconvincingly of a dream-like vision of a dragon asleep in a motorbike sidecar. Then, he threatens to thump Herbie Dragons for suggesting that *he*, the bearded man, might have been involved himself. Fielding, after interviewing several incoherent mummers, now out of costume, decides that they were all drunk, which is probably true. He asks them not to leave the country because he may need to call on them again.

-o-o-o-

11) Whitby Jet Wyrm

The Norton, having carried them to the seaside haven of Whitby, is secure under cover, for in the evening the rain had changed its mind about Norway and a squall had been building. Now, in the dawning day, the weather is competing with the entire Whitby fishing fleet for a berth in the harbour, while bobbing boats jostle with each other in disagreement over territorial rights. The deep, dark night has gone and a wet, grey day takes over, the wind now blowing horizontal rain across the town. Umbrellas are rendered useless, raincoats marketed as 'stormproof' are put to the test and unsecured garden gates are clattering on their protesting hinges.

Bella peeks out from their second-floor bedroom window, the sash rattling in its ancient frame, the wind shrieking fitfully, banshee-like. Water streaming down the glass distorts her view of the harbour.

Rangvald thinks: *'no wonder a lot of dragons live underground.'*

There's a muffled call from outside the bedroom door: "breakfast."

Bella ushers Rangvald into the adjoining bathroom and George turns the brass knob to open the bedroom door.

"Turned out nice again," suggests the young lad who's brought their breakfast, on a tray big enough to carry a banquet. After helping to wrestle the tray through the narrow bedroom door, George thanks him absently.

The lad closes the door behind him. Bella turns back from the window and sees that George is deep in thought as he places the tray on a corner table. He's in a morose frame of mind, brought on more by the Fielding factor than by the treacherous weather.

"At least this weather should put the police of the trail for a bit," says Bella, trying to lift George's mood, tousling his hair.

11) Whitby Jet Wyrm

"They never come out in the rain. They'll be holed up inside somewhere, drinking tea and sharing ginger nuts... Leastways until it passes."

"Do you reckon, Del? Maybe we *should* do the right thing and give ourselves up after all. Burning a book isn't quite a hanging offence, surely."

"Depends on the book, I suppose."

At this, Rangvald pops his head around the bathroom door, picking up on George's glum mood: "Don't be silly, George. If that detective turns up again, I'll give him what for. Anyway, *you* didn't damage that book. *I* did... and they wouldn't manage to lock me up for long, unless the prison door had a magic clasp."

"Right, George," Bella announces in an upbeat voice. "It's time to decide what we're going to do now that we're here. You mentioned that you'd found reference to a dragon in the town. Tell us more."

"Well, Bel," George replies, his mood lightening a little at the prospect of another search, "this beast, by all accounts, had cruel dominion over Whitby, a village as it was then, and often caused trouble on a whim. The people enlisted the aid of Benedictine monks who built the abbey in an attempt to ward off the evil creature, but it attacked and tried to destroy their sanctuary. The tale goes that the prayers of the monks were stronger and the wyrm was banished to the sea, where it nursed its grievance. After that, every seven years, the beast returned to shore and tore at the rocks, trying to destroy the abbey. Then, thanks to Henry VIII, the abbey was partly demolished. So I suppose, in a roundabout sort of way, King Henry unwittingly did a bit of good for a change. The wyrm didn't have much to destroy after that, though even now it's rumoured that on stormy nights, more stones are torn down mysteriously from the remaining walls. The question is, is the wyrm really still out there at sea? I wonder if there are any clues up at the abbey?"

"I bet that poor creature *is* still out there," says Rangvald. "I can feel it in my old bones. And I bet it isn't the ogre that you're all making out. It may even be one of my relatives. As for Benedictine monks... I never heard of them."

"That's because you'd been locked up for a couple of hundred years before they came along," says George, feeling a little more combative now.

"Well, when this rain stops," says Bella, "let's make our way up to the abbey and see how the land lies up there. Rango, you'd better keep your distance. People may think you're this ancient creature."

"But I *am* an ancient creature, Bella."

"But more benevolent, I hope."

"Like I said, Bella. People often give dragons a bad name... even when they're friendly."

They make preparations and as the rain subsides, Bella and George decide to first walk the town looking for dragon clues. Acknowledging Rangvald's claustrophobic tendencies, it's agreed that he should fly out swiftly before the rain dies, when most people wouldn't be out and about, then keep his distance from the town until dusk before returning to their lodgings.

"Head out to sea for a bit, Rango," George suggests, "and see if you can spot any signs of the Whitby wyrm, while *we* ask around the town."

"Are you sure you're not just going to one of those pubs without me again, George?"

"Of course we're not, Rango. Trust me."

"Look, George. As you know, I've not been near that much water for many, many years. Are you trying to get me drowned?"

"No, you'll be fine. It'll be just like riding a bike. And there'll be remote places along the coast where you can settle for an hour or two."

11) Whitby Jet Wyrm

"Nobody rides bikes on water, George," Bella suggests.

"Well, you know what I mean, Bel."

"I shall go, reluctantly," Rangvald concedes, "but if I have to come back inland then I will, regardless of who may see me."

The town is becoming more tourist-orientated these days and George and Bella stroll, under a brightening sky, along the backstreets past several shops: a boutique selling miniskirts and large, floppy hats; a newsagent's; a holiday souvenir shop shut up for the closed season; and a drably awninged tobacconist's shop displaying all manner of pipes... briar pipes, Meerschaum pipes, clay pipes and unambitious pipes. There are boxed cigars of all manner of origin. There are table lighters, stormproof lighters and pipe-cleaners and all kinds of smoking accoutrements. George spies an ornamental pipe, the bowl carved in the form of a hideous monster with red eyes and fangs drooling painted blood.

"Look at that, Bel. Isn't it delightful?"

"It's dreadful, George. I've never *seen* anything so ugly."

"Well, I've got to go in and enquire about it."

"But you don't smoke a pipe, George."

"That's not the point, Bel. It's a work of art. And anyway, if I ever do take up smo..."

"No, George. Not while I have a say in the matter. Even if you bought a normal pipe."

"Well, I'm going to ask after it at least."

A tiny entrance bell tinkles and the pair are inside the dismal little shop that reminds them of the now infamous shop back in London owned by Herbie Dragons.

The tobacconist, a man with a nicotine-stained complexion, springs up from behind the counter.

"Yes?" he enquires, monosyllabically.

George is taken aback a little and, after a short pause, says: "I was wondering about the pipe with the dragon's head?"

"I'm sorry, sir. We don't have a pipe with a dragon's head."

"The carved one. The one with the goggle eyes and the blood."

"Oh, *that* one. That's a vampire, not a dragon."

"A vampire?"

"Yes. Surely you've heard… Bram Stoker and the abbey and all."

"Sorry? I've no idea what you're talking about."

"Dracula, George," explains Bella. "Bram Stoker wrote Dracula. Whitby is famous for it."

"Well, *I* didn't know. Our books only cover dragons and the like," apologises George, half to Bella and half to the tobacconist. "But do you know about the Whitby dragon… or, more correctly, the wyrm?" he adds, questioning the shopkeeper.

"Well not really. I'm quite new here. I only took over the shop in 1945, at the end of the war. But old Dufkins, six doors down will know. Last time I looked, he had a little jet wyrm in the window."

"Jet?"

"Whitby's famous for that too, George," Bella informs him. "Jet's a gemstone formed from wood compressed over millions of years."

"Isn't that coal, Bel?"

"Well, yes, George, sort of. But I think jet is compressed more, and for longer."

"Well, I never knew that. The things you learn. I bet this Dufkins will know about the Whitby wyrm then."

They thanks the nicotined tobacconist and head for the sign that announces '*Dufkins' Emporium*'.

George and Bella soon find the shop with the wyrm in the window and, after negotiating another tinkling bell, this time are greeted by a jovial, rotund chap in his green and white striped summer blazer despite it not being summer. Bella is tempted to ask for ice creams, but controls her mischievous

11) Whitby Jet Wyrm

impulse.

"Oh yes, sir. I know about the wyrm. Ever since I moved here in 1960, I've learned all there is to know about that wyrm."

Despite him having been here fifteen fewer years than the tobacconist, he's professing to be an expert in all things wyrm. Yet, for all this, he can tell the couple little more than they already know.

"Just remember, though," Dufkins adds at the last. "Don't get mixed up with no vampires. They're much more dangerous and devious than wyrms. They say that vampires can't enter your house unless you invite them in, but *I've* known them to invite themselves in for a bite on odd occasions." He says this, chuckling to himself, then laughs heartily, exposing rather pronounced upper canine teeth.

George negotiates the purchase of the jet wyrm, for the princely sum of four pound five shillings, and thanks the jovial, toothy Dufkins. They beat a hasty retreat and rejoin the street outside.

"Well, that was a waste of time, wasn't it," Bella says to George.

"Apart from this little gem, Bel. It's face reminds me of Rango."

"Don't suggest *that* to him. You know how sensitive he is."

Back at the lodgings, they find that Rangvald has somehow managed to return to their room without setting off alarm bells: "I just flew in through that open window that looks out over the yard," he says. "No one saw me… I was very careful to avoid that."

"I hope so, Rango," says Bella "Where did you get to?"

"I headed south, down the coast about five miles and came to a bay. There was a village, but I daren't go very close, so I flew around over the sea a lot. Then, unusually, my wings seemed to get very tired, so back I came. I didn't see any sea creatures either though."

"That'll be Robin Hood's Bay," decides Bella. "I know that my auntie often used to go there for her holidays when she was younger. She says it's a very nice place. A bit hilly though. We could go there ourselves, George."

"Maybe another time, Bel. I don't think it has any dragons."

"Well, when we get back home after this epic search for mythical creatures, George, we have some serious things to get on with. We need to settle down and get sensible jobs if we're going to make a go of our relationship. You'll have to put dragons behind you, at least for awhile."

"But we haven't found the truth behind Boris yet."

"I don't think we ever will, George. You're going to have to find a new quest to keep you occupied. How about stamp collecting or building an electric train set?"

"I'm not an eleven-year-old, Bel."

"I know, George. I'm pulling your leg."

"What about me," protests Rangvald. "I'm rather enjoying all this searching and flying around different places, Bella."

"I'm afraid you'll have to find a new life too, Rango. Somewhere where you won't get into trouble with people."

"It's people that are the trouble. Not me."

"Well, there's always China, Rango," George suggests. "England's a bit crowded, and there's a lot more room over there. There are lots of hills for you to live under... or over as you seem to prefer."

"Thank you very much. *I* know when I'm not wanted," says the disgruntled dragon.

"It's not that we don't care, Rango," says Bella, attempting to lift the dragon's morale. "Quite the opposite. You know from experience what it's like to be persecuted. Over in China they revere dragons. You'd be held in high esteem."

"Yes, but they're ones without wings. Still, I suppose I'll have to think about it then."

"Oh, dear," says George with a sigh. "It seems our adventure

11) Whitby Jet Wyrm

is coming to an end, Bel. We've travelled the length and breadth of England and not really found what we've been looking for. And we seem to be fugitives from the law for our trouble."

"Most adventures are a bit like that, George, apart from the fugitive bit. Remember, 'It's better to travel in hope than to arrive'… you told me it was Robert Louis Stevenson who said that, when *I* thought it was Oscar Wilde."

"Well, he must have been a spoilsport. That's all I can say."

"Reflecting on our travels though, George. We've met lots of interesting people, and a few dragons too. I wouldn't have missed that for the world."

"Or even for the World Serpent," smiles George, conceding that it's all been a bit of an adventure worth having.

With that, George and Bella go down for their evening meal, promising to smuggle food back for Rangvald. In the dining room there are only two other guests; a rather staid, middle-aged couple who acknowledge George and Bella with a nod and a smile. On the mantel piece George spots a tiny jet figure of a wyrm; the spit of the one he'd bought from the shop.

"If you don't mind me asking, miss?" George enquires of the waitress. "Do you know where that little jet figure came from?"

"Oh, yes," she says, enthusiastically. "They sell them on the Saturday market. Two pounds each. They're lovely, aren't they."

"Thank you," offers George in a deflated voice, largely because he'd paid four pound five for his.

Turning to Bella, as the waitress attends the other two guests, George says: "Right then. That settles it. You're right, Bel. As soon as we've had a look around the abbey, if we don't find any real clues as to where Our Boris's story lies, we'll head back home and make that new life. And I'll collect stamps if that makes you happy."

"Just British and Commonwealth?" teases Bella, stifling a

snigger. "But let's see what we can find up at the abbey ruins before we throw in the towel."

The waitress brings their meals; chicken and chips with a salad garnish and a warm glass each of Liebfraumilch. They pick at the meal dejectedly, pondering the impending end of their madcap adventure. They each stash away much of their chicken for Rangvald in 'draggy-bags' provided by the waitress. Looking at each other with a smile of resignation, they listen in on the conversation of their fellow diners.

"Well, Marjorie," says Cyril, "that was a bit odd at lunchtime in the teashop. That detective chap and his furtive friend asking if anyone had seen a young couple with a dragon... A real, live dragon. I ask you. As if anyone would have seen a living dragon. I think the pair of them were on drugs. They soon went away when everyone laughed at them."

George splutters, midway through a large gulp of his Liebfraumilch. Bella looks up in disbelief.

"Too right, Cyril," agrees Marjorie.

"Please excuse us," says Bella, as she and George stand and shuffle out from their seats and make for the door.

Marjorie nods in acknowledgement.

"There's nowt as queer as folk," they hear Cyril say as they leave the dining room.

Back in their bedroom, they give Rangvald his chicken contraband and ensure that he has a dish of water.

"Blimey, Bel. Here we go again. How have they tracked us down this quickly? Someone must have seen Rango. Or maybe someone heard us talking about Whitby."

"I told you, George. I was too far away from anywhere to be seen," insists the dragon.

"I hope you're right, Rango. But either way, Fielding seems to be more astute than we thought. He must have a sixth sense."

"It's that Herbie fellow, George. He has the smell of dragons about him. We dragons can sense that kind of thing."

11) Whitby Jet Wyrm

Bella, hands on hips, strikes a determined stance: "Right, George, It's decision time. You were wondering if we should pack in this dragon lark and get back to normal life, whatever that is. So, either we hand ourselves in, and accept that we may go to prison for years for illegal entry to a castle, which is probably still a treasonable offence, or we make another dash for it."

"Well. *I'm* certainly not handing myself in," protests Rangvald. "After centuries locked up, I'm rather enjoying my freedom, even if I do spend half my days in a motorcycle accessory."

"I can understand that, Rango," George says, sympathetic to the dragon's spirit.

George turns to face Bella, ponders for a moment, mirroring her hip-handed stance then, with a clap of his hands, declares: "We make a dash for it, Bel. I want to visit Knotlow, down in Derbyshire. There *are* rumours of dragons there... and it's on the way home anyway."

Rangvald belches approval with a tiny lick of flame.

"Right then, George," says Bella, hands now transferred from hips to holdall. "Let's pack, pay and proceed, before Inspector Fielding comes in to bat and makes his arrests."

In a flash, they're packed and making their way to reception, ready to apologise for leaving at such short notice. Rangvald is out through the window and circling high above Whitby harbour waiting for directions, a remote speck to any would-be spectators.

"Oh, no you don't!" demands Harry Fielding, dashing in through the front door, followed by an out of breath Herbie. "At last, we have you cornered. Now where's that flying freak you've been hiding from us."

"You'd better not call a dragon that sort of name, Harry," Herbie hisses. "Some dragons may conduct criminal activities, but all deserve respect. As you well know, sometimes they have short tempers and long tongues… fiery tongues. And they can easily find out where you live, Harry."

Harry hesitates, taken aback briefly by his companion's reprimand, then makes his intended statement.

"George Crosby and Bella Drake, I'm arresting you on suspicion of aiding and abetting book burning. You do not have to say anything but anything you *do* say will be taken down and may be given in evidence," adding with a whisper, as if Hector Parrott may be listening in: "If you tell us where the dragon is, you could get a few years off your sentences."

"Oh, what's the use," sighs George. "I didn't really want to go to Knotlow. The dragon there sounds very similar to Rango's Micklewhite at Bignor. I wouldn't be surprised if *he's* a pile of bones too."

"I suppose you're probably right, George," Bella says, sympathetically, acknowledging that his passion for dragon searching has hit the proverbial buffers. "I can't imagine we'll go to prison. Not without a body for evidence. Rango will fend for himself if we're carted off back to London."

"You'd be better to come clean, my dear," suggests Fielding, in a patronising tone. "We'll pin it all the more heavily on you if we haven't got *him*… err, it." He hesitates, thinking: *'What am I talking about? I'm suggesting we're looking to pin a minor crime on a mythical creature that appears not to be mythical anymore. I didn't join the force to chase fire-breathing fantasies.'*

"Excuse me, sir," calls a voice with some urgency from the doorway. It's P.C. Simpkin. "Headquarters have radioed telling you to phone D.C.I. Parrott urgently. Here's the number, if it's not in your notebook."

"What *now*? Can't he see that I'm busy on his wild goose chase?"

"Not really, sir. He's in London."

"You know what I mean, Simpkin."

Fielding asks the girl on reception to pass him the phone.

11) Whitby Jet Wyrm

P.C. James comes in and together Simpkin and James handcuff George and Bella rather ceremonially.

"Yes, sir... I understand, sir... No, sir... Right, sir," Harry says down the reception phone, with a submissive pause between each comment, as Parrott fills him in on requirements. He puts the phone down. Herbie Dragons looks on expectantly.

"Right, Simpkin. Right, James. You can take off those cuffs," announces Fielding and, addressing George and Bella, says: "I've been told that you can go. Apparently it's come to light that the book at Arundel was damaged in a minor fire caused by a heater which was left turned on. It was placed too near to a curtain. Thankfully, it didn't burn the whole place down... that could happen far too easily. If you ask me, people who live in castles should be more careful. We can't go destroying our heritage, can we now."

"Does that mean we won't be charged for illegal entry, Inspector?" asks Bella.

"Apparently not, my dear. The owners are too embarrassed. They don't want the incident dragging through the courts. But let me tell you this... if that dragon of yours causes any more trouble, I'll be down on you like a few hundredweight of bricks."

"He's not really *our* dragon. He's a free spirit. Well, he is now. Now that he's not bogged down by a book."

Herbie Dragons sneers and skulks, seeming to think that Rangvald doesn't deserve his freedom. He follows the three police officers out. The receptionist repositions the phone on her desk, looking for all the world as if she's witnessed an impossible scene from an episode of *Z Cars*. George and Bella look at each other in happy disbelief, pay the bill, pick up their luggage and head for the Norton.

Out on the street once more, Bella says to George: "You haven't phoned your parents again, have you."

"Oh. Sorry, Bel. It's hardly surprising though, is it? Let's get on our way first, and clear our heads on the road. We'll stop at the first village. There'll be a phone-box for sure."

"And don't forget Rango, George. He'll be up there, circling, waiting for us to appear. We'll have to have a heart-to-heart talk with him. See what he really intends to do now. He'll have to go his own way, surely?"

"I suppose so," George answers, pensively. "It'll be hard parting, after all these miles.

"He's a sweetheart really, isn't he, George?"

"He is Bella. He definitely is."

-o-o-o-

12) The Whirled Serpent

As soon as they set off, they can see Rangvald circling high above, to be mistaken for a bird, a hawk perhaps, by anyone glancing casually skyward. As Bella kicks through the gears and they make for the outer reaches of Whitby, heading south, the dragon follows, still circling, but following nonetheless. They've decided to head for Leicester, there to catch up with George's parents. Then, they'll look for a house suitable for the two of them to move into together. Bella will need to tie up some loose ends in Cambridge, but they now have every intention of setting out on that new journey together. Maybe, once they've found that common ground, they'll strike out on adventures new; to far-off lands exploring the strange delights of the man-made and the natural world.

It's not until they reach the quiet village of Old Malton, some thirty miles along their route, that they spy a convenient telephone-box. George dismounts and ferrets in his packed bags for loose change. Rangvald sees that the coast is clear and swoops down to join Bella, perching on the vacated pillion. Bella smiles at the reunion. Rangvald snorts a burst of white smoke, but resists flame, Bella having pointed to the bike's petrol tank.

"Well met, Rango. You must be tired again, flying all this way."

"No, Bella. We dragons can fly many miles, most of the time. And I'm building back my strength more and more since I've been able to stretch my limbs again. I think when I got tired over that Robin Hood's Bay place, it was to do with anxiety, but I'm over that now."

"Good. We have another three hours or so to ride before we reach Leicester and unless you want to be parcelled up again in the sidecar, you'll have go cloud-hopping all the way."

"That's easy," boasts Rangvald. "We dragons are tenacious. In the past, I've flown across whole countries without a rest."

George's mum answers the phone and he presses button A to connect.

"Hello, mum. It's me, George."

"George. How nice to hear from you. Me and your dad have been wondering where on Earth you might be again. It's been a while since you last phoned."

"I know mum. I'm sorry. I've been in Whitby just now."

"Well, *I* wouldn't be sorry if I'd been in Whitby. It's a lovely place. A bit bleak in the winter, mind you. You didn't talk to any vampires did you?"

"No, mum. A tobacconist warned us about the vampires."

"You've not been smoking, have you, George?"

"No, mum. I was enquiring about dragons."

"Oh, that. I don't see the point myself, truth to tell. I mean *they* smoke a lot, don't they?"

"Only when they're breathing fire, mum. Anyway, how's dad?"

"Oh, he's fine. His usual self… if that's fine."

"I'm sure it is mum. Look, we're travelling back down now. To Leicester. To you. Me and Bella. We may need to stay over for a night, then we'll be going to Cambridge for a while."

"Bella? That's the girl you met, isn't it. The one with the motorbike. I hope you're not bring any dragons with you."

"Maybe a little one, mum."

"Well, I hope it's house-trained. Are you sure it won't get you into more trouble with the police?"

"No, mum, it won't. That's all been sorted out. I'll explain when we get back. By for now. Love to dad."

"Bye George. Phone me when you get near us. I'll put the kettle on."

"No mum. When we get to you, it'll only take a few minutes to boil a kett…"

12) The Whirled Serpent

George realises that she's put the phone down. He hangs up and gets back to Bella and Rangvald.

"How are they both, George?"

"Fine, Della. I told mum to expect three for tea."

"Tea, George? I don't particularly like tea," Rangvald complains.

"Coffee then perhaps, your Lordship," jests Bella. "Or maybe Champagne?"

Rangvald looks at her quizzically.

"Never mind," she adds in dismissal of his frown. "Let's make tracks, George. It could be nightfall before we get to Leicester, if we don't burn some serious rubber."

Rain stays away and traffic seems to be shy of the roads they're on. By mid-afternoon, only having stopped once for the convenience of a public toilet, they make the outskirts of Leicester. Rangvald has flown all the way, encountering no more than a flock of geese and then a light aircraft piloted by a now very startled pilot. The dragon stays high aloft, awaiting a signal again from Bella or George.

"Pleased to meet you, dear, offers mum Crosby on seeing Bella at the opened front door."

"Me too, love," pop Crosby says.

"Hi, both," Bella replies, smiling.

"Why didn't you phone again, George. I haven't put the kettle on yet. I'll go and do it now," says mum.

"I hope you've got some money left in the bank, George," are the words pop Crosby greets his son with. "Women can be very expensive," he adds with a mischievous wink in Bella's direction.

Bella smiles: "Rest assured he has, Mr. Crosby. We've been living on bread and water," she parries.

"Good," say dad, assuming without a further thought that they really *had*. "Now, where's this dragon mum's told me about. I'd like to meet a dragon. If it's not too big, that is. You'd better tell us all about this fire business down in Sussex too. I'm glad to hear that's all blown over."

"Err, right dad. I'll go and make sure he's not smoking before I bring him in."

"Good idea, George. Perhaps best if you bring him into the back garden. I've got the hose connected. And Mickey Hebblethwaite next door went out to the shops up town a little while ago. He won't be back for ages yet. It's just that, as you know, he's always popping his head over the fence wanting to borrow something; a spanner here, a shovel there."

"Good thinking, dad. I'll wave Rangvald down and ask him to keep the flames under wraps. I'm sure he'll behave himself."

"You mean he understands words? Can he *talk* too?"

"Yes, he can talk, even though he's very old. I think most dragons can talk, if they have a mind too, though some of them haven't had a good relationship with man. I'm finding out that some of them just go on the rampage... against my earlier understanding of them."

"A bit like people then, son."

"I suppose so, dad. There he is, look... that speck up over Mickey's house."

With that, George unzips a breast pocket on the jacket of his leathers, pulls out a white handkerchief, flicks it, then whirls it around vigorously above his head. Rangvald drops into a peregrine dive and, in the blink of an eye, he swoops low over Mickey's roof, negotiating the fence and landing with a flurry on pop Crosby's water butt.

"Blimey!" exclaims pop. "If Mickey had've been in, he would've come head-over-fence into my cold frames borrowing a cloche, before he could even ask the favour."

George laughs out loud at the dramatic impression Rangvald has made on his dad. Pop, grinning, offers a smile.

"He's a lively little blighter, isn't he, George. I can see why

12) The Whirled Serpent

you're into researching dragons. It reminds me of when we used to collect frogs… only *they* didn't have wings."

Rangvald looks sideways at Mr. Crosby senior, unsure as to whether or not to trust him, but even before Mrs. Crosby has brought out the tea, the two of them are launched on a philosophical conversation about the growing of melons and gourds.

As the evening deepens to night, they risk letting Rangvald into the house. By ten o'clock, Mr. and Mrs. Crosby have retired to bed and George, Bella and Rangvald are ensconced in George's bedroom.

"It's the box-room for you, Rango," declares George. "Bella and I want a little privacy."

"A box-room isn't as small as I think it might be, is it, George?" Rangvald asks.

"No, Rango. It's more than big enough for you. Far better than a sidecar, which is the only alternative."

"I could always sleep outside."

"I don't think so, Rango," insists George. "Mickey will be back home by now. One ill-advised fiery peep from you and before we knew it, he'd be asking to borrow pop's hose-reel."

Early next morning, George and Bella are making ready to travel on to Cambridge.

"You can come with us, Rango," explains Bella, "but you're going to have to find your own way in life at the earliest opportunity. You can't go on avoiding the Mickeys of this word forever. I'm sure you'd be best to fly east… the further the better."

"Well, there's gratitude for you. I rescue you both from all sorts of difficult situations and you want me to go as far away as possible.

"For *your* sake, Rango," say George. "Not for *ours*. You know it makes sense. The Orient is far more tolerant of dragons than the Occident is. We'll miss you greatly, but there's nothing else for it. Cambridge could be full of dangers for you. There are hundreds of libraries there. If there's a Samantha Battlebury in one of them, just say hello to her in the rare books section and you could be trapped in a book again before you knew it, even accidentally, for centuries."

"I have no intention of going *near* another library, George... either occidentally or orientally. But I suppose what you say makes sense. I shall miss the two of you though."

"I know, Rango, I know," Bella acknowledges sadly.

When George and Bella reach Cambridge, they make their way to her digs where she'd cancelled the milk, ensured that the fridge had been left empty and that her magazine deliveries had been suspended. She'd neglected to have her post redirected though, and a fair wodge of it lay on the hall floor requiring attention; binning or paying. They've pick up emergency milk and instant coffee from the corner shop, intending to shop properly in the morning. They bring in all their bags and baggage. Rangvald is sneaked in from the sidecar under a coat. He'd elected to ride on this leg of the journey.

"What an amazingly beautiful place this is." remarks Rangvald, having fleetingly viewed many of the architectural delights from the sidecar.

"Well, I'm glad you like it. I try to keep it clean and tidy."

"No, I mean the city, Bella. All those glorious buildings. What are they all for?"

"Most of them are universities, Rango. Places of learning with dining halls and chapels. And libraries... remember what we said about the libraries."

"We never had anything like that when I was young, Bella." say Rangvald, in awe, but shuddering at the mention of libraries again.

12) The Whirled Serpent

"Maybe not, Rango. But I imagine you had all sorts of ways of learning about the true necessities of life. I'd say you can waste an awful lot of time with your head stuck in a book."

"Was that meant to be funny, young lady?"

"Sorry, Rango. It just slipped out."

George chuckles, neither Bella nor Rangvald seeing the funny side of this last response.

"Come on, George. Wake up," encourages Bella who's shaken off her dreams and is more than ready for the challenge of a new day. "We have some shopping to do."

George stirs from deep sleep. Earlier, he'd half-woken, restless from a fantastical dream featuring hills and caverns and dragons and launderettes and neighbours borrowing shovels and eccentric characters with some mysterious connection or other with the shadowy world of fiery creatures. Then he'd realised that it wasn't really a fantasy at all… just a tumbling from his brain of the events on their journey around the country. He'd fallen back to sleep, making up for the interruption.

"Shopping, Bel? What shopping."

"Food. We need food, George. Then we're going to have a long talk about our future; what to do with our lives after our weird and wonderful journey around this England. And what to do about Rango? He really *does* need to find his own new life now too."

"Right," says George, sleepily. "I'll do it first thing in the morning. I promise."

"It *is* morning, George. Wake up. It's a lovely day. Morning is escaping."

Meanwhile, Rangvald shows the merest hint of stirring. He's dreamed about motorbikes and sidecars and car thieves and policemen and seascapes and long-lost relatives. Bella opens his box-room door and sees a restless dragon tangled up in the candlewick bedspread.

"Good morning, Rango. Time to stretch you wings. George and I are off in search of food. When we get back, we need to have a long chat about your future."

"Right, Bella. I'll do it first thing in the morning," he answers blearily.

"It *is* morning, Rango. Wake up. It's a lovely day."

Out in the streets of Cambridge the weather is fine. The clear, pale blue, winter sky sets off the rich ochre tones of the stone buildings as the sun rises. Traffic consists more of bicycles than of cars. Gowns and mortarboards bear witness to term still being in, though about to break for Christmas and New Year. University scarves proliferate. Some of the river punts, that have lain moored and idle overnight, are being prepared for keen winter customers.

The shops have all opened and the couple are in and out of them with gusto. Bella knows them all well, and George is finding it hard to keep up; fresh baguettes in the bakers', fresh ground coffee and marmalade from the coffee shop, cheese, butter, biscuits and fresh fruit from the market and several tins of baked beans from the co-op."

"Just a visit to the butchers' now, George, to get something for Rango. Then back for that chat."

George nods compliantly, still sleepy. On their whirled tour of England looking for Jörmungandr the World Serpent, he'd been wide awake, raring to go for much of the time, urged on by the thrill of the chase; *them* chasing dragons or Harry Fielding chasing *them*. Now, with both chases over, he seems to have lost that adrenaline rush... for the time being at least.

Bella and George settle in the lounge on the generously-cushioned sofa. The mingling aroma of coffee and fresh bread set them in good stead for a long talk. Rangvald is parked in a convenient corner, grappling with the chicken meat that Bella

12) The Whirled Serpent

had decided he'd like. She was right.

-o-o-o-

13) Tail Ends

A week later, and the university term has ended. Rangvald is ready to fly, after spending some bitter-sweet days carefully exploring Cambridge with Bella and George, always avoiding people, sometimes avoiding daylight, and in particular avoiding libraries.

George and Bella have found a new place to live and are hoping to move from her current digs soon after the holidays.

"You know, Bel," says George, "it seems like years since we met, yet it's less than two months."

"Time's a funny thing, George. Sometimes I feel it's only last week that I was running around the garden with Ken as children; those idyllic summers and long summer holidays, snow on Christmas morning, Ken catching frogs and digging up worms. Then at other times I feel as if I've been here for a hundred years and more; ready to draw my overdue pension, hobbling to the shops, wondering why I haven't taken up knitting. Then again, it seems about right; travelling the country with some young bloke, wearing bike leathers, sneaking into castles, meeting dragons and thinking that it's only the castles and dragons that have been here for long ages."

At the mention of worms, George is reminded briefly of his schoolfriend Danny Page's habit of biting bits off them. He shakes off the thought and turning to Bella's comments says: "And isn't it odd, Bel, that we met quite by chance through my deciding to search for dragons and you just happening to have got the sack and being there looking for a job in the Information Centre. And if you hadn't been ready to come gallivanting around the country on a mad adventure, then just think of what wouldn't have happened?"

"Well, George. *That* must have been a day when it seemed about right. A day for living in the moment. And look where it

13) Tail Ends

landed me. Where it landed us both."

Rangvald looks up from his chicken, casting a sideways glance as if to say *'what on Earth are they talking about?'*

"The thing is, Bella. I suspect I've still got itchy feet. We never *did* fathom out where Our Boris might be, did we. All those dragons still lurking under hill and over dale as we whirled around England, yet barely a hint of any World Serpent. It's as if he never really existed in the flesh. Maybe all the dragons in the world, big and small, fiery and watery, needed some form of deity to explain their existence. Like humans seem to need a God."

"You're getting a bit deep now, George. I'd prefer to think of him as a particularly big dragon that got fed up and rode away around the world on an enormous Harley-Davidson, still out there somewhere, stopping at petrol filling stations to sustain his progress, chasing his tail on a never ending quest for freedom and along the way frightening half to death anyone that sees him."

"*Now* who's getting a bit deep, Bel. *I'm* saying he might not exist at all and *you're* saying he's some sort of globe-trotting Hell's Angel."

"You're both wrong," declares Rangvald, who's finished his chicken and is now paying full attention to what his two emancipators are saying. "He exists, unquestionably; I knew dragons who'd *definitely* seen him. He's quite benign and minds his own business, or else *people* would have seen him too."

"Ah, but there are people who say they've seen God, Rango. They usually say *he's* nothing if not benign too. Unless you've met him yourself, how can you be sure."

"Well maybe you should keep on searching, George. Find your Boris and your God for yourself, then you'll be able to tell others that you've seen them... but my guess is that they wouldn't believe you, even then. As for me?... I'd believe you."

"Look, George," Bella says. "Don't let Rango encourage your

feet to itch more than they already do. Maybe we should assume that we've followed our own parochial World Serpent... the world being England. After all, we *did* go full circle. But let's give this settling down lark a try now, and see how you... see how we feel in a few years' time. Let's concentrate on a bit of 'seems about right' time, shall we?"

"I guess so, Bel. You can only have your head in the clouds for so long, I suppose."

"Well, that's not true for a start," says Rangvald brightly. "I can keep my head in the clouds for ages when I want too."

"That's because you can fly, Rango."

"It's a good job you *can*, Rango," says Bella, "because you can't stay here. It would be nice if you could, but it just wouldn't work out. People would go crazy, seeing a dragon in the area, especially if they saw you more than once. If they saw you once, they'd convince themselves they were imagining it. If they saw you twice they'd think they'd gone mad. A third time and they'd probably call in the police. Luckily, I don't think you've been spotted this last week, but you never know."

"Not that Fielding fellow, Bella? I couldn't face *him*, especially if he had that Herbie with him. Anyway, I've decided to get off to China, like I always wanted to."

"Not China *Town*?" says Bella, reminding him of his previous excursion.

"No, Bella. Not China *Town*."

"I know what you mean, Rango," says George. "We'd have been better off if we'd never gone to the *Herbie Dragons* shop, though I suppose his books did give us a few leads. Bit of a mixed blessing really. It's that fate thing again isn't it, Bella."

"Well, yes, George. And it's a good job they decided that a misplaced heater caused that scorching incident."

The next day, after breakfast, Rangvald is perched on the sill of a second floor window. The sun has given way to a blanket

13) Tail Ends

of dark, brooding cloud and heavy snow is falling.

"Are you sure you won't wait for this snow to ease?" asks Bella. "You have a long way to go."

"Don't be silly, Bel. We dragon's can brave *any* weather. My scales are more than a match for this."

George steps forward and, to Rangvald's surprise, places his well-travelled bobble-hat on the dragon's head.

They each say their goodbyes. Bella laughs and cries at the same time, and she and George both wave, as their dragon companion flies up high, circles once breathing fire, and is gone.

In truth, the phone call to Harry Fielding from Hector Parrott had been instigated by someone higher up the police food chain who'd decided the available budget wouldn't stretch to more time spent chasing castle interlopers, especially as Herbie was costing a fortune in consultancy fees… always one for a main chance, that Herbie. The higher authority had merely told the castle owners that the trail had petered out. Harry's papers, and all the reports and such had been filed away as a cold case, awaiting some future researchers like George and Bella to unearth them, and merely speculate on whether there was any truth in the legend of Rangvald, the 'Book Worm'.

~The End~

14) Epilogue - *Ten Years On*

George and **Bella** are well settled in Cambridge and enjoying life there, not hankering to travel around the world, but occasionally revisiting some of the places they'd landed in on their adventure around England. They continue to use the mighty Norton Dominator with its sidecar and they're content to take in the scenery, and the architecture, and the pubs. Sometimes, quite by accident, they come across characters they'd met on their tour; mercifully not Harry Fielding or Herbie Dragons.

They rarely come across any hint of a dragon at all; just as with mumming plays, if you're not looking for them, you don't often see them. In any case, the fire of their dragon enthusiasm is spent, and they have other interests, though George has never taken up stamp collecting.

Most of George's inheritance has been spent on setting up a comfortable home, and now that he has a regular job in one of the college libraries, he finds plenty of scope for researching all manner of things... not dragons, but all kinds of exotic and fascinating subject. This very week, he's been asked to appear on television to expound his theories on the geology of the moon.

Bella has attended art classes for several years and, when she's not working as the regional manager of a well-known charity shop chain, she's busy organising exhibitions of her watercolours. Life's good, and they wouldn't dream of changing it for the World Serpent.

-o-o-o-

14) Epilogue ~ *Ten Years On*

As for those Characters who George and Bella encountered on their strange adventure?

They have inevitably continued on their own paths through life. Most of them are largely oblivious to the true existence of dragons and other 'mythical' beasts, each following the destinies laid out for them by the ever-spinning world:

Natalie has found her youth, though not in the form she'd expected. A young visitor to the British Museum café sat down next to her one day at the very table where she'd chatted with George. His name is Ollie Moore, a twenty-five year old aristocratic Irishman who, back home in Ireland, keeps exotic birds of prey. His favourite bird is a merlin called Grace. Some say Natalie married him for his money, but he was almost stony broke. They now live happily together, back in the Emerald Isle, supported by her state pension. She grows the best snapdragons in all of Ireland.

Jonny never *has* met with a dragon, or anyone in particular called Arthur, perhaps because he never eats his bogeys. However, he *has* become an airline pilot and flies around the world many times each year. He never gets back home for tea on the day *before* he's set out on a flight. However, he's bought his parents, **Ethel** and **Cecil**, a villa in Torremolinos and visits them there whenever he gets a chance, when he often can tell what his mother is going to say before she says it.

Danny Page, having gone over to Ireland to *avoid* snakes, decided he likes them after all, so he started a campaign to re-introduce them to the country, but his son, Patrick, would have none of it, telling him it could be dangerous. After that, Danny decided to take up traditional Irish dancing, thinking: *'there no harm in that, surely'*.

BOOK WORM ~ *The Curiosity of George Crosby*

Samantha Battlebury has worked her way up through the hierarchy of the Council's public services department to become head of all the city's libraries, thus ensuring that the supplies of gloves are of the whitest of whites and that all the pencils are HB.

The 'Leprechaun' eventually found what he was looking for in the pages of the library's ancient comestibles section and now enjoys soups of the utmost traditional authenticity. As for anything else the little man may have been looking for in life, no one will ever know... but then, no one could be happier than him as he flits around Leicester in his black plimsolls.

Fred and Agatha Crosby have moved to Mablethorpe. Fred sits on the beach on knotted handkerchief days in the summer, surveying the horizon, but coming back to where he started from when Agatha has fetched ice creams. George and Bella visit often, remembering that all roads lead there. Fred has left his best set of spanners and his favourite shovel to Mickey Hebblethwaite, back in Leicester, for fear he might otherwise follow them to the seaside.

Malcolm and Annie have spent a lot of time on the bus, and almost as much time in the pubs of Geddington. Once, they went as far as the Green Dragon over in Brigstock. Now, sadly, they only get to the pub occasionally, since arranging transport from their sheltered housing is rather difficult for them.

Ken has married an opera singer called Carla and has moved to Italy with her. He's sold his faux Gothic house for a tidy sum, but has ensured that he's kept his leather sofa, his Victorian smoking jacket and his much prized record collection; all of these, he'd arranged to be transported to their villa in the Italian

14) Epilogue ~ *Ten Years On*

lakes. Bella doesn't see him at all now, but they keep in touch by telephone.

Old Harry, with his rosy cheeks and seriously bushy red beard, still haunts the Jolly Sailor, deceiving people as to his identity and occasionally purloining a wallet. Over the years, his jasmine and turmeric brew has got him into more trouble than his sticky fingers, though occasionally it's got him *out* of trouble. As for the Orford Sea-dragon... Harry's always ensured that he keeps far enough away from the beast to maintain possession of his rationed fingers.

Jacob, ever the less-than-jolly treacle-meister at the Jolly Sailor, is still serving scrumpy and other strange brews to his customers and advising them on the pros and cons of talking to old Harry.

Carlton Buncle is still at the Georgian hotel in London, a semi-retired retainer. He has ever growing problems with his memory and is often found wandering along Fleet Street, looking for the door of his bridge club where he's meeting with 'the others'. When he's most confused, he can be heard asking passers-by if they've seen any of the Devil's dragons or God's unicorns lately.

Lucy now performs most of Carlton Buncle's previous duties at the Georgian hotel in London, though she still makes sure he's not too distressed when he returns from an eventful bridge meeting.

Herbie Dragons may be 'closer' to the World Serpent, Ouroboros, than anyone has dreamed of. His bookshop holds more secrets than even the wildest imaginings would allow, and he still has an unfathomable, long-standing bone to pick with Rangvald.

Aunt Vicki has recently taken the plunge and extended her lease to include the two floors above her original basement business. She now boasts three departments: 'Victoria's Plunge' 'Vicki's Ground Coffee' and 'Vicki's Upper Crust'.

Ben, Vicki's ex-husband, has branched out recently too. Off the back of the psychedelic period, he took up a shop in Carnaby Street and, whilst the powder blue leathers are no longer de rigueur, he finds that the seventies 'riot of colour' brigade still want clothes that echo the flamboyance of the sixties.

Barry, a.k.a. *Bazza*, has toned down his chauvinistic attitude to women somewhat. This change is partly due to the lesson instilled by Bella with her 'six-foot three, bloke-bashing girlfriend', but mainly thanks to his conspicuous quiff having been replaced by a conspicuously receding hair line. Even the sideburns have receded.

Joe, the farmer has died. He reached the ripe old age of ninety-nine and in the six years since he died, **Elsie,** and her stepson, **Tommy**, have been in early retirement, she now being seventy-nine and he being eighty-four. They might have carried on working longer, but Tommy's leg finally gave up the ghost at Joe's funeral… just when he needed it. He had to wait for his new N.H.S. leg for two years… he was hopping mad. The two of them live in the farmhouse still, and have employed a young lad of seventy-one to look after the farming duties.

Joanie is a little more crooked than she was, but still hobbles out to sing and play for the Knucker. She's taught him a few more tunes and he still delights in her visits. The curtains still twitch along her route to the hole, but even now, very few

14) Epilogue ~ *Ten Years On*

believe that the Knucker inhabits the Knucker hole, or else they're too frightened to say they do. Elsie still keeps in touch with Joanie.

Madge and **Peregrine** go to the cinema twice every week now and, since they moved in together along with Maggie the cat, Peregrine doesn't see the need to sit in the launderette any more. The downside to this is that he finds it hard to concentrate on his Beano without the soporific spin and hum of the washing machines and the driers. The upside is that Madge ensures their blankets are washed and dried to perfection. Every time Peregrine glances at the ramparts of the castle, he breaks out into a cold sweat at the thought of Harry Fielding's interrogation techniques, but the cold sweat is replaced by a hot one at the thought of Rangvald's fiery breath. He's disposed of his old keys.

Mark Stark had taken his wife, **Muriel**'s advice and decided to appeal his dismissal. The tribunal panel found in his favour, deeming the taking of rubber bands as a substitute for his failed belt to be reasonable. Otherwise, they argued, he could have caused an embarrassing incident with the female staff. His 'fart-brain of a boss' had been sacked for unreasonable aggression, despite his own nose being blooded by the plaintiff. Mark Stark was offered the boss's job, and took over at nearly double the salary he'd been drawing, so Muriel had been able to give up the cleaning work. The shingles on their front porch are no longer threatened by dragon claws.

Harry Fielding, a pivotal name to conjure with: He's broken all ties with Herbie Dragons, for apart from the Dragon-Meister's peripheral help in *not* achieving a conviction of the Arundel arson gang, Harry has had his fill of dragons. He'd contemplated leaving the force to set up a detective agency in partnership with **Simpkin** and **James**, but realised that the overheads would impact on his net income too heavily, so he's stuck with it and tolerates **Hector Parrott** as best he can. He's never received the prospective promotion, so at least remains un-demotable.

Ernest Van Kampe still sells more petrol than campervans. He tends to shy away from stocking any psychedelia, since the sight of brightly painted vehicles now gives him an instant migraine headache. He won't allow a single gas camping stove anywhere on the premises, suspecting that it may not have been the dragon that was the primary driver of the fire that got rid of his car thieves.

Derek Cattermole felt the need to up sticks from Chichester and move nearer to his place of work, in Orford, at the *Atomic Weapons Research Establishment*. The White Horse had splashed out on a leaving do for him and ordered in extra KP salted peanuts. Given the speed at which he usually consumes them, he felt the need to take two dozen packets with him to Suffolk. The nature of his work there is still a mystery, though the the Sea-dragon seems to have developed a liking for peanuts. **Deirdre**, the pub landlady, remains as busy as ever, despite the fact that she's lost her only real regular customer in Derek.

Allison has embarked on the cataloguing of extensive archives of some stately home in Sussex, while **James** is still the cheery greeter insisting to all and sundry that 's'alright, in't it'. Their much treasured copy of *Jörmungandr - the Tale of the Tail of a Serpent* has been recategorised under 'Modern Classics'.

Beryl is still pounding the beat in Lyndhurst thinking that Martin Blake and Maurice Burke are two different people.

14) Epilogue ~ *Ten Years On*

Major Martin Blake, at ninety-five, is still of the opinion that W.P.C. Beryl gets everything wrong, and he's probably right. He tells any and all of his visitors to the care home that he'd had two people come to his front door who didn't know the first thing about dragons, and another couple who'd actually found the Holy Grail. The staff are happy to let him tell his stories.

Benjamin Green, a.k.a. 'Green Ben' has passed away, short, dumpy and smiley to the last. Old Bernie Brown died too, and never did move to the village. This has left Blue Ben to reign over local folklore without the previous colourful confusion over names, though the few inquisitive people who come looking for dragons think that Blue Ben is a he, not a she… after they've established that 'he' is not the sticky-out-bit.

Wilfred and **April** are still running the local postal services single-handed, together apart, in their strange way. Second post takes it's toll these days on old Wilf, but he soldiers on. As for that 'bloody **Agnes** woman at number seven on Church Lane'… She seems to wait longer than anyone else in the locality for parcels.

Anne Dromeda still star-gazes on cloudless nights. She sometimes meets with her old schoolmates who'd caused her to dispense with her real name of Smith. On such occasions, she's recounted more than once the night when bandages, police cars and the *Macclesfield Caving Club* featured heavily, not to mention a little dragon that caused havoc among them all. Her friends have asked more than once if she can get them some of the drugs that *she's* obviously taking.

Eric Battersby, **Sid** and **Carol** still visit the caves up on Alderley Edge on suitable occasions. The *Macclesfield Caving*

Club has gone from strength to strength, now boasting nine members. At regular meetings of the club at headquarters, the three founding members occasionally recount the night when they encountered a couple of dragon hunters, a nurse and police cars, not to mention a little dragon that caused havoc among them all. The other members of the club have asked more than once if they have any of *their* drugs to spare. As for the legend of King Arthur, the club have tried, to no avail, to extract from the rock the shard of metal that George had cut himself on. They believe that the knight of long legend is still awaiting some future future to return.

Alf, the landlord of the Upholland pub, has invested in a new jar of pickled eggs and sells them freely now to all and sundry. They seem to have had a resurgence in popularity, partly because they can be seen more clearly through the fresh glass jar. **Billy** and **Cedric** are no more, and **Boadicea** too has gone the way of all things. As for **Boady**? She has a new greyhound... a *white* greyhound. It has a single black patch around it's right eye, meaning that Boady is keeping one eye on the future.

The Mummers have been continuing their indulgence in the art of entertainment these last ten years though they've modified their several plays to exclude Saint George and the Dragon. They'd thought about introducing King Arthur as a character, but thought better of it. In deference to modern sensibilities, the doctor character is now female, Beelzebub is portrayed as the Chancellor of the Exchequer and Father Christmas is Father Winterlude... it's just *not* like the old days. To cap it all, they cast a watchful eye on the heavens and cringe momentarily every time an aeroplane roars within earshot.

Dufkins, the man with the souvenir shop in Whitby, had

14) Epilogue ~ *Ten Years On*

concurred with the nicotine-stained tobacconist that trade would benefit from diversification, so these days the tobacconist has added dragons to his stock list and Dufkins has added vampires to his. Trade is so good that they're planning a luxurious family holiday together in Transylvania, and plan to claim the cost as business expenses.

Marjorie and **Cyril**, George and Bella's fellow diners in the Whitby hotel, who'd briefly witnessed part of Fielding's police hunt for fugitives with a dragon, still believe that 'there's nowt as queer as folk', but they don't know the half of it. To this day, they proudly display their little jet wyrm, bought from '*Dufkins' Emporium*' for the princely sum of four pound five shillings, which reminds them of that odd little encounter.

Mickey Hebblethwaite, back in Leicester, has the tightest nuts and the most comprehensively shovelled loose materials in the neighbourhood, thanks to Fred Crosby's parting bequests. He now relies on his *new* neighbour for various pieces of equipment. Currently, he's borrowed a set of stepladders and a trestle table and is embarking on a bit of home decorating.

-o-o-o-

And, as for the 'mythical' beasts?

Who can really tell whether or not dragons and their brothers and uncles and nephews really and truly *do* exist? And if they do, could more of those that George and Bella came across have been related to Rangvald, the Book Worm?

All those beasts; the dragons, the drakes, the serpents, the wyverns, the wyrms? Much has been cited and said of them over the centuries yet, just as gods and aliens remain tantalisingly out of reach, they are real enough for some people to believe in and for some to embark on lifelong quests for them in all their disparate incarnations.

As for the mythical creatures sought, and sometimes found, by Bella and George? They were and are real enough for the couple who met by chance in Cambridge on that auspicious day. Enough for them to raise a glass to:

    The Orford Sea-dragon
    Ouroboros, Jörmungandr, the World Serpent
    The Lyminster Knucker
    Rangvald, the Arundel 'Book Worm'
    Micklewhite, the Bignor Dragon
    The Bisterne Dragon
    Blue Ben, The Kilve dragon
    The Upholland Dragon
    The Loschy Dragon
    The Whitby Wyrm

Apart from poor Micklewhite, not even George and Bella are certain what might have happened to each of them, though rumour has it that their Rango has dropped by on the odd, clandestine occasion to wish them well.

14) Epilogue ~ *Ten Years On*

King Arthur and his knights remain conspicuously quiet.

-o-o-o-

Printed in Great Britain
by Amazon